ABOUT THE AUTHOR

KIM WILKINS was born in London, and grew up at the seaside north of Brisbane, Australia. She has degrees in literature and creative writing, and teaches at the University of Queensland and in the community. Her first novel, *The Infernal*, a supernatural thriller was published in 1997. Since then, she has published across many genres and for many different age groups. Her latest books, contemporary epic romances, are published under the pseudonym Kimberley Freeman. Kim has won many awards and is published all over the world. She lives in Brisbane with a bunch of lovable people and pets.

THE YEAR OF ANCIENT GHOSTS

ALSO BY KIM WILKINS

ADULT
Rosa and the Veil of Gold
Giants of the Frost
The Autumn Castle
Angel of Ruin
The Resurrectionists
Grimoire
The Infernal

YOUNG ADULT
The Pearl Hunters
Nightshade: A Gina Champion Mystery
Witchsong: A Gina Champion Mystery
Moonstorm: A Gina Champion Mystery
Fireheart: A Gina Champion Mystery
Bloodlace: A Gina Champion Mystery

CHILDREN'S
Ghost Ship: The Sunken Kingdom I
Tide Stealers: The Sunken Kingdom II
Sorcerer of the Waves: The Sunken Kingdom III
The Star Queen: The Sunken Kingdom IV
Space Boogers

WRITING AS KIMBERLEY FREEMAN
Lighthouse Bay
Wildflower Hill
Gold Dust
Duet

THE YEAR OF ANCIENT GHOSTS

STORIES BY
KIM WILKINS

T≋
p≋   Ticonderoga
      publications

for Olafr, min leof

The Year of Ancient Ghosts by Kim Wilkins

Published by Ticonderoga Publications

Designed and edited by Russell B. Farr
Typeset in Sabon and Charlemagne Standard

A Cataloging-in-Publications entry for this title is available from The National Library of Australia.

ISBN 978-1-921857-45-4 (limited hardcover)
     978-1-921857-46-1 (trade paperback)
     978-1-921857-47-8 (ebook)

Ticonderoga Publications
PO Box 29 Greenwood
Western Australia 6924

www.ticonderogapublications.com

10 9 8 7 6 5 4 3 2 1

CONTENTS

INTRODUCTION

" . . . woven together elements of history, mythology, horror and magic . . . "

— Kate Forsyth

INTRODUCTION

KATE FORSYTH

The first time I met Kim Wilkins, I told her she looked like the evil queen in my novel.

She laughed and took it as a compliment which, indeed, it was. Maya, my evil queen, has blue eyes and a black bob just like Kim, and ensorcels people with her beauty and charm.

It was a hot oppressive evening in Melbourne, and we were shouting above a noisy crowd while waiting for the announcement of the 1997 Aurealis Awards for Speculative Fiction. My first book *Dragonclaw* and Wilkins' first book *The Infernal* had both been short-listed for the Fantasy Award.

The Aurealis Awards are the premier prize in Australia for fantastic fiction. Writers of fantasy fiction are rarely shortlisted for any other kind of award . . . which is a short-hand way of saying we both wanted to win. Badly.

That night Kim's book not only won the Fantasy Award, but she also walked away with the prize for Horror Fiction as well. To add insult to injury she was looking absolutely gorgeous in velvet and a starry tiara while I was barely able to waddle, being eight months pregnant.

I bought *The Infernal* that muggy night in Melbourne and began to read it a few weeks later, pacing the floor with early contractions and desperate for distraction. I became so instantly absorbed that I, incredibly, forgot about my coming baby. I emerged hours later, petrified, shaken, exhilarated and without a contraction in sight. The Infernal had literally scared them away.

I have read and loved every one of Kim's books since. She is one of my all-time favourite writers, someone whose books I wait for impatiently and rush out to buy as soon as they hit the bookstores.

These are the thirteen things I love most about Kim's books
1. the way the pages just fly by while I'm reading, as if turning themselves
2. her characters—all so very different, with frailties and terrors and flaws that make them feel so very real
3. the vividness of her settings, so beautifully drawn I can see them clearly in my mind's eye
4. her limpid and sensuous prose style that sings with effortless grace
5. her ability to weave together two separate time periods without ever letting her narrative threads fall slack
6. the way her stories illuminate the past so I feel as if I have travelled there myself
7. the way the real world utterly fades away, so I am completely lost within the world of the book
8. the way each book is utterly different from any book she has written before
9. I feel so much while I'm reading Kim's books—in turns, they chill the spine, bruise the heart, make my eyes sting with tears, my skin crawl, my pulse quicken, I laugh, and cry, and gasp out loud.
10. This means, at the end of each book, I feel as if I have suffered and fought and survived just like her heroines, and I am a much wiser person because of it
11. She knows so much, about so many things—I come away from each of her books feeling like I have learnt so much
12. because she constantly surprises me
13. her fearlessness

In this collection of short stories and novellas, Kim proves herself one of the most gifted and versatile writers Australia has ever produced.

The title story, "The Year of Ancient Ghosts", is an utterly chilling and suspenseful set in modern times. A grieving mother and her young daughter come to stay in the Orkneys—the place where her husband grew up—and find themselves haunted by eerie ghosts from his past.

The next piece "The Crown of Rowan" takes us far back into the past, to a land that seems much like England in the 8th century. It tells the story of a young queen who has taken a secret lover and must do all she can to protect her unborn child during a time of turmoil and war. It left me hungry for more—I'm desperate to know what happens next and can only hope that Kim fulfills her promise of turning it into another novel.

"Dindrana's Lover" is set in the time of King Arthur and his knights and contains a true frisson of supernatural horror, while "Wild Dreams of Blood" returns us to the modern day with a most unexpected twist.

The final story in the collection is "The Lark and the River", a heartbreaking story of love and faith and magic that is utterly perfect in its creation and execution. Set just after the Norman conquest, in a small English village where old superstitions still hold sway, it tells of the love between a Norman priest and a young Saxon woman whose family adheres to the old ways. It left me with tears in my eyes.

In all of these stories, Kim has woven together elements of history, mythology, horror and magic to create something utterly new and utterly beguiling. All I can say is: I WANT MORE!

Now, please.

SYDNEY
FEBRUARY 2013

THE YEAR OF ANCIENT GHOSTS

THE YEAR OF ANCIENT GHOSTS

"Further than history / the legends thicken . . .
Further than death / your feet will come"

— George Mackay Brown, *Further than Hoy*

I

Shards of bright pain and bright light spear into the cloying vacuum. He struggles upwards; he has something important to remember.

"Try to be still. You've had an accident."

His tongue swells against his teeth.

"Don't talk and don't move. We're taking you into surgery."

The darkness yanks him towards it. Surrender. Beyond this threshold is the big black; an end to the pain. But there is something else. Something waiting, as it has waited for nearly twenty years, tangled in seaweed and teeth and veins.

His voice breaks from his throat, a blood-soaked gargle. "Jenny! Mary!"

The light blinks out.

II

We came late to Orkney after all, when the lambing snow was melting off the crest of Hoy. Lachlan would have been dismayed. *It's April*, he might have said. *The book is meant to be called "The Year of Ancient Ghosts", not "The Nine Months of Ancient Ghosts"*. But Lachlan wasn't around to be dismayed. A council bus had taken care of that, clipping the back of his bicycle three days before we were due to leave.

We came anyway, Mary and I. We came late.

The three of us had been meant to stay at the croft where Lachlan spent his childhood. That there were only two of us added more sodden weight to the inescapable sadness. We ploughed over the black water on the ferry, and the waves and the wind were relentless. I knew the weather and I would get on: we had much in common. I had not imagined that I would find myself in this position: single mother to a two-year-old, mourning my husband on a remote island off the tip of Scotland. But then, I wasn't the one with the imagination: that was Lachlan, my husband.

Mr McBride met us off the ferry. I'd only seen a photograph of him when he was younger—Lachlan had it in a frame on our bookshelf—wearing a yellow cable-knit pullover with his dark hair curling over the back of the collar. The elderly man who waved from the bottom of the walkway bore so little resemblance to the man in the photo that I assumed he was waving at someone behind me. But then he said, "Jenny!" and I managed to recognise the heaviness of his brows and the tilt of his mouth under his white beard.

"Hello," I said, coming to a stop a few feet in front of him. I wasn't sure of the protocol: we had never met. We had spoken two or three times on the phone. He was from Lachlan's past, not mine.

Mr McBride seemed to feel the awkwardness too. He crouched with an audible knee-click in front of Mary and said, "And you must be wee Mary."

Mary, defiantly cold in only a little pink fleecy pullover and track pants, dived behind my legs and pressed her face into the back of my knees.

"So she's a little shy," he said.

"I assure you, that's the last word I'd use to describe her," I said. "She'll warm up."

Already Mary was tipping her head out from behind my legs, stealing curious glances at Mr McBride.

"Oh, well," he said, straightening up, but it sounded like "Och, weel". "Sorry about the weather."

"Thank you for coming to collect us."

"Couldn't have you making your own way up there. Not with your bags and with the wee one." He smiled at Mary, who smiled back.

"Wee," she said, laughing.

I hefted my suitcase and Mary's stroller and knapsack off the luggage rack and Mr McBride felt in his pocket for his car key. Then he stopped, reached out his hand for my wrist, and said softly, "Look, I don't know what to say. I'm sorry. I'm just . . . I'm so sorry for your . . . for Lachlan."

The sadness, as it always did, winded me unexpectedly. I don't know how many times I'd thought I was doing okay, only to have some small thing remind me and then . . . that familiar hollow punch to the belly. I took a deep breath. "Thank you," I said, because there was nothing else to say, and he was sad and uncomfortable.

"Well. I'll get the car."

The cottage sat a half-mile from the water's edge, its deep front windows directed out over Scapa Flow to the island of Hoy. Viking language, Mr McBride told me, for "high island". It looked like a sea monster's back rising treeless out of the churning blue tide.

"I've fixed you up with some tea and bread and so on," Mr McBride said as Mary ran from room to room chatting to herself happily. "But if you want anything else there's a grocer near the roundabout. I can take you there tomorrow if you like."

"Thank you. I'll be fine. I'll need to fill the time somehow and you have enough to worry about. Can't be running around after me."

"I can, Jenny, if needs be. Just until you settle in."

"Mama!" Mary called. She emerged from her new bedroom cradling a soft doll that wore a tartan raincoat. "Mama, look!"

"Aye, now. That's from Mrs McBride," he said, crouching. "She's very sick and can't leave the house to come down and welcome you herself, but maybe you'd like to come up and see her some time soon? That would make her very happy."

Mary was too busy pulling the raincoat off the doll to answer him.

"She'll have that naked in two seconds," I said. "None of them keep their clothes on. Not even in this weather."

Mr McBride laughed. "Don't worry: spring will be upon us soon. We'll have sun and blue skies. You'll see." Then he raised his bushy eyebrows. "Won't be anything like that Australian beach you live on, though."

A pang, remembering the untroubled sun and the warm ocean back home. But home, now, was a very different place. Hollow and cold in the shadows. "It's nice to be somewhere different," I said.

"Aye. I understand. Now, the little miss has found her room. This one is yours." He pushed open an internal door and I moved in ahead of him.

"It's been waiting for you since . . . ah . . . since before."

Since before. When there was need for four pillows and two empty bedside tables. My heart clenched.

Mr McBride strode to the dresser, picked up a little book and handed it to me. "This isn't easy, but you'll be wanting to see this," he said.

Its thin pages were fastened with rusty staples. Childish handwriting on the front declared it "written and illustrated by Lachlan McGregor".

"*The Fisherboy*," I read from the cover.

"First wee book he ever made, stapled together out of cardboard," Mr McBride said, then he chuckled. "Combined his love of stories with his love of fishing. Clever lad was only five. Mrs McBride has saved it all this time. Brings it out to impress dinner guests. 'This was the famous Lachlan McGregor's first wee book'. She was longing to show it to him." A short, uncertain silence. "You should have it."

I laid the book gently on the dresser. I didn't know if I wanted to keep it or if I wanted it to go back to Mrs McBride, who had preserved it so proudly all these years. "It's lovely."

"He was always special."

"I know."

"Strange wee boy. Full of stories. Full of mystery. Folk around here used to say, he's not for this world, that lad. Not for this world." Then, checking himself, realising he might be stirring my sadness, he cleared his throat. "I'm glad you're both here. I think you made the right choice."

And that did cheer me a little. A number of people—including my own parents—had thought coming here the very worst decision under the circumstances. "Thanks," I said.

"I'll leave you to it."

· · ·

Mary had always been a good sleeper. When we brought her home from hospital, she was already sleeping six hours at a stretch at night. I was the envy of my mother's group, whose shadowy eyes and twitching moodiness told of sleep snatched in fragments. Lachlan's theory was that she was just so exhausted by being awake: curious, smiling at everyone, poking everything; and then, later, crawling everywhere, grasping handfuls of the cat's fur, pulling things over on her downy little head. By the time evening fell, she didn't so much sleep as black out.

So her cry on that first night at the croft made me wake in alarm. I didn't know where I was. My phone, docked beside my bed with the time showing, told me it was three in the morning. I pulled back the covers and got up, whacking my shin against the chest of drawers. The floorboards were cold on my bare feet.

"It's okay, Mary," I croaked. "Mama's coming."

I felt my way down the hall to her room. She sat up in bed crying. Crying hard, as only the very young can cry.

"Sh, sh," I said, sitting next to her, pulling her against me.

"The mean lady," she said. "The mean lady."

"Just a dream, sweetheart. You just had a bad dream."

"Bad dream."

"Yes, the mean lady isn't real."

I could feel her heart ticking fast against her little ribcage. I stroked her hair and she began to calm. I almost asked if she wanted to come and sleep with me, but not for her comfort, for mine. If I was ever going to recover, I had to get used to sleeping next to Lachlan's empty side of the bed.

Mary snuggled back under the covers, and was soon breathing deep and evenly. I sat with her for a long time. Her curtain was open, and I could see mist over the ruined farmhouse next door, lit softly white by the moon. I couldn't hear the sea through the closed windows and thick stone, but I knew it was out there, ever restless and in motion.

· · ·

The morning was heavy with mist. The view disappeared outside the window, but then began to reappear in the middle of the day. Distant, white sunshine. I wrestled Mary into a padded anorak that was two inches too long for her arms, and then got her settled in the stroller for a walk down to the shops. I knew where the shops were because Lachlan, in his obsessive poring over every detail of our stay, had mapped out the route. As it turned out, he'd failed to account for several sets of stairs. I bumped Mary down them backwards where I could, or lifted the stroller and struggled where I couldn't. Finally, we were on the dark grey flagstones of Stromness's narrow main street. The damp little houses were all crammed up against each other, spotted grimly by age and weather. The harbour smelled dank and briny, and the air was chilly.

The supermarket's warmth was welcome, but the aisles confused me. I didn't know where to look or what to buy. Everything was *different* from back home, so I bought random things that caught my eye: cheese and leeks and tomatoes and dried pasta and a bag of jelly babies; things that I didn't know if I needed or could use. Mary fidgeted violently in the stroller, whining all the way home. Once there, I decided that we were jetlagged and needed extended time in the sunshine, however filmy that sunshine might be.

The path down to the beach wound past old croft land, muddy ditches and stone fences falling into ruin. The cold came on the wind, which rose and fell off the sea in a slow dance. Mary was already struggling out of her anorak and running ahead in her t-shirt, blithe to her goosebumps.

When we saw the beach, she pointed and looked at me doubtfully. "Swim?"

"No, darling. Not here."

Mary loved to swim. In summer, we swam in the sea every afternoon. Forbidding a swim was a tantrum-throwing offence, but even Mary seemed to see the sense here. She shook her head. "No swim."

I took her hand and we picked our way down onto the dark grey rocks, moulded by the centuries into sharp geometrical patterns and festooned with tough, slimy seaweed. She found a rockpool and crouched next to it, little fingers poking the algae that drifted like soft green hair within. I stood beside her, gazing out over Scapa Flow, missing Lachlan sickly.

He should have been here. Lachlan McGregor, author of the international best-selling children's series *Sea Orphans*, had been commissioned in a six-figure deal to write his first adult work: a memoir of a year in the place he left behind at eighteen. A place that was as thick in his blood as it was terrifying for him to return to. Something happened here to Lachlan, twenty years ago, something that even he couldn't remember.

Now nobody would ever know what that something was. The book would not get written.

"Come on, Mary, let's walk for a bit."

She rose without protest and we picked our way back up to the stony beach. The stones were round and smooth and many different shades of grey, so we played a game to see who could find the roundest and the biggest. Of course, mine were all wonky and I led Mary to the roundest ones every time, until she was squealing with delight at having beaten me on so many occasions. By the time our pockets were full of stones, we had managed a good half-mile walk along the beach and the sun was making me feel more human.

Then we found it. A huge, perfectly egg-shaped stone.

I collected it in two hands and held it up. "Look, Mary," I said in faux-reverent tones. "A sea monster egg."

Her eyes went round. Her mouth dropped open.

"Shall we take it home?"

She shook her head vigorously, and then I remembered she'd had bad dreams the night before and I felt like a rotten mother, putting ideas of monsters in her head. "It's okay, darling, I'm only joking. It's just a rock. There's no such thing as sea monsters."

"Put it down, Mama," she said, pointing at the ground.

I dropped it with a thud and grabbed her hand. "Shall we go home for some lunch?"

"Hot dogs?"

Mary's favourite. Why hadn't I thought to buy any? I vowed to start a shopping list the moment I got home. "Sorry, sweetie. We haven't any hot dogs. How about a cheese sandwich?"

But she had spotted a length of old rope a little further up the beach and run off to investigate, so I assumed lunch was not high on her list of priorities. I watched her. She seemed so untroubled and I wondered if she ever missed her father. I didn't talk about him or remind her about him because I didn't want her to be upset, and I didn't want her to see me upset. I realised, dimly, that this probably wasn't the right way to go about grieving. I was getting it all wrong.

My stomach gurgled.

"Mary! Come on. Back to the house."

We picked our way back over the beach, the sun bright on our hair and the wind cold on our cheeks. Halfway up the path to home, an elderly woman in a tartan skirt and black cardigan was walking a fat sausage-dog. She saw us, gave us a smile, then realisation flashed in her eyes.

"Oh, you're Jenny McGregor?" she said, stopping and turning.

"Yes," I said. In fact, I was and always had been Jenny Sanderson, but since Lachlan's accident I had stopped minding if people assumed I'd taken my husband's surname.

She extended her hand. "I'm Nora Kirkby. I live right next door to you. Kevin McBride told me you'd be coming soon." She smiled at Mary. "Hello."

"You have funny teeth."

I blushed. "Mary, that's not polite."

"Och, it's fine. Don't trouble yourself. I dinnae look after my teeth, sweet pea. You make sure you brush yours, okay?"

Mary put her knuckle in her mouth.

"Listen, Jenny, I hope you don't think me too forward," Nora Kirkby said, her eyebrows taking on the expression of pity I had seen so often in recent times. "But I'm just so sorry to hear of your husband's passing. My husband died six years ago and I cry about it every day still. But your Lachlan, he was a young man with a young family. It's a tragedy. If you need a shoulder, I'm just next door. Drop by any time for a pot of tea."

My mouth opened and closed silently for a few, creaking seconds. How could I tell her?

"Are you all right?" she asked.

"He's not . . . Lachlan isn't dead."

Nora Kirkby tilted her head to one side curiously, waiting for me to explain, but I couldn't. I just said again, "He isn't dead," and grasped Mary's hand and walked away fast.

Because articulating it was impossible. No matter what words I used, all anybody would ever hear was that I'd abandoned my husband in a hospital thousands of miles away in Australia.

Not dead. Dead to the world. Dead to all sense and sound. Nothing could rouse him. And every time I went to see him, he looked worse. With every minute and hour he grew greyer, smaller, like a fruit shrivelling in time-lapse photography. Mary cried and trembled whenever we drew close to the hospital. He frightened our baby. He frightened her. I couldn't take her back there again. Lachlan wouldn't have wanted me to.

The call would come, no matter whether I was in Queensland or in Orkney. The call that it was over would come and until then, I was closer to Lachlan here than I was next to his husk in hospital. I knew it in my soul.

"We walking fast," Mary said, huffing next to me to keep up.

"How about we go into town and see if we can find somewhere that sells hot dogs?" I said to her.

Her rosy cheeks lit up in a smile. The smile that was the only thing keeping me hanging on.

. . .

Lachlan feels the hot breath of the ship behind him. He swims on, muscles burning, choking on huge lungfuls of water, all the while knowing he cannot escape. The ship will surely catch him. He risks a glance over his shoulder. The ship bears down, its mast and sail obscure the moon in the molten indigo sky. The dragon on its curling prow grins at him cruelly.

And he sees her. He stops swimming, turns around and peers into the fast-moving mist. Waves wash over him, the ship speeds forward, but the dark figure on the ship is uncannily familiar. His memory churns like a big wheel in water: who is she? An image of milky skin and liquid eyes flashes across his brain.

Then the wind drops suddenly and the sail on the ship goes slack long enough for the moonlight to shine directly on her. No milky skin. No liquid eyes. Seaweed hair and barnacle teeth. His heart catches on an icy hook. The wind picks up again and he turns, swimming away with rubber limbs, while the ship casts its black shadow over the water, over him.

"I've found your child!" she screams, cackling, over the wind. "I've found Mary!"

III

The McBrides had their heating on too high. I shrugged out of my coat and scarf, but I'd worn a heavy pullover and the dry heat made my skin prickle uncomfortably. The house smelled like vanilla, a fact that was not lost on Mary.

"Hello, blossom," Mr McBride said as I hung Mary's little anorak behind the door.

"Is there cake?" she asked.

"Right this way," he said, leading us into the sitting room for our first glimpse of Mrs McBride.

She sat noble and erect on the settee, dressed in a floral blue nightgown. Her hair was dark brown apart from two white streaks on either side of her head. I'd seen two photographs of her as a young woman. Neither of them prepared me for how handsome she would be in person, even now in her late sixties. She smiled and I felt as though I should curtsey.

"Welcome, welcome," she said in her thick Scottish accent. "I cannae get up, but it doesn't mean I'm not pleased to see you."

"It's so lovely to meet you in person," I said, moving forward to clasp her hand in mine. Her fingers were soft and powdery. "This is Mary."

"Och, wee Mary," she said.

Mary was entranced by this striking older woman. She came to stand in front of her and said, "I'm Mary."

Mrs McBride laughed. "So am I."

Mary looked puzzled.

"Mrs McBride's name is Mary too," I explained. "You were named after her."

Mary held up two fingers. "Two Mary?"

"Yes, two Marys."

She grinned, delighted. "Is there cake?"

"Coming right up," Mr McBride said, disappearing through a swinging door into the kitchen.

"Can I help with anything?"

"No, no. Sit."

I sat in an overstuffed velour armchair and watched as Mrs McBride chatted softly to Mary, who stood half-twirling in front of her, hands clutching the hem of her dress. The McBrides had been Lachlan's foster parents from his fourth birthday, until he'd run away to Australia at eighteen. He hadn't seen them since, but if there was any ill-will on the McBrides' part about Lachlan's sudden disappearance and lack of contact, they were hiding it very well. Perhaps the dozens of phone calls between them over the past year had repaired the damage the long, unexplained silence had caused.

Mary had climbed up on the couch next to Mrs McBride and was snuggled against her side. Mrs McBride gave me a smile and said, "And how are you, Jenny? How are you managing?"

I didn't know how to respond. My usual reply, to a person I'd just met, would be that I was managing fine and it was difficult, but I had hope that things would improve. But there was something about the way she looked at me, with her lucid grey eyes, that made me want to tell her everything.

"It's horrible," I said, simply. "Horrible."

"I understand," she said, and I truly believed she did understand. In a matter of minutes, both Mary and I were under Mrs McBride's spell. It was impossible to imagine that this fiercely attractive woman with such fire-and-ice clarity and composure could be sick. Dying of a heart condition. Too much activity, even lifting her arms too high over her head, could be fatal.

Mr McBride emerged with the afternoon tea and set it carefully on the coffee table. Victoria sponge and a pot of tea. My mouth watered. Mary waited patiently for her slice of cake, then crammed it in her mouth so quickly that half of it wound up on the thick rug.

"Mary!" I admonished, but the McBrides were already laughing it off, telling me stories about how messily Lachlan ate as a child, and I relaxed into an afternoon of gentle conversation and reflection. Mary was happy and settled. It was such a relief. Being the single parent of a two-year-old was very hard work, especially a strong-willed—some might say naughty—two-year-old like Mary. The wind moved in and rattled the eaves, and clouds covered the sun, but we were warm—a little too warm—and cosy inside.

But eventually, the matter of Lachlan's sudden flight from Orkney came up.

"You know, I never imagined I could be so happy as I am now," Mrs McBride said, "with Lachlan's wife and child sitting here in this very room, where so often I have thought of him and wondered how he was. Where he was."

"He thought of you too. All the time. He had photographs of you about the house . . ." I trailed off lamely. It was for Lachlan to tell them why he had run, why he'd not contacted them for so long.

"You needn't sound apologetic, dearie, I never blamed him for leaving, nor for not staying in touch. I knew, when the time was right, he'd come back."

The McBrides exchanged a glance. I tried to read it, but couldn't. But it was almost as if they were checking, silently, with each other whether or not a subject had been broached that ought not have been.

I trod carefully. "If it's any consolation, he often told me he didn't know why he left either. Something happened, he said, something he can't remember." I corrected myself, "Couldn't remember. And he had an urge to be as far away from Orkney as he could possibly go. That's how he ended up on the other side of the world."

Mrs McBride nodded slowly. "Lachlan was always a strange lad. A little unpredictable, a little fey. Especially after . . . the incident."

"When he nearly drowned?"

Mr McBride harrumphed. "A long time ago, now, dear. My memory isn't so good."

I wasn't completely convinced he wouldn't remember such a traumatic event. "He was fishing in his rowboat and somehow fell in the water," I said. "That's what he told me."

"Yes. That's right." Again the exchange of glances between them. Mr McBride climbed to his feet and fetched a framed photograph off the crammed mantelpiece. "Here," he said, showing it to me. "That's our Lachlan and his boat, out on Scapa Flow just in front of your cottage, where we lived at the time. It was his favourite place to fish. That's where it happened."

I looked at the photograph of the still silver-blue water, and the young boy sitting in the rowboat wearing his blue rainproof jacket. His face was turned towards the camera, but he was too far out for his features to be properly visible. I didn't recognise him as Lachlan at first, and then something about the grip of his hands on the oars registered with me as incredibly and viscerally familiar. I remembered Lachlan's hands on mine as we stood at the altar of the little church we were married in. I shivered.

"How old was he?" I asked.

"In this picture? About ten. But he was twelve when he had his accident."

"He was in the water a long time," Mrs McBride said softly. "He shouldn't have lived, at least not without . . . permanent damage. But he was fine, thank the stars."

I turned this over in my mind, thinking of the shell of Lachlan breathing slowly on its own back in Australia. And I remembered Mr McBride's words when we first met: *folk around here used to say, he's not for this world, that lad*. Perhaps he wasn't. Perhaps he was destined, somehow, to have a short life, and I should just be glad that I got to spend some of it with him.

The weather had changed in the room, somehow. This talk of the past, of Lachlan and his two near-fatal accidents, had brought the clouds inside. A silence fell. Mary looked up from the carpet, where she was playing with her naked rag-doll, and frowned.

"Mama?"

"I should go," I said, handing the photograph back. "I don't want to wear you out, Mrs McBride."

"Och, I'm not that easy to wear out. But you should get on before the rain sets in." She leaned forward in her seat, and it was the first time I saw difficulty in her movements. "Now, Mary, would you make an old woman happy and come to see me once a week?"

Mary nodded enthusiastically, and held up her dolly to make it nod too. "Two Marys."

Mrs McBride looked at me and said, "I'd love some time alone with the wee one, if you need to get chores done. Or just have a break."

My heart swelled. I hadn't let Mary out of my sight since Lachlan's accident: she had become like a precious gem that I couldn't trust the world to keep safe. But the idea of some free time, some time just to think and be me, was intoxicating. At that moment, it felt like exactly what I needed, though I'd not known it.

"Yes," I said gratefully, then remembered how ill she was. "It won't be too much for you?"

"No, I have a perfectly good husband to do the dirty work." She smiled broadly.

"My love," Mr McBride said with a grin.

"She's Lachlan's daughter, she's my namesake, and the closest thing I'll ever have to a grandchild. And I haven't long left on the planet. I'd love to have her."

And so it was settled. Mrs McBride would take Mary every Monday for the whole day.

•   •   •

The evening seemed very long. Mary was tired well before night had truly set in, but I knew better than to try to get her into bed when there was still light outside. I sat her in front of the television where she ate her fish fingers quietly, dipping them solemnly in her mashed potato while Iggle Piggle danced about in the Night Garden. I'd bought a bottle of wine at the store earlier in the day— Australian wine to remind me of home, but also because I suffered from that innate snobbery all Australians feel about their wine—so I poured a glass and watched the television with her. Then another glass. And another. And then it was night.

I bathed Mary and tucked her into her night nappy, then read her a book and sang her a song. I have no musical ability—once again, that was Lachlan's domain—but she insisted I sing her another, and then finally I took her down the hall so she could climb into bed.

"Night, night, darling," I said, kissing her cheek.

"Mama?" she said, in a frightened voice.

"What is it?"

She pointed at the window. I looked. Saw nothing.

"What's wrong?" I asked.

"The old house," she said.

I realised she was pointing to the old farmhouse next door. Its roof had long since fallen in, and it did look creepy standing there half-ruined in the misty dark. I got up and closed the curtains firmly. Mary usually slept with the curtains open at home. She liked to look at the stars while she went to sleep. "There," I said. "No more old house."

I lay down next to her for a few moments to stroke her hair. She was quiet for a long while and I thought she'd gone to sleep, but then she said softly, "The mean lady lives there."

The mean lady. I remembered the bad dream she'd had. It must have really got under her skin. "There's no mean lady, sweetheart. And it's just an old house." I nearly told her that tomorrow we would go over and have a look at the old house, in the comforting light of day, but decided it might frighten her if I said it now. "Go to sleep, now," I said. "You're tired."

I lay there until I was sure she was asleep: it didn't take long. I was half-drunk and tired myself, but I sat down on the little sofa and watched television for a while, drinking the last of the bottle of wine. Night deepened. Another cooking show. I supposed I should cook something for myself but weariness was seeping into my bones and I slipped off into sleep.

When I awoke, a completely different show was on and my neck was sore. I glanced at the clock on the microwave. It was one in the morning. The timed heating had gone off, and cold had seeped through the stone walls. My mouth felt dry and tasted salty.

Time for bed.

I stood, reached for the remote, then heard it. A bumping noise along the side of the house.

I switched off the television. Listened as hard as I could into the silent dark. The thump of my heart swelled in my ears. I'd imagined it.

Then I heard it again. A bumping, scratching sound along the eastern wall of the house. I realised the sound had woken me. I went to the window, pushed it open and looked out, expecting to see some kind of strange Orkney wildlife. But I saw nothing. The cold was thick and insistent, so I closed the window.

Now the sound came from the other side of the house, with a slither. Near the door.

The skin on my scalp prickled, and the arches of my feet felt hollow. I wondered, fleetingly, if I might be having a bad dream, but reality was everywhere. The smooth wooden floorboards under my socks, the smell of fish fingers trapped in the air, the rattling wind against the window panes.

I went to the door. The noise stopped. My heart thudded and my ears rang.

I told myself not to be a quivering fool, like a girl in a 1980s horror movie. With a confident pull, I opened the door and looked out.

Nothing.

I stood there for a moment, in the cold damp night air. Rain was moving in. Soft, light drops. Boldly, I stepped out of the house, walked down to the front corner and surveyed as far as I could see. The farmhouse next door was shadowy and still. My hair grew damp. I went back inside and locked the door.

One last check on Mary. She was sleeping peacefully. Her breathing was even and soft, and it made my heart feel warm.

I decided on a hot shower and, as I stood under the scalding water, I turned over what had just happened in my head. Wildlife? Local kids? Stones and wood settling? Sometimes things weren't explicable. That didn't mean they had to be frightening.

That's what I told myself over and over as I tried to get to sleep.

. . .

I packed far too many things to take to the McBrides' house with Mary, and I left them far too many instructions.

"Now you'll have to remind her to wee," I said as I showed them the spare change of clothes, the little lunchbox full of cheese cubes, the three favourite stuffed toys. "She's not that long out of nappies and she forgets. If she has a tantrum, just ignore her if you can. Don't let her touch your breakable things; she hasn't yet learned to be gentle. And if she—"

Mr McBride hushed me with a gentle hand on my forearm. "Off you go, lass. Enjoy yourself."

Mary turned round, dark eyes on me. "Off you go, Mama," she said, mimicking the Scottish accent. "We going to play."

I took a deep breath. "You have my mobile number."

"We won't need it, dear," Mrs McBride said, inviting Mary to sit by her on the settee with a pat. "Untangle some of your knots. We'll see you about five."

I left the heated house and found myself outside on the grey street, by myself.

By myself. *Untangle some of your knots.* I was surprised that my knots were so visible to others. I'd thought I was doing a wonderful job of hiding them.

I walked. Not the shuffle-stop-shuffle-drag walk I had to do if I walked with Mary. Just walking. Striding, turning the world underneath me with the power of my feet. Sunshine broke through the clouds. I walked along the street and up the close towards the cottage, but I didn't go inside. I kept walking. I hadn't realised what a hunched, soft thing I'd become since Lachlan's accident. I walked the path that led along the sea front, even where it crumbled away to rocks or mud. My body warmed. I shrugged out of my jacket, then realised I was a long way from home and hadn't any water to drink. So I turned and started striding back, eating up the ground beneath me.

It felt wonderful. As though I was back in my body again for the first time in months.

I stopped at the bottom of the path to the cottage, and turned to look out at the water. Out there: that's where Lachlan had sat in his little rowboat and smiled back at Mr McBride for the photograph. I half-closed my eyes, picturing him there. A dark-haired, long-legged boy who loved fishing and making up stories. A cold wind picked up and shivered across my skin. Out there was also where Lachlan had fallen into the water, and been under a very long time. He should have died. But he hadn't died, he'd gone on to grow into a tall, lean man with spectacles and a large collection of superhero t-shirts. He'd written a modest children's story about an orphanage under the sea for mermaids and mermen, and it had turned into a sensationally popular series of six books, all of which had somehow been compressed and adapted into one Hollywood animated film. "It's all so mad, Jenny," he'd said to me, time and time again. The night of the movie's premiere, we had stood together on the red carpet—I was six months pregnant with Mary and felt decidedly glamourless next to the Hollywood types—and he'd leaned over to me and whispered in my ear, "It's all so mad."

"I know," I'd said.

Then he smiled and said, "And a little bit magic."

Mad, and a little bit magic. Like the fact that Lachlan hadn't drowned that day. Perhaps even like the fact that he was still—somehow, bafflingly—alive after being literally hit by a bus. I found myself smiling. Perhaps he would pull through somehow. Perhaps it was a mad enough and magic enough thing to happen. Smiling and crying now. Rain in the sunshine.

I turned and headed back up the path, tired and thirsty. I could see the cottage in the distance and, off to the west, the ruined farmhouse. I'd seen several ruined houses around the island: the legacy of a system of crofting that had passed out of common use. They were pretty, almost a part of the landscape. I headed for it, intending on a short reconnaissance to see if it might be safe to take Mary there so she would stop worrying about it. The roof had completely fallen in, and there were only gaping holes for windows. No, not a place to bring Mary, simply because of the uneven piles of broken timber and sharp heaps of fallen stone. Lots of old bird nests in the remaining beams: with so few trees around, that was no surprise. I leaned in the window and tried to imagine which room of the house this had once been. A kitchen? There was a fireplace and hearth, but no other identifying features.

And seaweed. A pile of seaweed in the middle of the fallen debris. At least half a mile from the beach. Not so much a pile of seaweed, either. A nest.

Oh no, I wasn't going to bring Mary here. Because if she asked, "How did the seaweed get here?" I had no answer for her at all.

. . .

I woke deep in the night with Mary standing at the foot of my bed.

"What is it, sweetie?" I asked groggily. Had I remembered her night nappy? Did I have a sodden set of bedsheets to deal with?

"Can I sleep with you?"

I threw back the corner of my covers. "Of course, come on. Bad dreams again?"

In the gloom, I saw her shake her head. She said nothing, but cuddled up hard against me. Mary liked her own space usually. It was rare for her to ask to sleep anywhere but her own bed.

I kissed the top of her head and she put her arms around me so that her ribcage was up against my breasts. I could hear her heart ticking fast and hot, but still she said nothing.

Then I heard it for myself.

Bump. Slither. Bump bump. Scratch.

The same noise I'd heard the other night. Mary read the immediate tension in my body, and clung to me tighter. She was wordless with fear.

I held her tight and willed my heart to slow, my muscles to relax. "It's okay, darling. It's probably just an animal of some kind that's lost its way back to the sea."

The stiff shake of her head told me that my explanation was unconvincing. I was on the verge of descending into shrieking horror myself, but being a mother meant I didn't have that luxury. Instead, I held her and she held me as the sound circled the whole house, then finally, finally, stopped. We both listened into the dark for a long time afterwards, but it didn't come back.

Mary didn't loosen her grip on me, even after she fell asleep.

. . .

We both slept late into the morning. I opened my eyes first, and gazed down at Mary for a few moments. Her soft, warm cheek and her long, dark eyelashes. She breathed softly and evenly. I extricated myself very gently from her embrace, and she rolled over and settled back to sleep.

I rose and pulled on my woolly dressing gown. Daylight made the events of the night before seem unreal, as though I'd dreamed it all. Of course there was an explanation; I just couldn't think of it. I promised myself to ask the McBrides. Did seals, perhaps, come this far up on land? Were there local teenagers who liked to play pranks?

I went to the kitchen to switch on the kettle, put on a load of washing, got about my daily business. Mary rose, seeming untroubled by the night before, and watched television for half an hour while I made a proper shopping list. I think we both felt comforted by the mundanity of the chores, by the sounds of electrical appliances and cheerful children's cartoons.

The washing machine finished, and I pulled out the towels to hang outside on the line, as it had turned into a sunny morning.

It was only on the way back from the line that I saw the long streaks of damp something on the flagstones near the front door. I felt myself frown, even as my brain was cheerfully telling me it was nothing, nothing at all.

Two long damp streaks. I stopped and studied them for a moment. Then bent to look closer. A smell of fish and brine. I touched the substance and my fingers came away sticky. I stood again. The trails of it went all the way down the flagstones to the end of the house, then disappeared on the grass. I followed it down, then around the house to the other side. More gooey streaks.

And on Mary's window, two slimy handprints.

I forced my steps to be even and slow. Inside, Mary was watching Peppa Pig and eating an apple.

"Did you like sleeping with Mama last night?" I said, my cheery voice brittle.

She turned, remembered horror shadowing her face, and nodded solemnly.

"I think you should sleep with me every night. What do you think? That will keep us both warm."

She nodded again, and I went to the cupboard under the sink to find the window cleaner.

. . .

That day was the mildest day since our arrival. The wind stayed low so the sun was actually warm, and by the afternoon it was pleasant to sit outside on the long wooden bench by the front door. Mary was busy playing with the rocks that we'd collected on our last trip to the beach. She had her crayons out and I presumed she was drawing faces on them. I was reading a book and hoping the warm sunshine would defrost my bones; but they were cold with fear, not chilly air.

We'd been outside nearly an hour before I realised that Mary was working with her crayons and stones in a very focussed way. She'd choose one, then draw on it, then stand and walk around the outside of the house until she found the exact right place to put it down.

"What are you up to, Mary?" I asked.

She finished drawing on her latest stone and proudly held it up for me to see. In red crayon, she'd drawn something that looked like a tree with only three branches.

"Is it a tree?" I asked.

"It's a ruin."

"A ruin?"

"Mary showed me. This one is called 'a-kiss'."

I looked closely at the drawing and then it dawned. "Oh. You mean a rune?"

"Yes, a ruin. This ruin will keep us safe. Mary said so."

"You mean Mrs McBride?"

"She lets me call her Mary." And she was off again, placing the stones around the house.

Why on earth had Mrs McBride taught Mary about runes that magically kept houses safe? I knew there was a lot of Viking history in Orkney, so perhaps she'd told Mary a story about runes, and now here she was after a night of strange noises, safe-guarding our cottage.

Then she packed up her crayons and stopped stock still, looking at the ruined farmhouse.

"Mary? What is it?"

But she didn't answer. She just set off determinedly towards the farmhouse. No doubt to draw crayon runes on it as well.

"Hold on now, miss," I said, putting my book aside and chasing after her. "You can't draw on the house, it might belong to somebody."

Mary looked at me dubiously. "No roof," she said, and it was a fair point.

And I thought, wax crayons won't wash off in the rain: why not have some safety runes on the farmhouse? What harm could it do? It might make Mary feel safe.

"All right," I said. "I'll help you."

I don't know if it was madness, or if it was magic; all I know is that we didn't hear any strange noises for many, many weeks. And time made the chill fade and we forgot that we had ever been so frightened.

IV

Lachlan is still in the water, but the moon is gone and the clouds have shredded and dissolved. The sea is still but for the deep currents that lift and drop him bodily, like great lungs breathing while sleeping. Above him stars. Huge handfuls of stars. He'd forgotten how many stars there were in the sky. Large and small stars, bright and dull stars. He watches for a while, carried on the currents. Lift. Drop.

Near the horizon, the stars aren't so visible. A lurch of hope. Is dawn coming at last? It seems forever he has been out here in the sea at night. He decides he will swim towards the horizon, towards the dawn, in the hopes it will come faster.

Seaweed tickles his legs. A chill of primitive fear.

Because the seaweed isn't seaweed, he realises, as it circles his leg and tightens. He is yanked backwards, and another tendril curls around his waist and holds him ever tighter, until his breath is flat in his lungs. His struggles to get away are met with more tentacles, some fine and some thick, all with the velvet-jelly texture of the inside of fish skin. The water bubbles and breaks around him; something is pushing its way to the surface.

Lachlan freezes with fear, for surely this can only be the Stoor Wyrm of Orkney legend. A massive coal-black head breaks the water; a liquid black eye blinks at him.

Then two tendril-fine tentacles emerge from the water directly in front of him, creep their way up his chin and tickle his nostrils.

He tries to shake his head.

The tentacles worm into his nostrils. The pain is blinding.

But on the horizon, the sky grows light.

Lachlan finds a shiver of strength somewhere in the depths of his granite immobility. His left hand breaks free, he yanks the tentacles from his nose.

"The dawn comes!" he shouts at the sea monster. "The dawn comes!"

The pupil in the Stoor Wyrm's eye dilates, and the tentacles are suddenly withdrawn. It submerges, sending up a wave that chokes Lachlan momentarily. He can swim now, he can swim towards the shore where grey light is spreading.

She is waiting on the shore.

"I'll bide my time," she says to him, her lips unmoving but her rotted voice loud in his head.

He swims until he can stand, then trudges onto the stone-peppered sand. She hasn't moved, and he sees she is surrounded by a ring of white rocks with runes painted on them in red. "Hello, Irsa," he says, her name jumping like sprung metal into his head. But then the exhaustion overwhelms him and the big black is coming back. He collapses on the ground.

Voices, a long way outside him, say, "His tubing is all messed up. What happened?"

"Could he have pulled it out?"

But then nothing, slipping back into the abyss between over here and over there.

. . .

It was the first week of May, and I was feeling unwell. Nothing serious: just a dull pain when I swallowed and a warm, damp feeling behind my eyes. I walked Mary up to the McBrides' house and left her there, intending to go back to bed to doze and read for the day. But when I let myself back into the house, the phone was ringing. I immediately assumed it was Mr McBride, and Mary had disgraced herself somehow. But I was wrong. It was my mother.

"Jenny, it's me."

My heart ran with hot and cold chills. Because if Mum was calling me—rather than sending me emails or ignoring me all together—then Lachlan must be dead.

I sat down, hard, on the floor, my voice trapped in my throat.

"It's all right," Mum said, quickly. "He's still alive."

"Oh," I said and, curse me, I felt an awful nausea as relief was snatched away. Because even though I couldn't bear the thought of Lachlan dying, the thought of him being suspended in a vegetative state forever was unbearable too.

"But I think you should come home."

"Why?"

"He removed his feeding tube."

"That's not possible." Hope and fear, hope and fear, light and dark across my heart.

"Well, they left him alone for an hour and came back in and his feeding tube was out."

"So nobody saw him do it?"

"No."

"And has he . . . done anything since?"

A short silence. Then, "No." In her voice, I could hear that she regretted telling me this way, giving me hope.

"Then why do they think *he* did it?"

"Because nobody else did."

"Perhaps somebody removed the tube to change it and forgot. Or wouldn't admit it." But I could feel my body, bending back there. Back to the sunny warmth of my homeland and the stupid, pointless, impossible hope that somehow Lachlan would get better.

"You're too far away," Mum said. "You should be by his side. If he could hear your voice. Or Mary's voice . . ." She trailed off. We'd had this argument, so many times.

I thought of Mary. She was happy here. She loved the McBrides, she loved collecting stones on the beach and counting the stairs down to the main street, and she loved Hobnobs and English jelly babies. Returning home wouldn't be returning to sunny warmth and comfort. I would be returning to the emptied-out house, to the soup-scented hospital. No, I wasn't going back. Not on the puffed-up hope borne of an intern's mistake. I told myself, one more sign. If he exhibits just one more sign of coming to consciousness, I'll go back. But not this time.

Because in the month since I'd been here, I'd learned so much more about Lachlan than I'd ever known. Mr McBride had taken Mary and me on a Lachlan McGregor tour of the Orkneys. Trout-fishing in Loch Harray, collecting daffodils by the roadside, picking our way across the causeway at low tide to the Broch of

Birsay to look at the Viking ruins, picnicking between the standing stones of the neolithic Ring of Brodgar as the heather ripened to purple around us: all things that Lachlan loved to do in his youth. Both Mr McBride and I found we could say his name more readily now, without wincing, and Mary was entranced by these stories of "your daddy".

She started asking me questions about him. "Was Daddy a fireman?"

"No."

"Did Daddy have big muscles?"

"No, but he had long legs and could run very fast."

"Did Daddy like broccoli when he was a little boy?"

"I'm sure he did. Now eat yours."

"Did Daddy love another lady before you?"

"I don't really know. He never said."

Then one night, as I tucked her into my bed, she admitted to me that she had forgotten what colour daddy's eyes were.

Blue-grey. Like the sea.

. . .

Predictably, soon after I recovered from what turned out to be a virus, Mary came down with it as well, so a large portion of mild and sunny May passed with one of us coughing all night. The days grew very long and I surrendered to Mary being up until ten most nights, then sleeping until nine the next morning. Breakfast at ten meant lunch at two, and dinner sitting outside in horizontal evening sunshine. I rarely thought about the strange noises I'd heard, or Mary's dream of the mean lady and her fear of the ruined farmhouse. It seemed to have happened in a dim, liquid past, in the grip of jet lag and grim weather.

The soft sunny weather was so different to back home, and could shift in an instant to a chilling mist of rain. But I kept up with my walking on the days Mary went to the McBrides. I loved it. I didn't get tired. I could walk ten miles and barely get puffed. And so it was on the first Monday in June that I decided to walk to Loch Harray and back, and found myself outside the *Angler's Arms* hotel at precisely lunchtime. I'd already been to town that morning to buy presents for Mary's birthday on Wednesday— her first birthday without her father around—and a boozy lunch seemed like it might help massage the knots of grief that thought had tied inside me. A board out the front advertised a soup-and-sandwich special for five pounds, so I went in.

The soup was some rich and wicked concoction of broccoli, cream, and stilton, and the sandwiches were cheese and Branston Pickle. I could only finish half my food, but I enjoyed my two glasses of white wine and the temporary lazy lifting of my cares. I sat by the window, looking out at the blue loch, and listened to the lilting accents all around me as people drank and laughed and talked about their lives. I'd noticed Mary starting to pick up a Scots accent from the McBrides: rolling her r's and asking for "fesh fengerrs" for dinner, or saying "d'ya ken?" instead of her standard "do you know what?" It was sweet, but I wondered if it would last when we finally went home to Australia. At the end of the year, or when Lachlan died: whichever came first.

My afternoon bubble was burst. I went up to the bar to pay, and the landlord, a bearded man in his sixties, examined my credit card carefully.

"Och, you're Australian then?"

"Yes."

"My son and grandchildren live in Australia. In Sydney."

"I'm a little further north than that. Usually."

He laid down my credit card receipt to sign. "You know one of your most famous writers comes from Orkney?"

Of course he was talking about Lachlan, and I opened my mouth to say, "Yes, he's my husband," but I didn't. I wanted to know what people said about Lachlan when they weren't being careful.

"Is that right?"

"Lachlan McGregor, the children's writer. *The Sea Orphans.* I knew him as a lad."

"You did? What was he like?" I handed back his pen and receipt.

He leaned forward conspiratorially. "Weel, to be honest with ye, he was an odd wee boy."

"In what way?"

"There was tell of him walking with ghosts." Then his face broke into a grin. "If you believe in ghosts."

A slow chill grew in the base of my spine. "Walking with ghosts?"

"He had an accident. He should have died. But he lived, and thereafter folk around here used to say they saw him talking to his self. Or talking to a ghost."

I shook my head with a smile. "Yes. Well. Few people believe in ghosts, as you say."

"Old Evelyn Flett certainly did. She marched over there to his house—his foster parents still live on the island—and demanded they get him seen to by a priest. I don't suppose they ever did. Not seeing as Mary McBride herself was just as odd as Lachlan, what with her hocus pocus."

A million questions sprang on to my tongue then, but there wasn't a chance to ask any of them because a huge crash from the kitchen had him saying, "Excuse me," and hurrying off. Someone within the kitchen swore loudly about broken plates, and the patrons of the lounge chuckled softly and went back to their conversations.

Lachlan walking with ghosts. Mary McBride's hocus pocus.

The sun shone all the way home, as I turned these thoughts over and over.

. . .

So my defences were down when, approaching the cottage, I saw something I'd never seen before.

There was a point at the crook in the path where I was up high enough on a hillock to see directly up the inside line of the long, rock wall that separated our cottage from the ruined farmhouse next door. A few feet inside the overgrown grounds of the ruined farmhouse, perhaps thirty feet from our cottage on the other side of the fence, was a standing stone. One I'd never seen before.

This should have been nothing. This should have been unnoticed and unremarked. But I had a head full of ghosts and hocus pocus and white wine.

I stopped in my tracks and considered the stone from a distance. Then headed down the path and stopped to look over the wall, my hands resting lightly on top of the cool, hewn rock. The standing stone was about four feet high but the same shape as the towering monoliths at the Ring of Brodgar. That was unsurprising, as they, like this stone, had been brought up from the beach where the tide wore the stones into uniform shapes: wide at the top with sharp angles, and narrower at the bottom. I'd seen stones like these used as gateposts on farms.

Somewhere inside, I had a photograph I'd taken of Mary from the hillock, looking down towards the cottage. If I could find it, I would know for sure.

I hastened inside and booted up my laptop, where all my photographs resided. I scrolled back through the library to the date we'd first arrived, then slowly clicked forward, one photograph after another.

Here. Mary smiling for the camera, the long line of the wall visible behind her. The stone wasn't there.

So why was it there now?

My stomach itched. I slapped the laptop shut and went back outside, climbed through the crumbled part of the wall that separated my garden from the old farmhouse's. Past the old farmhouse—sideways glance to check our runes were still in place—and I approached that stone with a determined stride, even though my heart was ticking in my throat.

I crouched in front of it, examining the ground for footprints or drag marks. Perhaps somebody had put it here. But why here? And who? Nobody had lived here for decades.

Finally, I lifted my eyes to look at the stone itself. It wasn't smooth and dark like the ones on the beach, it was spotted with lichen and barnacles, and eaten by time. A rune, not unlike the ones Mary and I had drawn on the farmhouse, was etched into its face. I stretched out my fingers and brushed it, then withdrew them superstitiously. This hadn't been hauled up from the beach overnight. This was ancient. I was looking at something ancient.

All of the little chills and fears of the past months coalesced in that moment. Because, with a little shift in heat and atmosphere, I knew that the ancient thing was looking back at me.

. . .

Even though it seemed mad, I did what I had to do. On the way home from picking Mary up, I bought a can of white spray paint from the hardware store on Victoria Street. That evening, when Mary was finally asleep and the sky was a velvet blue that wasn't quite night, even though it was nearly ten, I gathered up my courage in both hands and went down there to that stone. I would much rather have done it in the light of day, when shadows and the sound of the sea were my only company; but I didn't want to be seen defacing what might be an ancient monument. I shook the can until it rattled, checked all around me, then I kneeled and spray-painted protection runes across both faces of the stone. In the silence that followed, as I was climbing to my feet, I thought I heard a harsh hissing noise coming from the stone.

I recoiled, fell on my behind, scrambled to my feet. Perhaps I was imagining it, and it was just the spray can drizzling, but I didn't want to be anywhere near that thing. I ran back to the cottage, and bolted the door behind me. Still, I could sense its malignant throb, right through the safety of the stone walls.

. . .

In the morning, Mary wanted to go down to the beach. Even though I didn't want to walk past the stone, I dared myself that I would. The morning was crisp and clear, not a morning for shadowy fears. The runes worked last time, I told myself, so they would work this time. But as the stone came into view, my spine prickled. I could see, even at this distance, that my runes had vanished.

Worse. The stone had moved. Ten feet closer to our cottage.

My whole body convulsed coldly. If I'd had any remaining doubts that my hysteria was creating these ideas, I released them. Mean ladies in dreams who lived in seaweed nests; Lachlan talking to ghosts and Mrs McBride practising magic; an ancient stone that grew overnight and moved when I wasn't looking: all of this was part of Lachlan's lost memory, I knew it. As he wasn't here to unlock that memory, I had two choices: to unlock it myself, or to go home.

I turned Mary around and told her we were going to take a different route to the beach from now on.

V

The mist comes all the way to the ground. It is pale and grainy, not quite white but not quite grey, either. The gritty sand beneath Lachlan's feet is murky grey, the same colour as the water. It is as though he stands inside a black-and-white photograph. Even his own hands, in front of his face, are robbed of their human flush by the mist.

The cold is damp in his chest. He cannot tell where the water ends and the beach begins, and when he turns around, he isn't sure which way he is facing. He is lost, and he is afraid, because he knows the water becomes deep immediately. One step in the wrong direction and he will be back in the sea that he has just struggled out of. A silence comes with the mist, and a smell of ozone and brine. He shivers with all of his ribs and guts. He needs to get off this beach and back to land, back to life, but the mist obscures everything. It drifts in front of his eyes so he cannot see where his feet stand. It creeps in his ears and makes him forget himself.

"Lachlan!" Her voice is strident, cutting through the mist so it swirls in the wake of her words.

It is Irsa. But who is Irsa? Why does he know her name?

"You promised me!" she shrieks.

Promised what? The answer is just *there* behind his eyes, but he cannot drag it into his brain.

A dark shape coalesces in the mist. She emerges, slowly, hideously. She is a thing of both flesh and seaweed, she is barnacled like an old rock and rotted like an old fish carcass.

"Look what you did to me," she hisses. "Look what you did to me."

"I don't remember."

"You loved me once."

He tries to feel that love, hoping it will open up the path to memory; but all he comes up with is an image of Jenny, the first time he'd seen her, her long dark hair falling over her face as she bent over her notebook in their shared philosophy tutorial. First week of university and there she was, the love of his life. But this monster in front of him? No. He doesn't love her. He has never loved her. He would remember love.

"I don't know you. I don't know what you're talking about."

"If I had your daughter here, would that help you remember?"

The paternal instinct within him hardens like iron cooling in a mould. "Don't you go near Mary."

"What can you do?" she laughs. "You can't even find your way out of the mist."

She withdraws. The ringing in his ears tells him the big black is approaching again, bearing down on him. He tries to fight it. He must find a way to the other side, to Jenny and Mary. But the big black weighs too much; it always weighs too much.

. . .

I barely slept, and was up the next morning early with my laptop open, searching through websites about runes. It wasn't clear which had been written by scholars and which by stoned wiccans, but they all seemed to agree: the rune that was inscribed on the stone before I'd defaced it meant destruction, disaster, the danger of elemental forces.

"Mama?"

I looked around to see Mary, awake far too early, watching me.

"Good morning." I moved so my shoulder blocked the screen, but she had seen it. She came to sit in my lap and pointed to the rune.

"How-claws," she said.

I glanced back at the screen. *Hagalaz.* "Did you read that?"

"Mary told me."

Mrs McBride and her runes again. "A-kiss" and "how-claws". How many others had Mary learned?

I flicked back to the screen that showed the whole futhark, the Old Norse runic alphabet, and said, "Did she tell you these ones, too?"

"Some," Mary said, pointing a few out and leaving a smudgy fingerprint on my screen. "And my ABCs."

I chuckled. So Mrs McBride had been teaching her the runes alongside the normal alphabet. All the things a little girl turning three tomorrow needed to know. But then my laughter died on my lips. Mrs McBride knew these runes: was she somehow involved in the strange stone moving closer to our cottage?

I knew it made no sense. Not only was she mortally sick, but she had no reason to frighten us, or put a magic spell on us, or whatever it was. But then how deep did her anger with Lachlan really go? Why were they so very keen for us to come here, when Lachlan could no longer accompany us? I remembered those glances they'd exchanged, the first time I'd met them. I remembered the creeping suspicion I felt, and I suddenly found I no longer trusted the McBrides much at all.

Mary had gone to the toy basket and pulled out her baby doll. I knew I should insist she go back to bed for another hour or so of sleep, but I was too busy looking up a name in the Orkney phone listings online. Evelyn Flett: the woman who had confronted the McBrides about Lachlan's ghost.

· · ·

It was tricky with Mary around, and I wasn't about to ask the McBrides to sit her, but Evelyn Flett was very accommodating once she knew who I was and what I wanted.

"I'll come to you," she said on the phone that morning, while Mary was distracted by the television.

"Mary sometimes doesn't go to sleep until ten," I said.

"Then I'll come at ten. Nobody else is going to tell you the truth about Mary McBride."

The day dragged on. I couldn't concentrate on anything. My mind whirred like an overwound machine. On just one occasion—when I was dusting the furniture—I forgot the dread for a few blissful moments. But then it was back: the stomach-loosening awfulness of my situation, caught in some supernatural witchery that I couldn't understand.

Mary, tired from being up so early or perhaps sensing my distress, threw endless tantrums all day. Her juice had too many "bits" in it; I wasn't playing baby dolls right; she didn't want *this* episode of Peppa Pig; she was not going to eat *that* sandwich and was even less likely to eat *that* dinner. Ordinarily, I would have stood my ground and made her sit in the naughty corner until she pulled herself together, but I had no energy for it. So instead, I let her open one of her birthday presents a day early. It was a set of pink and purple building bricks, and it kept her busy for all of twelve minutes until two of the bricks wouldn't fit together right and she flung them across the room.

She was out like a light in my bed just after eight.

Which gave me nearly two hours to wonder what I was going to ask Evelyn Flett, and if I'd even believe her answers. I cleaned up the dishes, folded laundry, tried to watch some television. But finally, I went to my bedroom and lay down on top of the covers, to watch Mary. She was very still, except for the rhythmic rise and fall of her ribs. I was overcome by an intense vulnerability borne of love and fear in equal measure. As though my skin had been whipped off. "I'm sorry, my love," I said quietly, in the dark. "I'm sorry." Sorry that her life wasn't the ideal I'd dreamed for her: growing up by the beach with two parents alive and well and there to keep her safe. I felt my own flimsiness acutely; my mortal lack of shielding power. I had two pale arms and I knew two runes; I couldn't even tell if the couple who had been babysitting her for months were actually a danger to her. "I'm sorry," I said again, tears hot on my face.

A soft knock at the front door told me Evelyn Flett had arrived. I wiped my tears away and straightened my clothes.

"Hello," I said, looking at the small, white-haired woman who stood in front of me in a cable-knit cardigan and tweed skirt. "Thanks so much for coming."

She nodded, twisted her lips in what might have been a smile, and came in. She surveyed the whole room before sitting down at the dining table. "The wee girl is asleep?"

"Yes, she went off early tonight. Can I make you a cup of tea?"

"Aye. That'd be grand." Her eyes kept travelling the room. "I haven't been in this room for a long time. Not since Kevin and Mary McBride lived here with young Lachlan."

"They let it out as a holiday cottage now," I explained. "Lachlan rented it for the year. Before his . . . accident."

None of the usual sympathy was forthcoming. She folded her thin, veiny hands together on the table and waited for her tea.

Finally, when I sat down with her, she said, "I took no pleasure in hearing of Lachlan's accident, but I must confess I didn't follow the news. Last I heard he was still in hospital."

"Yes, he's still in hospital."

"Then why are you here?"

"He isn't conscious and he scares Mary."

She nodded. "Weel, and now you're finding there's things around here will scare wee Mary more than her sick Daddy."

"Yes. Yes, exactly."

"Do you believe in mermaids, Jenny?"

I was taken aback. "I . . . no."

"Nor do I. But I do believe in ghosts."

The wind had picked up outside, and I half expected my lights to go out and that I'd have to bring out the candles to have this conversation. But no. Rattling panes, but lots of comforting electric light and fridge noise.

"Where do you want me to start?" she asked.

"Mary McBride. She's been babysitting my daughter—"

"She won't hurt her. But Mary McBride's always dabbled where she oughtn't. Everybody knows it but nobody will say it, because she's sick now and nobody wants to speak ill of the soon-dead.

Quite a few of the young lassies, back in the day, went to Mary McBride for love potions and baby charms. I even heard tell that a few people went to her to ask for revenge on their enemies."

"So she's like a village witch?"

Evelyn sniffed. "Makes her sound a little too interesting. I'm sure she'd like the term, though. But she stopped all that. After Lachlan left. She stopped it all. She loved that boy too hard, d'ya ken? Given he wasn't hers to love. When he went, her spirit dulled a little. Like tarnished silver."

I turned this over in my mind. Evelyn sipped her tea and fixed me in her gaze.

I ventured, "The landlord at the Angler's Arms said something about Lachlan and a ghost."

"Will you believe me if I tell you?"

"I'll try."

She stood and walked to the front window. "Out there," she said, "a lass drowned. I should say, her father drowned her. On purpose."

I recoiled at the idea. "That's awful," I said, coming to stand next to her.

"Yes, I suppose it was. But it happened a thousand years ago, and our sympathy thins out when that much time has passed." She kept her eyes on the window. "D'ya ken, everyone thinks history is remembered in books, but it's not. It's remembered in people and places. My granny told me when I was a peedie girl about Irsa the fair, just as her granny told her. You won't find her written about in any book, but her story is here just the same." Her voice became quiet. "Just the same."

My mind was reeling from trying to connect up all of these ideas, but I sensed I needed to let Evelyn take her time to get to the point. "All right, then," I said, "tell me about Irsa the fair."

She folded her arms and kept her gaze fixed on the window. "The story goes that she was the fifth child of a man named Einar Hlodvirsson, the brother-in-law of the ruling jarl. Einar had four sons, and then his beloved wife died giving birth to Irsa. Irsa grew up to be fair, so fair that there was rivalry over who would marry her. But she was also the very image of her dead mother, and it is said that her own father turned his eye to her.

"Now, nobody knows what made him do it. Nobody knows if he tried to force himself upon his own daughter and she refused; if

— 55 —

he was angry with her for causing his wife's death in the first place; or if he simply couldn't bear to look at her daily and feel such immoral feelings, but it is certain that he was seen rowing her out there and lowering her into the water—gently, if the stories hold true—then pushing down on her head till she went still."

A deep shiver moved up through my body, sending icy tentacles along my ribs.

Evelyn turned and smiled a tight smile at me. "The water out there is very cold, Jenny."

"I can imagine."

"I don't think you really can imagine how cold." She shook her head. "And speaking of cold, I've let my tea go cold. I don't suppose you'd make me another? A little less milk this time. You should get yourself a teapot, lassie. Real tea is made with leaves, not bags."

Feeling like a social failure, I made her another cup of tea and brought it to her. She sat on the couch and indicated I should sit next to her.

"Now there are many mixed-up old legends in these parts about drowning. If you live in a place where there's more water than land, then lore about drowning prevails. The Vikings—and don't forget the Orcadians a thousand years ago were Vikings—they used to believe that if you drowned, you'd become a thing in the water trying to drown others for company. Draugar, huldrefolk, mermaids, selkies. Fin folk, all of them. Finmen and finwives, living in their underwater villages." She paused, sipped her tea, then leaned in a little so I heard what she said next very clearly. "The finwives, well they needed a mortal husband if they wanted to stay beautiful. So they'd come up on land and tempt likely young men to come back under the water with them." She leaned back. "That's the legend. But as I said, I don't believe in fin folk. People drown, and those who die young often come back as ghosts. That's where the legends come from."

She fell silent for a long time, drinking her tea, her mouth turned down a little in disappointment with it. I realised that I didn't like her. I compared that to how I'd felt the first time I met Mrs McBride, and understood that perhaps I'd chosen to trust the wrong person.

"You think this woman became a ghost who haunted Lachlan?"

"He fell in the water just in the same place she drowned," she replied. "And he should have died. D'ya ken? They searched for him until the sun went down; and the McBrides accepted he was gone. I'll never forget Mary McBride's face: her heart was ripped in two, sure he was dead. But the next morning, he shows up at home, all fine. Wet through, but all fine. Says he cannae remember much, but he's hungry and wants some hot cocoa and jam toast."

I compared this with the version of the story Lachlan had told me. He fell in the water and then remembered nothing in the weeks that followed, and had distinct holes in his memory from that time until he came to Australia six years later. He'd always assumed it was from the accident. I remembered Mrs McBride telling me Lachlan had been in the water "a long time". Not all day and all night. She hadn't told me that.

"Now your Lachlan, he was always a strange lad. Off in his own world. But after that, he grew a reputation around here for wandering up and down the beach talking to himself. Later, long after he'd left and become famous, they all started speaking of his strangeness fondly. Saying, I always knew there was something special about him. But at the time, I wasn't the only person saying the McBrides needed to get him seen to. Mary McBride held her ground. Always stubborn as a goat, that woman. We were in school together, and she was stubborn and fond of the sound of her own voice even then."

I didn't answer. I didn't want to jump to defend Mrs McBride in case Evelyn Flett decided not to tell any more of her story. The heating had switched off, and the room was growing chilly. I curled my feet under me on the couch and wrapped my hands tighter around my warm mug.

"And so," she said, with a sigh and her eyes turned towards me, "we come to Lachlan's ghost.

"I was out walking my wee doggie—may God rest his merry soul—when I saw Lachlan sitting on a rock with a fair-haired girl of about eighteen. Lachlan would have been fourteen at the time, but already a strapping lad. Handsome and long-legged. Well, you'd know that. It was late afternoon, dusk. The sun was setting over Scapa Flow, a big orange ball. And I walked up towards them to say good evening and also because I was curious who this fair-haired girl was. Then she vanished. There one minute, the next . . . nothing. Lachlan kept talking as if nothing had changed. Talking to her. Not to himself, as everyone thought."

"Was that the only time you saw her?"

"Yes, it was. But it was enough. I hied it up here to see the McBrides and I said, 'You need to get that lad seen to. You need a priest or an exorcist or you need to get him out of Orkney'. He was the age for boarding school somewhere in Caithness or even down in Edinburgh. I don't know why they didn't send him but as I said, Mary McBride is a stubborn one and she loved him overwell." Here she raised a crooked finger in the air. "I might not be God's favourite sheep, Jenny McGregor, but I know when something's evil and I saw it that day."

My scalp prickled.

"It was Irsa's ghost, sure as anything. A lonely ghost biding her time before she took him with her. Under the sea. Forever." Here she nodded once, a full stop on the story. "So, there it is."

There was a time in my life when I wouldn't have believed a word of this story. When I would have dismissed Evelyn Flett as a mad old lady who'd had a hallucination and couldn't admit it. But now wasn't that time. I believed every word.

"Have you seen her, then?" she asked me. "His ghost? Has she come back looking for him?"

"I . . . I don't know." The mean lady. Not a fair-haired beauty. "There's a stone with a rune on it that wasn't there when we arrived, and a seaweed nest in the farmhouse, and there were noises . . ." I trailed off. My own desperate voice made me sad and frightened all at once.

Evelyn Flett's jaw tightened. "Go home, lassie. You don't belong here. You belong with your husband, and if you should be so blessed as to see him recover, you tell him never to come back here. Never. For as much as these islands are a beautiful, cold treasure in the sea for most of us, for Lachlan McGregor they will always be haunted; and you've got a wee bairn to protect."

She was right. I had heard enough now. Mary and I needed to be far, far away from this place. "Yes," I said. "Yes, I'll call the airline in the morning." The idea of doing such a simple thing gave me immense relief. The horror grew mild: it was nearly over.

· · ·

When I came to bed, Mary was sleeping right in the middle, in the starfish pose. I gently nudged her out of the way, then lay for an age unable to sleep. I dozed and drifted, and Mary's little limbs kept ending up in my face or ribs. Finally, longing for sleep, I went down the hall to Mary's bed, which she hadn't slept in for months. The sleepy buzz sank heavy through my limbs, and I drifted off gratefully.

Not much later, I felt a cold in the room. I woke, pulled the blanket over me tighter then realised it ought not be that cold. I sat up. I could hear the sea.

That meant a window must be open. Or a door.

Galvanised, I shot out of bed and into the hallway. The front door of the house was wide open. I turned, ran to my bedroom. Mary was gone.

On bare feet that bruised themselves on the cold stony ground, I ran into the driveway, my heart exploding out of my chest. But there she was, standing a hundred feet away in her pink nightie, looking out to sea.

"Mary!" I called, as I ran towards her.

She didn't turn. As though she hadn't heard me at all. The light unsettled me, the half-dreaming light before dawn. My eyes went to the place where I had last seen the stone. It wasn't there. But I did see two pale, gnarled hands, wreathed in seaweed, creeping over the rock wall. I ran for Mary, scooped her up against me without looking at those hideous hands, and bolted for the house. Sobbing.

We were inside with all the lights on before Mary woke in my arms, looked at me strangely. "What's wrong, Mama? You crying. Bad dream?" She reached up to stroke my hair, the way I stroked hers if she had a bad dream.

"Yes, yes, my love," I said. "But it's nearly over."

. . .

Of course I didn't sleep after that. I bolted the door and hung the key up high so if Mary went sleepwalking again she couldn't open it. I locked down all the windows, then got up and checked them all again. Then I lay with my arms locked around Mary until the weak sun came up and I no longer had to try to sleep.

I could see out the front window of the cottage that the stone now stood on my side of the fence. Rage bubbled up inside me. I flung the door open and strode down there in my slippers. "Leave us the fuck alone!" I screamed at it. I tried to push it over with my foot, but only ended up slipping on the dewy grass.

Today. We were leaving today. I climbed to my feet and stalked back to the house. I had the ferry tickets booked before seven, and two suitcases packed before seven-thirty, and all the packing crates out of the storage shed by eight, when Mary padded out of the bedroom with a huge smile on her face.

I was distracted. I said, "Good morning," but went on sorting what to pack and what to ship.

"Mama?" she said, still smiling.

The penny dropped. It was her birthday. Today was Mary's birthday.

"Oh, happy birthday, darling," I said, pouring all the sweetness into my voice that should have been there. "Big girl today!"

"Big girl," she said.

I went to the cupboard over the fridge where I'd hidden her presents, and she ripped into them with unabashed vigour. Then we ate breakfast together while she played with them, and I tried to think how I was going to tell her that we needed to go home today.

I decided on casual and non-threatening. "We might go back on the big boat today, Mary. What do you think? We might go home to Australia now. Back to the beach."

She frowned. "Not today. I have a party."

I nearly swore. I'd forgotten the party that the McBrides had insisted on—just the four of us—at their place this afternoon at three. Right when the last ferry was due to leave.

"Of course! The party. Well, maybe we will have to miss the party."

Her face fell. I took a puncture wound to the heart. Her first birthday without her father, and I was going to deny her a party with what were effectively her grandparents.

Then it all fell into place. We would go to the party this afternoon, and we would just stay there at the McBrides. They'd have us, of course, when I explained what had been happening. Mrs McBride especially. She probably knew just what to do to keep us safe.

"You know," I said, "missing the party is a silly idea. We'll go on the boat tomorrow instead. But that means we have to pack everything up today. Will you help?"

She nodded, and made a show of putting her new toys into a suitcase. Five minutes later she pulled them back out to play with them. I kept my head down and kept working. My body was exhausted, my mind couldn't think in straight lines. But we were on our way home and that was all that mattered.

. . .

I heard the horn of the *Hamnavoe* ferry, over the seagulls and oyster-catchers, as we walked up towards the McBrides' street. It was leaving without us, but it would be back and tomorrow morning we would be on it, on our way back to mainland Scotland, and from there to home. I felt the fearful pull in my heart, knowing it was moving out of the harbour and away, stranding us here, and I regretted very much my decision to stay one more night. But I took comfort knowing that Mrs McBride had more understanding of the situation than she let on, and would be able to protect us.

I held Mary up so she could press the doorbell and we waited. I'd tried twice during the day to phone the McBrides to organise our staying with them, but nobody had answered. I'd presumed Mr McBride was out buying cake and Mrs McBride was resting up in advance of the party, and I didn't want to disturb her.

We waited, and time drew out, and I knew in my heart they weren't there. But Mary insisted we ring again, and so we did. And waited a very long time.

Mary turned her enormous eyes up to me. "Why would they miss my party?"

"I don't know," I replied. Fear and lack of sleep had made me jumpy, crazy. "I don't know."

She pointed to her little backpack, which had her pyjamas in it. "No sleepover?"

"I don't know," I said again, and now I was crying because I didn't know where they were or what to do or who to trust.

"Let's wait," Mary said, still not giving up on the idea of a party. She sat on the cold stone step and I let her sit there while I checked my watch and paced.

"I go look in the garden," Mary said, climbing to her sturdy legs and making her way around the side of the house.

She was gone a few minutes. It made me sad to think of her checking behind every hedge, wondering where her friends were.

Then she re-emerged with an upside-down mouth, and I bent to give her a cuddle.

"I'm sorry, darling. Maybe they forgot."

"I need to go wee."

We had to go back to the cottage. Dread walked my spine.

It was a misty afternoon. I tried ringing the hotels, but it was midsummer and everything was full. The stone hadn't moved since the morning, but I kept checking on it obsessively, over and over, while Mary sat at the table and drew pictures with her new drawing set. I wanted to collapse in a screaming heap, but Mary was only three and she had needs. I couldn't fall apart. I cooked dinner, I watched television with her, I tried to hide that I was frightened out of my mind. And I put her to bed at nine. She insisted on wearing her backpack, in case the McBrides called and the sleepover was still on. I let her. It was easier than arguing.

Then I locked all the doors and windows. I moved furniture against the door. I took one of Mary's crayons and I drew protection runes in the windows. I phoned the McBrides again and got no answer. I pulled an armchair into the threshold of the bedroom door and sat in it, rigid and alert, watching Mary sleep. Midnight. In nine hours we would be on the ferry. All I had to do was stay awake.

· · ·

Dreams have a grey mood and this one was no different. Jenny was leaving the cottage, but it was twilight and all the stars were winking into life and a cold wind licked her cheek. On the other side of the fence was the ruined farmhouse, and this was where she was moving to in her dream. Inside, all the furniture from their beach house was arranged just as it was at home. But the roof was open and rain had fallen, so that it was all spotted with mould and slimy with algae. She had so much work to do to clean this off, and it was too dark to see properly. Such an ache of sadness hung on her heart. These things would never be the same again. They were ruined. All her things were ruined.

· · ·

I woke with a start. Daylight.

The bed was empty. The bedroom window was open. One of the packing crates had been pushed up to the hook above the door to fetch the key down. Mary must have been standing right beside me while I slept. Slept when I was supposed to be watching her.

I ran to the door, hefted aside the chair and coffee table that had been blocking it, and emerged into the bright day.

"Mary!" I screamed, my voice tearing at my throat. "Mary!"

She was nowhere to be seen. And neither was the stone.

VI

I was raw, body and mind. I felt Mary's absence with every aching pore in my skin. They'd sent a lovely police officer who held my hand and tried to get sense out of me. Her patience, on reflection, was astonishing, considering how many times I said, "I don't know what's happening. I don't know if it's ghosts or fin folk or witchcraft or if I'm going crazy. I just know she's gone." She took notes with her free hand while her offsider examined the open window, the perimeter of the cottage, the track down to the water.

"Mrs MacGregor," the police officer said, "the most likely scenario is the simplest one. Mary has climbed out the window to go somewhere. Where would she go?"

"I don't know. There was a stone . . . it's gone now . . ."

"Did she have anything with her?"

I shook my head, but then remembered. "Her backpack. She wore it to bed. She was still hoping we'd sleep over with friends."

She scribbled this all down. "And have you called those friends?"

"Yes, I called them before I called you. But they aren't there. I don't know where they are. I don't know what's going on. I just want my baby back." Hot tears washed my face. There was no stopping them.

"What are your friends' names?"

"The McBrides. Kevin and Mary."

She stopped writing, gave me a sharp look, then her partner came in with a soft knock and an "excuse me". They conferred near the door for a few moments. I could hear them. They were talking about a water search. They thought my baby might have gone in the water, in the cold cold water, and my face fell apart with sobs at the thought of it.

The soft police officer came forward and took my hand again. "It's important you stay here, Jenny. Don't go anywhere. The most likely scenario is she will come back here. Don't give up hope."

"You're going to look for her in the water," I sobbed. "What if she's dead? What if I've lost her as well as Lachlan?"

"I know this is very hard. But you must stay here, so if she comes home there is somebody here for her. Do you understand?"

I nodded.

"There's another thing," she said gently. "I think you ought to know, Mary McBride died yesterday afternoon in a hospital in Kirkwall."

"She's dead?" *Two Marys. Please, please, don't let their fates be linked somehow.*

"I'm sorry. But it tells you why there's been nobody there. If Mary went there, she wouldn't have found any company, and she might have wandered off. We'll get some officers to search in that area, and we'll let the local community know." She squeezed my hand. "Keep hoping, Jenny. She's a wee girl who probably got a mad idea in her head."

"Evelyn Flett talked about fin folk who want to drown the living."

She smiled. "Evelyn Flett is quite, quite mad."

"But the stone—"

"The most likely is the most simple," she said again. "Now stay put, and we'll call you the minute we know anything."

I tried to take comfort in her words, but there was no comfort. I was desolate; meaning was breaking down completely. My baby was gone, something dark and supernatural was involved, and the one person I'd thought might be able to help was dead. I thought an hour had passed, but it was only five minutes. I thought five minutes had passed and found it was two hours. Life had lost all its neatness, its linearity. I was treading water in a swamp.

A knock at the door made me jump. Fear and hope. I threw it open to find Kevin McBride on the other side.

"Mr McBride?"

"I heard about your Mary."

"I heard about *your* Mary."

We fell into each other's arms, and we both sobbed. His woolly pullover was damp and smelled musty. I cried all over it. His cold, age-worn fingers gripped the back of my neck under my hair. Finally, we stood apart.

"Mr McBride, this may sound crazy, but I think Mary has been taken by a finwife, a ghost who once haunted Lachlan. Do you know anything?" I asked, "Anything at all that might tell me where Mary is?"

His pupils dilated, but then his shoulders sagged. "Aye," he said. "But I don't know if it will help you find her. Sit down."

We sat on the couch. My knees were trembling.

"When Lachlan was a lad, he was in love. The way only teenagers can be in love. But Lachlan was in love with a ghost."

"Irsa," I said. "Irsa the fair."

"We never knew her name. We never knew what he was doing. He was different after the accident. Distant, off in another world half the time. We didn't know he was . . . Evelyn Flett, she was the one who alerted us. She said she'd seen him with a ghost, down by the sea. Mary was on to it in a second. Finwives, they only want one thing from a mortal man. To marry them. If she doesn't marry him within seven years of falling in love, she turns into a hag. And to marry him, she would have taken him under the sea and he would have drowned.

"We told him all this. We warned him and we forbade him from seeing her, and he said he saw sense, and we had no reason to believe any different. Life went on. We didn't know that he was still seeing her."

"Why didn't she just take him under? If she had all that time?"

"He wasn't much more than a boy, remember. Maybe she was waiting for him to become a man. In any case, we found him out. My Mary, she knows things." He stopped, taking a deep shuddering breath. "She *knew* things. She followed the way of the seidhr: Viking magic. She suspected Lachlan was up to something, and she followed him and caught him out, but she never told him. We made a decision to handle things . . . differently."

"That night, when he came home, she asked him to kneel in front of her. He was curious, but we all loved each other well, so he did as she asked. I remember it so clearly, though I was stood in the kitchen door watching and feeling that little tickle of fear I used to feel when Mary got going with her craft. She put a hand either side of his head and she said a stream of words—words I didn't know—and Lachlan froze there on the floor in a kneeling pose. It went on and on, for nearly an hour.

"When he stood up, he had forgotten his ghostly lover. Mary later told me it wasn't too hard. He had so many holes in his memory from the night he nearly drowned—the night he must have met her—that Mary just connected the holes up into a trench. His love for the finwife was down there in the depths. What he was left with, though, was a terrible fear. A fear of what he'd forgotten, of something supernatural that he felt was hung about him. The next morning, he was gone. We didn't hear from him for twenty years."

"So that's why you weren't angry at him for disappearing."

"No. We'd made it happen. And it was for his own good."

How I longed to tell all this to Lachlan. But I couldn't. And nor could I imagine myself passing this on one day to my Mary. I was already certain she was dead, taken by the finwife—now a hag—perhaps in place of Lachlan.

"When Lachlan contacted us and said he wanted to come back, my Mary decided she would tell him everything. She thought that, now he had a wife and a child, he'd be safe. She thought that the finwife would have long ago forgotten him. It was such a burden on her heart, what she'd done to him, even though she did it to help him. To take away somebody's memories, to deny them their love . . ."

"She saved his life," I said. "Without her action, I would never have met him. We would never have had Mary." I would have been alone, without my two navigational stars, just as I was that very instant. I fell silent, hushed by the edgeless cold of a universe without them.

He leaned forward, touched the back of my hand with his knuckles. "The very first day your Mary came to us alone, we knew the finwife was about."

"The mean lady," I said.

"Yes, she talked about her. So my Mary prepared her."

"Prepared her? You should have warned me! Teaching a toddler to paint some runes on rocks is not preparing anyone."

"Now, if we'd told you would you have believed us, Jenny MacGregor? Or would you have thought us mad and not let us near Mary, and left her completely exposed?"

I shrugged, grudgingly.

"I need to tell you, our Marys spent a long time together in the garden, painting runes on rocks. The wee round rocks you see here on the beach. Dozens of them, and in each one, my Mary put a spell."

"A spell?"

"Spells that should banish the finwife from this world forever."

Hope lit in my heart. "Did you bring them?"

He shook his head. "They've disappeared from the garden. I checked before I came here."

I slumped forward, sobbing on my knees. She was gone. There was nothing I could do. Hopeless, helpless despair opened up like a black hole in front of me. I wanted to die. I would rather be dead than go through what I imagined would come next. The police finding her little body in the freezing water— *I don't think you really can imagine how cold*—or waiting for hours that turned into days and weeks and months and years, and never knowing where she was. My precious child in her pink rabbit pyjamas with only a thin pair of socks and her little red backpack.

Her backpack. I sat bolt upright.

"She has them!" I said. "Yesterday, when we went to your place for the party, Mary insisted on going round to the garden. Then she wouldn't let go of the backpack. She even slept with it."

The corner of his mouth twitched in a half-smile. "She has them?"

"I'm sure of it."

"Then Mrs McBride's craft may save wee Mary yet."

I leapt from the couch and started pacing. "This is unbearable," I said. "I can do nothing but wait and hope."

"Then I'll wait and hope with you," he said.

· · ·

"Daddy. Daddy, you have to wake up."

Lachlan stirs. His face is crushed into sand and stones. He spits grit out.

"Daddy. Daddy, please. Please, Daddy. I'm cold."

Electricity to his heart. He pushes himself up and looks wildly about the grey beach. The mist is thin, and he sees his daughter a hundred feet away, sitting hunched at the water's edge.

"Mary!" he gasps. He stumbles trying to stand, then he is on his feet, lurching towards her. He sees now that she is tied up in seaweed, her hands bound to her ankles. The primitive fury it arouses causes him to stumble again.

"Hurry, Daddy!" she calls. "The mean lady is coming back!"

His legs barely work. His blood barely works. He throws himself at her, skidding to the ground and ripping at her seaweed bonds. But then a crushing foot comes down on his wrist and another kicks his face sideways. Blinding, addling pain. He rolls over and Irsa is standing above him. Mary whimpers and inches away.

"Let her go!" Lachlan cries, undone by Mary's cries and the happy pink rabbits on her pyjamas.

"Remember me and I will let her go!"

"I remember nothing. I don't know who you are."

She throws him on his back and kneels across him, knees on the insides of his elbows. The rancid fish-like stench of her body makes him gag, and she leans her face close to his. "You forgot me so quickly," she says. "It was as though we had never loved. You didn't even try to come back to me. You left me behind and you were in love with another before my tears had even dried. And look what happened to me. Look!"

But Lachlan has his face turned away. He cannot bear to look. Some of her veins and teeth are on the outside. She is a nightmare made flesh.

"Look at me!" she spits. "Look at what you did to me!"

Then Mary's little voice. "Look at her, Daddy."

So he turns his eyes up, and he tries to make sense of the monstrous chaos that is her face. His gaze travels up past her neck—which pulses sickly like the gills of a fish hauled on to land—to her twisted, tooth-pierced eel lips and the gaping nostrils where her nose should be. And finally, to her eyes.

Finally. Her eyes.

It is a spark that ignites into a raging bonfire. He remembers her now. Her white skin and fair hair, her grey eyes and the pretty tilt of her mouth. He remembers the long hours they spent telling their hearts and minds to each other. He a boy, she a ghost, but lovers nonetheless. "Irsa," he says.

"You remember," she sighs, her weight lifting as she moves off him and sits on the sand. She bends her head to her knees and cries. "You remember."

"I do," he says, softly, wordless pity in his heart. "I loved you. You're right. I loved you."

She looks up, her monster's face drooping with sadness. "Then why did you leave me?"

"I forgot you somehow."

"It is awful to be forgotten."

"I'm sorry."

She stands, extends her hand. "Come with me now."

Suspicion prickles. "Where to?"

"Fulfill your promise. To be my husband."

Lachlan reels. "I already have a wife."

"She doesn't matter. Now you have remembered that you love me—"

"*Loved* you," he says.

Her whole body hardens. "Then if you won't come, I'll take the child."

He tries to stand but her foot is on his chest, and he has no strength left in his body. She weighs as much as Scapa Flow.

He knows he is defeated. It is time to go into the big black, so that Mary may go free and live her life. He opens his mouth to say he will go, but before he can, a little girl's voice pipes up out of the mist.

"Leave my daddy alone!"

Lachlan stretches his neck around to see Mary, just ten feet away, free of her bonds—he must have loosened them enough for her to work herself free—rummaging in her backpack. She pulls out a handful of stones and seems to be sorting them somehow.

"Mary, it's all right. You'll be safe. You'll go back to Mummy. I love you, darling. I've always loved you."

Irsa's foot grinds harder into his chest, her jealousy inflamed by this easy declaration of love. She leans over him. "You've made the right decision."

Smack. One of the rocks hits Irsa in the face. She puts her hand to her cheek defensively when another comes hurtling towards her and hits her in the forehead. She lifts her foot off Lachlan and turns her attention to Mary.

Mary pelts another rock at her, a determined expression on her brow. And as she does, Lachlan hears a voice far away on the wind. A familiar voice, though he can't place it, speaking an ancient, arcane language.

Irsa puts her hands over her ears. The rocks keep coming. Lachlan rolls away, struggles to his feet and comes crashing down next to Mary.

"You in the way, Daddy," she says, pushing him off her backpack. More rocks, a dozen of them. And as they rain down on Irsa and the strange voice floats down through the mist, Irsa bends lower and lower to the ground until she is crouching with her hands over her head.

That's when Lachlan recognises the voice. It is Mary McBride, his foster mother.

Little Mary has the last two now, and she stands and dares to move a little closer, carefully bouncing them off Irsa's spine. They lay all around her now, round stones with strange letters on them. And Irsa is perfectly still. Perfectly grey. Smoothing over, hardening, turning into a stone herself.

The mist begins to shred and roll. He can hear the big black returning.

Mary reaches for him, puts a hand on either side of his face, and says, "Come back, Daddy. Mummy is too sad."

"I'll try."

She reaches in her pocket. She has one more stone. She hands it to him. "Mrs McBride says get better."

The big black is upon him, crushing out all the light.

Nearly all the light.

· · ·

When the dark came in, I was out of my mind. A whole day she had been gone. Mr McBride, mindless with his own grief and pain, cried with me. I felt the scars forming on my soul already.

The phone rang shortly after ten. I leapt upon it.

"Hello?"

"Jenny, it's Mum."

A guilty pulse as I realised I hadn't contacted her about Mary's disappearance. I hadn't wanted her to say that she'd told me never to come here in the first place. "Mum, I'm sorry but I have to keep off the line. I—"

"He's awake."

A moment, unfurling. "What?" I gasped.

"Lachlan is awake. He's sitting up and asking for you and Mary."

I dropped the phone on the ground. Mr McBride, concerned, came to me, but I pushed him out of the way, hands in my hair, howling. Lachlan was awake. Mary had disappeared. Some cruel god had decided I couldn't have them both at once. I was mad with lack of sleep, with grief and fear. I ran for the door, intending . . . I don't know what. To run into the fields and throw myself on the ground and sob and laugh and scream and throw myself on the mercy of the gods or the moon and stars.

I flung open the door, and there she was, in her pink rabbit pyjamas, lying on the doortstep, fast asleep.

"Mary?"

She roused, looked up at me. "Mummy?"

I reached down and scooped her into my arms, choking on my tears. I didn't know what to say to her to express my immense relief and love and gratitude, but found myself saying, "Daddy's awake."

"I know," she said.

VII

Eighteen months later

The warm balmy days of summer have started. I've opened up the sliding doors to the deck and the sea-laden breeze washes through and stirs the curtains and I feel glad to be alive. Mary is quietly arranging her dolls in her doll house, Lachlan is downstairs in his study answering emails, and I am sitting on my lounge finishing reading Lachlan's latest book, his first novel for adults. It's called *The Fisherboy*, like that stapled-together book that I left with Mr McBride when we rushed away from Orkney to be reunited with my husband's living body.

The Fisherboy is a historical story about a young man, in the eleventh century, who falls in love with a nobleman's daughter named Irsa. Irsa, however, is caught up in a dangerous relationship with her father, tinged with incestuous desire. Irsa, as you've probably guessed, is drowned by her father and the fisherboy mourns her forever after.

I have told Lachlan every day how much I am enjoying his story, but I am lying. For every mention of this Irsa—of her beauty, her sweet laugh, her fire and intellect and vulnerability—sends a pang of jealousy through my heart. Never has a narrator been so in love with a character. How he can write like this about a woman who would have torn our family apart is beyond my understanding.

We don't talk about it. We hardly ever mention our year of ancient ghosts, mostly for Mary's sake. Mary seems to have largely forgotten: she's far more excited about the impending arrival of what she's sure is a little sister in my ever-expanding tummy. Don't misunderstand me: the love between Lachlan and me isn't dimmed. But I know now that it isn't as special as I'd once thought.

I remembered Mary's question: *did Daddy love another lady before you?* No doubt she'd overheard the McBrides say something. The answer was, of course, that yes he did. He loved another, and that love had burned within him—even if he hadn't known it consciously—for twenty years.

It was behind him now. But it would always be there.

I finish the last line of his book. This story has made reviewers reach for their handkerchiefs and their superlatives in equal measure. I am left cold. I close it, and I turn my eyes out to sea.

Did Daddy love another lady before you?

"You're finished?"

I look around. Lachlan stands, hopeful, behind me.

"Yes."

"You liked it?"

"I loved it." I reach for him, pull him down beside me. "I love you."

"And I love you. Isn't it a beautiful day?"

"It's almost perfect," I say. And I mean every word.

THE CROWN OF ROWAN

"I was cruellest to him whom I loved the most."
— *Laxdaela's Saga*

I

Blotmonath

There are seven kings in Thyrsland. My father is one of them, and my husband is another. In my belly, perhaps, I carry a third.

It is blood month, and outside my bower window I hear fear-moaning cattle on their way to slaughter. Every night this week, I have smelled blood on the wind: faint but unmistakable, worming under the shutters. And I've turned my face to my pillow and held tight to avoid retching.

My sister's hands are cool, pressed against my belly, sliding down hard towards the bone. Ash hasn't seen me naked since we were children, when we shared the same bath before midsummer feasts. Her face is a mask of concentration: her eyebrows are drawn together, which makes her look cross. And yet Ash is never cross. She is as bonny as the sun.

She lifts off her hands and smiles, smooths my skirts down again. "You are definitely with child," she says, leaning in to hug me, her long dark hair becoming caught in my mouth. "Darling Rose, I'm so pleased for you."

Even though I was expecting this answer, the world swings away from me a moment and I see myself from afar. Small and soft, a snail without a shell. Then I am back, and it is hotly true: a child grows within me, somebody who will one day think and speak and rule over Netelchester when my husband, Wengest, is gone.

But Wengest is not the child's father.

Ash has turned away. The afternoon light through the narrow window catches the side of her face and she looks so very young. Too young to be away from home and studying; but she has gathered my fate, just as I gathered my older sister's. Bluebell, as the first daughter, should have been married off to Wengest, to weave peace between Netelchester and Ælmesse. But she flatly refused; she threatened to cut out her guts if pressed. Father's eyes could tell him that no husband would lament not having her. She is six feet tall, all long limbs and jutting bones. Her nose was smashed sideways in battle practice when she was eighteen, and each arm wears a sleeve of scars and tattoos. Which is to say, she is formed for war, and not for love.

So I was sent to Wengest, and Ash was sent to the Study Halls of Thriddastowe. She is learning to be a counsellor of the Common Faith. Part of her role is to tend to women in childbirth.

"When will the babe come?" I ask her, pulling myself up into a sitting position with my arms around my knees.

"If you last bled in weed-month, then the babe will come in milk-month." She laughed. "It won't just be the cows making milk, then."

I think about my breasts, the faint blue veins that appeared on them eight weeks ago. I knew then, of course. I had counted back the days. Wengest was away, meeting with the king of Lyteldyke, who has lately converted to the Trimartyr faith. He had been away a month and four days. He hadn't been in my bed for nearly a fortnight before that.

I know that he has not subsequently noticed those tell-tale lines on my breasts. He prefers to couple in the dark, believing somehow that passion reduces us, strips us of our dignity. But Heath had noticed them. Out in the fields far from my husband's hall: sunlight white and warm, caught under the ears of wheat as they shook in the breeze, dazzling in Heath's pale gold hair, bathing my bare white skin . . . He saw the veins, he traced them with his fingers, but he said nothing. I said nothing. The memory comes upon me fresh: my belly grows giddy, my heart pinches. Many say that love is a blessing; but to love a man one cannot have is surely a curse.

"You will be here for milk-month?" I ask Ash, aware now of my body's vulnerability, of what childbirth can do to women. Our mother died delivering twins. "You will deliver the child?"

"I will ask my elders at the study hall for permission to come."

"You are a king's daughter," I say, "you can surely do as you please."

"My loyalty as a counsellor is not to any king. It is to the great mother, to the horse god. In their eyes, no family is more important than another." She reads the anxiety on my brow and she shifts to sit on the bed next to me. "I will do my very best, Rosie. But even if I can't make it, you aren't to worry. You will be perfectly well, and your baby will too. She'll be bonny and strong, you'll see."

"*She?* You think it is a girl?"

Ash smiles, but I see her eyes flicker like a person about to tell a lie. I know that expression; I wear it often. "There is no way to tell, no windows to the womb." She shakes her head gently. "With four sisters, it's hard to imagine a baby boy. Forgive me. It might as well be a son as daughter."

My daughter. I have never been fond of children, but this creature embedded in my body is not just any child. It is *my* child. And his.

"Wengest will be pleased," Ash continues. "Will you tell him soon?"

I cannot answer. I am thinking, instead, of telling Heath what he surely already knows.

. . .

The wide Wuldorea divides my husband's kingdom from my father's. The river snakes through Thyrsland from its mouth on the south-east coast, up towards the great lakes of western Netelchester, on the border with tiny Tweoning, a little kingdom that has seen much war. The Wuldorea is brown today, engorged with a week of rain. Heath owns five hides of land bordered by her banks; five miles downstream from Wengest's hall and the rest of the town. When I stand at the western edge of his land, I can see Ælmesse, the kingdom of my birth. On a clear day, I sometimes imagine I can see the steep hill upon which my father's hall is built, the gleaming ruins of the giants' halls at Blicstowe— my home town, the most beautiful place on earth—though I know it is an illusion.

Heath's fields are dark and smell of earth and rain. I make my way up the line of elms between fields to the thatched round-house where Heath lives. A crow sits on bare branches above me, watching. I don't like to be watched; frost creeps over my skin. The crow clicks its beak against the branch, spreads its wings, and takes off into the white sky. Its wake shivers across the branch.

Inside Heath is sitting by the fire. Smoke catches in my throat and stings my eyes. The hewn carcasse of a cow is hung from the rafters to smoke for the winter. The shutters are closed against the cold, so the room is dark as it will be until the sun comes back in summerfull-month. The weak light from the open door shows me Heath's back and shoulders, his long gold hair. Then I close the door and only firelight illuminates us. He turns and smiles at my arrival, shifts over on the bench to make room for me. I slide into place and he catches me in his gaze.

Heath does not wear a beard, as most men in Thyrsland do. But it isn't true that he can't grow one. How many times have I heard that insult whispered? Even Wengest has said it to me. "My nephew must not be fully a man; twenty-five summers old, and still no beard."

I know Heath's secret. He shaves it from his face with a warm knife every morning, because when it grows it is bright coppery red. Heath is part Ærfolc; he is the half-breed bastard son of Wengest's wayward sister. The Ærfolc, who were driven deep into the north-west and across the sea a hundred years ago, are regarded by the people of Thyrsland with suspicion, hostility. Some of us, in the south of Lyteldyke, still use them as slaves. Their coppery hair and pale green eyes mark them. Heath, beardless, could barely be recognised as Ærfolc except if one is looking for the signs: threads of copper in his golden hair that are only visible in bright sunlight; an undercurrent of sea-green in his eyes.

"I wasn't expecting to see you today," he says, bringing rough fingers to my chin, running his thumb gently over my lower lip to coax a smile.

"It's so hot in here," I complain, unpinning and shrugging out of my cloak. It falls in a puddle behind me. Heath's home is small. The only furniture is this bench and a straw mattress. We have made love many times upon that mattress; the straw ticking scratching our bare skins softly through the thick blankets. My husband's hall is far grander than Heath's home; my father's is a hundred times the size. But I have known unutterable happiness in this warm room.

He sits and waits for me to say what I must say. Ever-patient Heath. The fire cracks and pops, the smoke catches my throat. Finally, I say, "I am with child. It is certainly yours."

His face softens; I have no idea what he is thinking. "What have you told Wengest?"

"Nothing."

"And you intend to keep the child?" he says, almost fearfully.

"I do," I say.

Heath rubs his chin, and I see he is hiding a smile. And now I am crying, because we made a child and he is glad, even though he knows he will never be recognised as the child's father. An image skids into my mind—a small boy at Heath's side, helping him load the sheaves on the cart, laughing in the autumn sunshine—and just as quickly I banish it. It will do me no good to harbour such fantasies and, in any case, Ash says the child will be a girl. And Ash *knows* these things even though she shouldn't.

I press my body into his arms and weep warm tears against the rough fabric of his tunic. "What is to become of us?" My voice is husky from smoke and from crying.

Heath kisses the trail of tears from my cheeks, and even in this dark moment the desire that arrows through me is bright and urgent.

He pushes me gently away so he can look at my face, and he opens his mouth and says, "Rose, we could . . ." But then he stops, and I am glad he has stopped, because I know he is going to say, *we could run away: we could find my father's family in the wilds of Bradsey, we could raise the child as our own and have six more and always be happy.* But we both know that such a sunlit scene blinds the mind's eye to darker truths. Ælmesse and Netelchester have been at war since the giants left Thyrsland, centuries ago. My father and Wengest's father were the first kings to bring peace between the kingdoms; and all of it rested on the marriage promise my father made to Wengest. If Heath and I ran away to raise fat babies in the wilderness, the sure result of our indulgence would be war. Thousands would die; many of them would be children. I want to shout and shake my fists and proclaim how unfair it is that I should be in such a position, forced into marriage, the fate of kingdoms weighing on me. And then I remind myself—as I always must—of my sister Bluebell on the fields of battle with my father, stained in blood and slipping over the spilled intestines of her fallen friends. A king's daughter knows duty. Bluebell would sacrifice her life for Ælmesse; how selfish I am to complain about sacrificing my womb.

Heath stands, pulls me up next to him. Then he kneels, his hands around my hips. He kisses my belly, and I can feel the heat of his lips through the cloth. I close my eyes and turn my face upwards. The mingled smells of meat, smoke, and mud seem stuck in my throat. He rests his cheek against my body, and I turn my gaze to him, tangle my fingers in his hair. And then the first bolt of true panic comes.

In the firelight, I see the red glimmer in his hair. It is suddenly clear to me that should my child have the faintest trace of the Ærfolc colouring, we will be undone.

Her hair or her eyes may tell a tale that should remain untold.

II

Motranecht

Wild snowy wind rattles the branches outside, battering the shutters, howling down the hill and plucking at the thatched houses of the village. Snow lies in uneven layers on the empty market square, on the roofs of barns where animals stand still and close together, on the bowerhouse and the blacksmith's forge. But here in Wengest's great hall, the freezing damp seems impossibly far away. The fire is huge and hot and bright, the smoke hangs thick in the air until it escapes, little by little, into the black cold outside. The occasional bold snowflake falls through the smoke-hole and melts in a hissing half-moment. All around me are the sounds of people shouting and laughing and drinking, the smell of damp clothes and roasting fat. It is the night we celebrate the great Mother, the deepest point of winter, the day when the sun rises the latest and sets the earliest.

I am wearing my best red dress for Mother's Night and, fittingly, it is strained across my waist as it never has been before. A loose pinafore pinned over it disguises my belly; but it won't be long before it is apparent to everyone who sees me that the king's wife is with child. Perhaps it is time I told the king.

Wengest is holding my hand loosely as he turns away to talk to his ageing uncle Byrtwold, who sits at the head of the table with us. My gaze travels the room. Beyond our table, other groups are arranged around the fire. The hall-staff work at the hearth, carving deer on spits, slopping gravy and parsnips onto plates. By the far door, a tale-teller is performing. I cannot hear his words, but I can see his exaggerated actions: an invisible sword, a dragon with hands for jaws. The warm, sweet ale has made me flushed and happy.

Of course, I am looking for Heath. Wengest has seated him at a far table, with a duke from the deep west of Netelchester. The duke's two daughters are with him; sullen skinny things. Neither of them great beauties. I think not.

Wengest's whisper is in my ear, his beard is rough against my skin. "Save us."

I look up. Uncle Byrtwold is holding forth at length, and under the influence of too much bog-myrtle ale, about the right way to knacker sheep. Wengest's closest retainers are silenced and glazed. I swallow a laugh.

"Uncle Byrtwold," I say in a sharp voice, "have you seen the way the hall-staff are carving that deer? I'm sure it is not right."

Byrtwold sits up, alarmed, peering towards the fire. "You are right, my dear. If they cut across-wise, all the fat will end up on the first twelve plates." He is on his feet in a moment, unsteadily. Wengest's hand shoots out under his elbow.

"You need to explain the process to them in detail," Wengest says, using his leverage now to propel Byrtwold away.

Then he is weaving off through the crowd, and restrained laughter blooms at our table. Wengest smiles at me, the firelight reflected in his dark eyes. "You are as wise as you are beautiful, my Rose."

This is surely the worst aspect of my betrayal: my husband does not deserve it. He is a patient man, and he loves me. The first time we met, I was struck by how handsome he was, how strong. He is not yet forty summers, and has thick dark hair and smiling eyes. The cold has made his skin florid, and his cheeks above his beard are dry and cracking. But he is by no means an ugly man, nor an unkind man. Had I not met Heath, I may very well have fallen slowly in love with him, as I expected to when our marriage was arranged.

I am overwhelmed by strong pity and lean up to kiss him, and he quickly pushes me away, glancing around. "Not so everyone will see, Rose. People do not like to think of their king as a man. Men desire, and desire saps judgement."

Such ideas about what kings and men should be is no doubt at the very root of the long-standing differences between my father's kingdom and Netelchester. For my father thinks that a king is first a human, and only through our shared humanity can we be a strong kingdom. Wengest believes kings are separate, different. Better.

I playfully put my arms around his neck and blow softly on his hair, and he looks cross for a moment and then laughs.

"Look you at my nephew, Heath," he says, his gaze going over my shoulder.

I turn, probably too quickly, my hands still linked behind his neck. I see nothing unusual. Heath is listening to the tale-teller, the duke and his daughters are eating their meals.

"I have been watching him all night, and I am suspicious," Wengest says.

My face grows hot. "You are?"

"I put him there with two women who would be perfect for marriage, and he looks at neither." Wengest frowns, disengages himself from my arms. "He cannot grow a beard, he does not enjoy the company of women. I hope he is not a cat-paw."

At that precise moment, a wooden trencher piled with meat and vegetables is dropped at my elbow. I become aware that the noise in the room has been dampened as people eat. Wengest has not invited me to reply, so I do not. But of course I am the person who knows best that Heath is far from being a cat-paw. Back at Heath's table, the tale-teller is finished and people around are clapping and cheering. The tale-teller turns and Wengest beckons him forward. He is a small but sprightly man with a wispy beard and a pronounced crook to his right shoulder.

"My lord," the tale-teller says as he approaches our table. "I have a tale for you."

"Tell on," Wengest says, breaking his bread to sop up gravy. "I could use some entertainment. Let it be a tale of adventure and men's courage."

But before the tale-teller can speak, a man dressed in white at the end of our table stands and, in a bold voice, says, "I can tell a tale."

The man, whose name is Nyll, is a pilgrim. I do not like him, but that is not his fault. He is friendly enough. But he is of the Trimartyr faith, a woman-hating death cult. Wengest is fascinated by this faith, but resists converting. Out of some strange pity or fear, he gave the pilgrim a half-hide near the river as book-land, and there Nyll has built a little house with a grass roof, where he writes his strange letters on his stretched calfskin and counsels those who have questions about the Trimartyrs. Winter has come, and he is still here. I know by this that he intends to stay until he achieves his object, which is my husband's soul and the souls of his people.

"You have a tale, pilgrim?" Wengest says, sitting back in his chair and swirling the drink in his cup. "I did not know pilgrims did such frivolous things as telling tales."

"Ah, my lord, but the Trimartyrs have the most glorious tale of all. That of the courage and sacrifice of the three martyrs so that we may all one day stand in the hall of the great god Maava."

The tale-teller retreats, bowing his head. Wengest shrugs his broad shoulders. "Go on then."

Nyll the pilgrim spreads his hands and clears his throat. "Listen," he says, straining to be heard over the noise in the room, "for Maava's word is great and good." A good tale-teller needs a strong voice, an ease with his own body. But Nyll does not know how to project his words, nor what to do with his hands. They clutch and unclutch in front of him. Undeterred, he continues. "Maava is the one god, the only god."

Already the group around him has divided. Those who are already sympathetic to the Trimartyrs are nodding, urging him on. Those of the common faith mutter to each other, they frown or roll their eyes. Some look murderous: to preach such nonsense on Motranecht seems evil. One god? When there are so clearly two? A mother: for growth, love, harmony, family; and the horse god: for war, diplomacy, thought, action. One for birth, and one for death: the two poles between which we all wander.

Nyll clears his throat again, and this time manages to imbue his voice with volume. He slips into verse, letting the words lead him.

Listen, the Lord Maava: mighty, good and great,
A message for men, cast off customs wilful and wild.

One god, only god, mortals must hear him,
For fate awaits all at end of life's lease,
Some in the Sunlands, the bad in the Blacklands.
Do not deny this told tale, and wail for wrong,
Listen, the Lord Maava.

At world's warm middle, moist garden of good,
Beyond before: the giants' grandfathers' times and tales,
Maava made two; twins proud to prophesy,
Babes in the belly of the loving Liava, who knew no men:
Virtuous virgin, birthed the babes, tended those twins,
In the honoured hall of the King of kindness, victorious Varga,
At world's warm middle.

I stifle a laugh. Perhaps if Wengest can believe that a virgin can get with child, then I need not worry about being discovered in my affair. I turn away from the pilgrim, and hum a tune in my head so I need not listen to the rest. I have heard the story before, and it is a cruel and sad one, of two little boys—the child prophets—and their mother, all cast alive upon a pyre as punishment for preaching the teachings of Maava. Nyll recites this verse with spittle-flecked relish. I try not to think about the mother, lying down and taking her children in her arms, knowing that she can no longer protect them from pain and death. When did I become so vulnerable to tales of cruelty? Since this child lodged itself inside me, I am a different person. I know not myself, I know not my future.

Nyll ends his tale by holding out the golden triangle he wears on a strap around his waist; the symbol of the three martyrs, of their pyre, of their bones standing among the cinders of their flesh. "Listen you, for those who take Maava as their god will travel upon their deaths to the Sunlands, where happiness is eternal; and those who do not will find instead the Blacklands beyond the clouds, to fall forever in fear and ice."

Everybody has stopped listening, even Wengest. Nyll tucks his triangle away on his belt, and returns to his seat, his elbows crooked awkwardly against the indifferent noise of people eating and talking, and not listening. The tale-teller leaps into the space vacated by him, launching into a tale of two brothers fighting over a dragon-maiden. Maava's fear and ice are banished by the return of firelight and laughter.

It is not simply the avid interest that the Trimartyrs take in cruelty that irks me; it is their law that women cannot rule. Four years ago Tweoning's queen, the mighty Dystro, was deposed and beheaded by the tide of the Trimartyrs. I wonder if Bluebell ever muses on Dystro's fate. I touch my belly lightly, unthinkingly. My own daughter, if Wengest converted, would not be queen. The thought lights up all my veins with a sense of injustice. A misplaced one, I suppose.

I become aware that Wengest is looking at me. Closely. Watching my hand moving softly over the outside of my pinafore. I drop my fingers quickly, he meets my gaze.

"Rose?"

"I am with child," I say, willing myself not to blush with guilt.

His beard splits with a grin. "Oh, my."

I cannot help but smile, his pleasure is contagious.

"When will it come?" he says eagerly.

"Ash says on midsummer," I lie. An early child is not unusual; he will not suspect.

Wengest stands, knocking over his cup. He reaches for mine, holds it aloft. The tale-teller falls silent. Wengest booms, "Listen you, all of you!"

I feel my face grow hot. I know Heath is looking, but I cannot meet his eye. Instead, I stare as hard as I can at Wengest, and a tunnel of blurred darkness forms around him.

"Let it be known," Wengest says, when the room has fallen quiet except for the whoosh of the fire, "that my wife Rose, the daughter of King Æthlric of Ælmesse, is with child."

A loud cheer goes up, and my eyes are stinging from staring so hard and from unshed tears.

"We expect the child on the very day of midsummer," Wengest boasts among the cheers and shouts. "An auspcious time for a king to be born."

"Or a queen," I say quietly, but he does not hear; or if he hears, he does not answer.

. . .

I do not know how close the dawn is when I finally slide into my warm bed. I let my head fall onto the soft lambskin and close my eyes. My mind still whirls. I feel the weight of Wengest's body as he lies down next to me. He often does not sleep in my bed, but tonight his excitement about the child has made him affectionate. He rests his warm hand on my belly and is silent for a long time. I am almost asleep, when his voice wakes me. It seems very loud.

"Rose, are you asleep?"

I open my eyes. In the dark, he is just a shadow. "What is it?"

"I need to ask you about your father. You know him better than I do."

I sit up, craving sleep. "Go on."

"Last time I spoke to Æthlric, he predicted he would soon be asking me for a hundred good warriors, to take up to the border of Is-hjarta in summerfull-month. I have had an idea, but I wonder how your father will take it."

"What is it?"

"Heath."

"Heath?" My heart beats a little faster.

"He shows no inclination to marry, so I shall put him to war. He has a strong arm and a good mind. It would be the making of him, as a man. But would your father object if I sent him an army led by a half-blood?"

My tired mind is so overwhelmed with thoughts and feelings that it freezes my tongue.

"Ah, I have offered you insult, too—"

"No," I say quickly. "My father would not object to Heath. My father does not harbour prejudice to Ærfolc—half-blood or full-blood."

Wengest's voice grows quiet, as though he is ashamed. "It is perhaps wrong of me to be partial towards my nephew. I loved my sister, so dearly."

"Heath is a good man," I say, guardedly. "But can he lead an army?"

A pause. A gust of wind hammers the shutters. "Ah, you are right. He has had only basic training for war. It is too soon to put him in such a position."

I relax, the black imaginings of King Hakon's northern raiders and their famed cruelty temporarily retreating.

"I will send him as second-in-command, behind Grislic."

Wengest kisses my cheek. "Good counsel, my Rose. I can sleep with a clear mind now."

But my mind is not clear. I am a fool. I should have said, *no, my father does not want a half-breed.* I should have said, *you are wrong to send a gentle man such as Heath to war.* I should have begged for Heath's safety; but I said none of those things, too concerned with protecting my secrets from discovery.

I turn over on my side, then my other side, then my back. The wind rattles the shutters, threads of snowy cold creep through. Hair works loose from my plait, and tickles my face and ears. I cannot sleep, I cannot sleep. I tell myself, perhaps my father will change his mind. Perhaps he will not ask for an army, after all. But these thoughts are small comfort in the face of the awful fear that my lover may soon meet his death, far far away from me.

III

Solmonath

I watch him from my bower window. Mud month has come and the snow has turned to brown slush. Rain falls on every cold inch of Thyrsland. And every day for the last six weeks Heath has been out in the war field with Grislic and a hundred other men. They throw spears at straw targets, they heft their great swords, they raise their wooden shields, they roar. From this distance, they are all small, dressed alike in mail shirts and iron helms. I recognise Heath only by where he is standing: at the front, beside enormous Grislic. Wengest has come down to the field today, in his rarely worn battle gear. My husband is not a warrior king like my father; or, indeed, Wengest's own father who was slain by raiders in his sixtieth winter.

It is too cold to have the shutters open, and my fingers have become ice on the window frame. Yet I watch a little longer, as I do every day. Now he is at Wengest's hall daily, I see Heath more than I ever have. But there is no private time for us. I have not had a chance to tell him how afraid I am for him. I suspect he is afraid too. Once I entered the hall to find him standing there, talking to Wengest alone. My heart caught on a hook, though it ought not have: Wengest is his uncle; he is partial to Heath. It is of no consequence if they speak to each other. So I joined them, and his eyes travelled to my belly and I know he was thinking what I was thinking: what if he never sees the child?

And I had the most despicable of thoughts. If Heath is away when the child comes, nobody will suspect. Should the child be flame-haired or sea-eyed, there will be disquiet yes. But nobody will point to Heath, for Heath will not be there. He will have dropped out of mind. People may see her colouring as dependent on the way the sunlight falls: an autumnal glow in fair hair, a blue gaze like my older sister's.

I banish the thought again. To see any benefit in Heath's deployment is to beg for special misery should he fall to the ice-men. I watch him a little longer: his grace, his strength.

A flash of colour in the distance catches my eye, and I peer into the misting rain. Riders are coming, and they are carrying the king's standard of Ælmesse. My father has sent them. My heart hollows, for it can only mean that Wengest was right to predict Ælmesse would ask for an army; and that Heath is surely going with them in only a matter of days.

I close the shutters and return to the fire. I pull up a stool and hold my hands out to the warm flame. My fingers ache as the ice melts out of them. I condemn myself for my selfishness. If I had not entered into this love affair with Heath, he might have married and Wengest would have left him alone on his farm. He would be happy and safe. Outside, I can hear running footsteps, people calling to each other. *Riders are coming. King Æthlric sends an envoy.* Tension and excitement infuses their voices. War is terrifying and thrilling: a hundred of the town's men—sons, brothers, lovers— are soon marching out to meet it. I close my eyes. My bower, with all its fine wall hangings and carved beams, disappears. Now I am just a woman, not a queen. The baby squirms inside me, pushes tiny limbs against the wall of my womb, then settles again. She knows no fear, she anticipates no loss.

More voices outside, the shouting on the war field has stopped. I open my eyes and return to the window, crack the shutter. The riders have pulled up their horses. The first rider is talking to Wengest. She wears no helm and her long, blonde hair is unbound. My heart leaps. It is my sister. It is Bluebell.

I fly from the room, forgetting my cloak. I am running, my heart thundering, all woes temporarily forgotten. Pregnancy has robbed me of much of my grace, but I hurry on, down the uneven road out of town and into the cold sludgy fields. She looks up and sees me and breaks Wengest off half-sentence with a sharp hand gesture. She has no love for him, and he none for her. He believes women do not belong in battle; she believes that kings do.

Bluebell dismounts with athletic strength and no elegance, and stalks towards me. A moment later she is bending to embrace me as the rain deepens. Her body is bony, the mail is cold and hard. Then she stands back, laughing at my swollen belly, reaching out a tattooed hand to touch it.

"Why are you here?" I ask, breath held against the answer.

"I'm here to fetch you and take you back to Ælmesse for summerfull-month." She tries to smile but it arrives on her face as a grimace. "Our father intends to marry."

. . .

The drinkhouse on the village square is warm, and flooded with sweet cinnamon steam and the pungent smell of fermenting yarrow. The rain intensifies. Bluebell's retinue sit at the hearth and order bread and meat. I take Bluebell to the king's table—a carved table with high-backed benches, tucked away from the noise in a corner of the room—so that we can talk uninterrupted.

Bluebell has few manners. She spends most of her time with warriors or with my father, so hasn't had the opportunity to learn niceties. She sits with her knees spread wide and her big feet lolling in the walkway, wipes her damp nose with the back of her hand, then raises her fingers and shouts to the young man with the tray of drinks, "I'm starving! Bring me food and ale." In height and colouring, she is my father's copy. In almost everything else in the world, she is my father's favourite. The rest of us have always known it and have each managed our jealousy silently. The idea that Father is to marry again is shocking to me, but to Bluebell it would sting like a betrayal. They are bone-achingly close. He makes no decision without her counsel; he enters no battle without her at his side.

"Who is she?" I ask, almost the moment we have sat down. "Is she a good woman?"

"I hate her fucking guts," Bluebell growls. "Of course."

"But how did they meet? I didn't know Father had any thoughts about remarrying."

The shutter next to us leaks, a slow trickle of water runs down the wall and pools under the table. Bluebell half-stands and slams the shutter with her shoulder. It crunches tightly. No weak light can make its way in. The small, close room is dim except for hot firelight. It could be morning or midnight.

Bluebell sits. "She came with a retinue down the river from Tweoning, on her way to visit her sister at the far coast. Her boat sprang a leak two miles from Blicstowe." She leans forward on her elbows, resting her chin in her hands and mutters, "Would that it had sunk."

I assess Bluebell as the rain thunders on the mud outside. I cannot trust her opinion; her jealousy skews her judgement.

"In any case, she made her way to town and Father offered her a place to stay," she continues. "It turns out that she's the widow of an old friend he knew in his youth. Her name is Gudrun."

"She's a widow? Any children?"

"A son. Wylm. A spotted eel, not yet fifteen." Bluebell's food and ale arrive, and disappear down her throat alarmingly quickly. As she chews loudly and slops her ale on the table, she describes to me our new stepmother. Gudrun is a pretty, soft-spoken woman who has lived among the Trimartyrs but retains the old ways of our common faith. I am curious to meet her, to see how far Bluebell's resentment of her is justified.

Finally, my sister slaps her hands against each other to wipe them clean, and indicates my belly. "Can you travel?"

"Blicstowe isn't far."

"A day and a half. Can you ride?"

"I . . . I don't know. I'll never fit into my riding clothes."

"You can't ride a horse in skirts. Two days then. You'll have to take a covered cart." She says the words as though they taste bad.

I feel weak and damnably feminine. Yet I am as relieved by the idea of a covered cart as I am ashamed to accept it. "Yes, that might be for the best," I admit.

The corner of Bluebell's mouth twitches in a smile. "I'm not riding with you. My men wouldn't look at me the same again."

I burst into laughter. The idea of Bluebell on an embroidered seat in a covered cart is entirely wrong. The baby responds to my laughter by squirming. I press my fingers against a tiny foot, poking me hard.

"What is it?" Bluebell asks.

I reach for her hand and pull her to her feet, holding her palm against my belly. The baby obliges by kicking her soundly. Bluebell's face is overcome by childish wonder.

"Is that the child?"

"Yes. She kicked you."

Bluebell presses her hand hard against my stomach, waiting for another kick. She knows not her own strength. The baby has gone quiet now, and eventually my sister sits again. "It was a foot then?"

"I don't really know. I think so." For a moment I feel sorry for Bluebell. She has no knowledge of the giving of life, only the bringing of death. She has often declared that she will never marry and bear children; though Ash and I suspect she has had lovers. I know that she is a fine warrior, a great leader, that she is addicted to the bloodrush of battle. But does she not deny somehow what the earth mother formed her for? So few women go to war, far fewer lead armies, because women are created for another purpose. As Wengest always says, crudely, *women have sheaths, not spears.*

But then I shake off my pity. She wouldn't want it. She has known glories and sorrows that I cannot imagine; she would consider me—trapped in the bower—to be living only half a life.

She raises her cup to her lips and drains the last drops from it. Turns and shouts for more. Then fixes me in her steely blue gaze. "You said *she.*"

"Ash said 'she'," I reply warily.

Bluebell's eyebrows arch. "I see."

"Though she tried to deny she meant anything by it." I shrug. "We ought not to talk of it. "

"I don't see why it should be a secret. If she has the sight, it will make her a better counsellor. Many counsellors in the faith are sighted."

"After twenty years of practice maybe: not in their first year of study. She might be thrown out of school. Nobody wants to be around a wild latent."

"She should be proud of herself." Bluebell drops her voice anyway. "I go to her, if I can, before every battle. She sees, she knows what will happen."

"Truly?"

Her voice becomes urgent. "Before we went to Skildan Bridge, back in winterfull-month, she told me to strike while the tide was still low. I marched my men for two days with barely a pause to get there at low tide, and praise the horse god that I did. The raiders had war ships waiting to come down the river on the next high tide. We had already spilled their blood before the other half of the army came. We picked off the reinforcements quickly and raided their ships." She thrusts out her arm and pushes up the heavy mail sleeve, to show me a gold armband—two fish eating each other's tails—jammed hard over the blurring blue tattoos on her forearm. Then she leans back, toying with her empty cup. "Ash is far from me now. Too far. As are you."

Outside, the rain has eased and the wind has begun to gust. I contemplate Bluebell's words. I had no idea that Ash's sight was so strong. But instead of feeling anxious for her—untrained latent sight can take a heavy toll, especially on young women—I am only anxious for myself. When Ash felt my belly, declared I was pregnant and accidentally told me the child was a girl, what else did she see? What else does she know about me, and about Heath?

"Something troubles you, sister?" Bluebell says.

I shake my head. "I am tired, that is all."

Bluebell rises, stretching long legs. With quick movements, she pulls her long hair back and winds it into an untidy knot. "We'll stay two nights and then head to Ælmesse. But first I have to speak with Wengest. Will you come? I find him so difficult to talk to."

"Surely. Though why must you speak with him?"

She doesn't blink. "Father needs an army. A hundred men to go with us up to the border of Bradsey. The Crow King and his raiders are pushing hard against the people there. We're going to go and crush them, send them back into the heart-of-ice. Where the dogs belong."

But I hear nothing beyond, *Father needs an army.* Because this is the news I have dreaded to hear. Heath is going away. To war.

Silence draws out uncomfortably. "Will you be going?" I ask at last, aware my voice is tremulous.

"Of course." Her chest puffs proudly, almost imperceptibly. "Father is staying home for the first time. I'm in charge."

A small comfort then. Bluebell will be there. Bluebell will look out for him. But, of course, she doesn't know he is important to me. I want to cry: I am so full of spidery fears and hot secrets.

Bluebell misreads the anxiety on my face and slings an arm around me, roughly pulls me close and slams her fist into her chest. "You need not worry, sister. No raider will cut out this heart. I'd cut it out myself first."

And I cannot tell her: it is not for her heart that I am anxious. Selfishly, it is for my own.

. . .

I wake earlier than the sun. Bluebell sleeps beside me, snoring softly. Wengest has given her his bed for the night, and he sleeps at the other end of the bower house. He has decided not to come to the wedding, because he must get his army ready for marching north. I know this is an excuse, that he trusts Grislic to prepare his men. But he is all too aware of Bluebell's disdain for his lack of involvement in war. He is trying to impress her, because she is so famed a warrior. And yet she remains unimpressed. I almost feel sorry for him.

I lie, stuck awake, for a long time. Outside, the darkness leeches from the sky. The wind has blown all the clouds away, leaving the world shivering unprotected under the stars. We are leaving this morning, after breakfast. My father's wedding feast will last a week, perhaps two. All my sisters will be there, clamouring for each other's company. Bluebell will ride early for Is-hjarta, but I will not get away before the end of summerfull-month. I will not see Heath again before he goes.

This thought throws itches into my belly. I sit up quietly, feel around in the half-dark for my clothes, and dress quickly and quietly. Bluebell sleeps hard, as does anybody who works vigorously and has a clear conscience. She doesn't hear me leave the room or the bower house; I doubt she will wake before the full rising of the sun. By then, I will have said my goodbye to Heath.

I walk, through the town and out the gate-house, calling good morning to the guards there. They are used to my long absences. The king's wife, it is well known, likes to walk and think. Perhaps, in whispers, they talk about how my father allowed his daughters to be too independent, far too clever for their own good. Yet they seem to have accepted my ways now, and I believe there is genuine fondness for me in the town. The birth of this child will be welcome and happy news.

I take the main road out of town and then cut across fields and skirt the edge of the wood. I see cows and sheep in the distance, farmers taking their first steps, yawning, into the day's work. The long walk warms my blood; I don't feel the morning cold anymore. I arrive at the edge of the river and follow it, staying in the cover of the trees. Finally, I am at the edge of Heath's farm and I make my way up towards the house. His fields have been freshly ploughed, and he is moving between the furrows, throwing handfuls of lime around him. The fields will be ready to sow soon, but he will likely not be here. Wengest will send a caretaker to watch Heath's farm in hopes he will be back for harvest-month. I pause, to burn the image of Heath into my mind. He is so beautiful, with his wide shoulders and his golden hair. He turns and sees me, half-lifts a hand in a hopeful wave.

I hurry towards him, and he catches me in his arms. I breathe in the scent of him: smoke and straw and faint sweat. He stands back and admires my belly, dusting his hands on his pants.

"You are growing apace," he says.

"There are just three months to go."

Sadness crosses his face. "I will not be here."

"I know."

We fall silent a while. Then I say, "I came to say goodbye. I travel to my father's hall at Blicstowe today. He is marrying a second time."

"I had heard it from Wengest," he replies. "But I had not guessed I would be so lucky as to see you a last time. Come inside, where it is warm."

He leads me into the house. The fire is hot but he doesn't go to the hearth, he sits on the mattress and I kneel, leaning on him. I am crying before I can promise myself not to cry.

"Hush, hush," he says, his warm lips moving over my face. "Your tears alarm me. They say you fear I will fall to the raiders."

I take a deep shuddering breath and stop myself. "My sister leads Ælmesse's army. Look to Bluebell. There is not a greater warrior in all of Thyrsland. In all things, look to Bluebell."

"Hush," he says again. "I won't speak of it." His lips are on my throat. I climb onto the mattress beside him. Lying against each other, we trace familiar patterns on each other's bodies. My belly is in the way, so I turn on my side and Heath presses against my back, his hot skin against me, his fingers gentle on my breasts, his kisses in my hair. The harder we chase desire, the more it eludes us. Instead, I turn against his chest and cry a little more and this time he lets me. I am warm, I am tired. I drift to sleep. We both do.

The next thing I am aware of is a loud voice at the door.

"Heath? Are you there?"

My heart jumps into my throat. Heath is scrambling for clothes, throwing the wool blanket over me and calling, "Who is it? What is it?"

"Grislic sent me. You are past an hour late for training."

I hear the door open, only a crack. "I slept late," he says. "I will come shortly."

"You will come with me now," the voice says. "Grislic insisted."

"I . . . very well." Then I hear the door close and I know that I am alone, that Heath has left immediately so no attention could be drawn to the figure hiding in his bed.

He is gone and I didn't say goodbye. I didn't say, *I love you.*

IV

Summerfylleth

Seven hours from home, my bones are aching and my ankles are swollen. The covered cart bumps along the rutted path and no matter how I sit I cannot get comfortable. Added to this, a miserable drizzle is falling so that I cannot even part the curtains to see outside. I hear voices from time to time, Bluebell laughing with her hearthband, but I am stuck in here with a sagging cushion and nowhere to put my feet up. Added to this discomfort, I am desperate to relieve myself but too embarrassed to ask because it is not yet two hours since I last stopped the riders for the same purpose. Travelling while pregnant, I now see, is a form of torture. My father should not have expected me to come. The very thought of having to get through another day of this, and then take the return journey after the wedding, makes me want to sob.

I have with me a wooden box packed with edible treats that Cook prepared for me: mince pies and sugared fruit. I am not hungry, but I pick at it and eat too much, until my stomach feels blocked and queasy. I am a lump, glued to the seat, the hours carrying me along in uncomfortable monotony.

Just before dusk, the hearthband stops. I pin back the curtains to peer out at the fading day. My knees are sore and my thighs are numb. The rain has cleared, and I see a nearby copse with sufficient privacy. My legs thank me for stretching them, my bladder thanks me for emptying it. When I return, Bluebell is nowhere in sight. Her retainers are gathered on the muddy road, arguing among themselves.

"Brygen is only two miles. If we don't stop there, we will not reach the next village before nightfall," one man says.

"I am not afraid of nightfall," another man says.

"And yet you are afraid of Brygen."

"The horses are tired. They need to rest."

"It will only be two hours more."

I glance around, searching for Bluebell. Two hours more! I cannot bear the thought. I need to convince Bluebell to let us stop in Brygen. I need a soft bed. There is my sister, slouching out from behind a tree, straightening her riding pants. I hurry over, but the men have spotted her too and are already calling, "Brygen or Dunscir, my lord?"

"Brygen is—"

Bluebell raises a long hand. "Dunscir."

Immediately the arguing ceases. Nobody is willing to disagree with Bluebell.

Except for me. "Please, Bluebell. I can't travel another two hours. I am raw. I must rest."

She turns to me, brows drawn down. Even I am afraid of her for a moment. "Rest? But you have been resting in the carriage."

"I cannot make myself comfortable. I am too big." I pat my belly for emphasis. I see that the expression on her brow is wavering. "Please." Her retainers are shifting from foot to foot. Even the horses seem nervous with anticipation.

"Very well. We will take the road up to Brygen."

"But, my lord—"

"My sister's comfort is all I care to hear about."

Silence.

"Let's go."

. . .

I deduce the reason for their reluctance to stop in Brygen almost immediately. The little village is dotted with empty, sagging buildings, the forest around seems to encroach on the hill upon which it is built, every third tree appears to be blighted with perpetual winter: leafless black branches raised against the whitening sky as the sun sinks somewhere behind clouds. Our inn is draughty and the food has the texture of sawdust. But when I climb into bed—leaving Bluebell downstairs drinking with her hearthband—I think of nothing but the soft lambswool. I drift to sleep within three breaths.

It is much later that I wake. A prickling in my bones. Bluebell is asleep next to me. I have no reason to feel unsafe.

But sleep will not come. A chill creeps under the shutter. My cheek is frozen. I sit up, but can see the shutter is closed tight. I rise, and find myself opening it and peering out into the dark.

The clouds have dissolved and a pale half-moon lights the scene. Down the hill, on the side of the road, a woman kneels next to a pile of dirt. Her figure is traced in shades of midnight and moonlight. She looks dreadfully familiar.

"Mother," I gasp.

But it cannot be mother. Mother has been dead for twelve years.

Bluebell rouses. "Rose? Is everything well with you?"

I turn, words falling from my tongue in a tangle. "A woman, outside on the road. She looks like mother."

Bluebell is out of bed faster than an arrow, but as I turn back to the window I can see already that there is no woman. That the road is deserted but for the skulking shadows of bare, sick trees.

A moment of silence passes between us, then Bluebell touches my hair. "It was a long journey, Rose. Come back to bed. Rest."

"I did see her."

She closes the shutter firmly. "Come back to bed," she repeats, tugging my wrist.

I follow her instruction and lie down next to her. I tell myself that Bluebell is right: I am tired. I cannot distinguish between sleeping and waking. And yet my heart stammers and my eyes will not close, even after Bluebell has let go of my hand and turned on her side to sleep. My bones are still prickling. Quietly, careful not to wake my sister, I return to the window.

She is there again, the figure that looks like my mother. And I know that this sending is for me. Not for Bluebell, or she would have seen it too. Despite the depth of the night, the cold of the moonlight, the eerie emptiness of the forest, I dress warmly and leave the room.

The front door of the inn creaks as I open it, and again as I let it fall closed behind me. The figure has not moved; she is hunched over the shape on the ground and I realise now that she is crying. I can hear her harsh sobs over the breeze rattling in the trees.

"Mother?" I say, but my voice is a tight, fearful whisper. I steel myself and approach. The shape on the road is a mound; a triangle—symbol of the trimartyrs—glints dully in the weak moonlight. A grave. My mother's spirit is bent over a grave. My skin shivers.

"Mother?" I say, louder now. Closer. She looks up. I stop in front of her.

"She will never be queen," she says.

"Who? Who is buried here?" Mortal dread flares in my heart: it is a presentiment of death.

"Nobody is buried here. Just her crown."

The flame of fear subsides a little. "Whose crown? Bluebell's? Will she be safe?" I glance over my shoulder, back to the inn, wondering if Bluebell still sleeps. When I turn back, it is not my mother at the side of the road, but a creature formed of sticks and mud, glaring at me. A mudthrael. I yelp, and back away.

"Wait!" it calls in a voice scraped from the bottom of a murky pond. It reaches its uncanny hands towards me, and distaste slithers over my skin. I see a dead branch on the ground, scoop it up and take aim—

But the creature flings up its muddy fingers and something gritty and darkly sparkling enters my eyes. I am instantly dislocated from the cold, wet road in Brygen: there is no mudthrael, there is no stick in my hand, there is no road, nor any trees. I am inexplicably *elsewhere*.

On a vast plain. A million miles away, there are mountains perhaps, beyond the fiery horizon. Wind buffets me, whipping my hair around my face. I gulp against the shock, pressing my toes hard into my shoes to ground myself. The mudthrael has thrown me under an enchantment, I must try to remember who and where I am.

The earth shudders, and I know that something terrifying is approaching. Sunset colours burn the sky. I am horribly aware of how open and exposed I am out here. "Bluebell!" I call, my throat raw with fear and effort. "Bluebell!"

But then I remember, I am not here at all, I am . . .

The shaking under foot intensifies, and my whole body resounds with the movement. A scant ten feet in front of me, a fissure appears in the ground. Paralysing fear turns my limbs to stone. I try to lift my feet, but they are part of the juddering ground. I am caught, heart and bones, in the thundering fear. Inch by crumbling inch the ground disappears in front of me and, from the black depths, a twisting firedrake rises.

Its eyes are bigger than my skull, its golden hide is spiked with bronze. The smell is fish and sulphur, dirt and old blood. It is the three-toed firedrake: the writhing shape on my father's standard, the symbol of Ælmesse's power. The drake spreads its jaw and spews curling fire above my head. My heart slams. I struggle against the glue that holds my feet to the ground, feeling the reflected heat of the firedrake's breath singeing my hair and stripping my cheeks bloody. I throw my arms up and call out in fear.

Silence, stillness, cold.

I open my eyes. The light has bled away. I am still on the plain, but it is late—so late. Past time for sleep, past time for death. My eyes search fearfully for the dragon, but it is now just a blackened skeleton in the distance. The churning sky is visible between its ribs. An icy wind creeps across the ground, tumbling ash over its gaping skull. Movement catches my gaze. A hand extended out of the ground, fingers spread apart. Ghostly white. It beckons slowly.

I move towards it. I have long ago forgotten that I am actually standing on the road in Brygen, under the influence of mudthrael magic. This dream is sharper than truth. The dragon bones are still and cold. Three feet from the tip of its tail, a dark pit of soil has been dug. A woman, buried in it except for her face and hands, glares up at me with icy blue eyes. I know this ritual of partial burial: it is a magic ritual of the under-religion, that shady cult that exists below the common faith and has been all but driven from Thyrsland. Her eyes terrify me; they seem to know my soul better than I know it.

"Who are you?" I ask.

"I am your father's sister."

"My father has no sister."

"He has a sister, and I am she. You may not know me, but I know you, Rose," she says. Her hair is mostly buried, but I can see that it is silvery-brown around her brow. "My name is Yldra. You know I am of your family, for I called the three-toed firedrake."

Shivering cold is eroding me inside. I cannot stay here; it will mean my destruction. And yet, I cannot remember where I am from. "How do I get back?" I ask.

Her mouth moves and no sound comes out. She tries again, and this time it seems as though her voice is far away. Reality glimmers back into my mind. This *is* a dream.

"You must kill Wengest as soon as you return from your father's wedding," she says. "Or Rowan will never be queen."

"Who is Rowan?"

"Your daughter. Kill him before the child is born."

"I am no killer."

And then it all dissolves, just like one of cook's sugar mice under hot beer. I am back in Brygen, mid-swing. I cannot stop my arms, the branch crashes into the mudthrael's sodden body, and the creature cries out and flies backwards, coming to rest in a heap in the middle of the road.

"Rose?"

It is Bluebell, running towards me, taking the branch from my hand and grasping my wrists. "What happened? What are you doing here?"

"I . . ." I point to the mudthrael, but it is just a pile of twigs and soil. "I have been . . . somewhere."

Bluebell looks closely at me. "Your eyes are wild and black."

"Mudthrael," I manage.

She glances around, alarmed. "This forest is known for bad magic," she says. "That's why my retinue didn't want to stop here."

Bad magic. The kind that everyone is afraid of, the kind that is brewed within the earthen huts of the under-religion. Mudthraels are fashioned and controlled by its devotees, and somebody sent this one to me: disguised it as my mother to tempt me out of my bed and throw visions in my eyes. But who? Bluebell is herding me up the road towards the inn, but I stop her.

"Bluebell, does our father have a sister named Yldra?"

"No."

"You are certain?"

"I am certain. He has no sister. Come, inside."

I allow her to lead me, but I am awash in confusion. I will sleep no more tonight.

. . .

My first glimpse of home comes late the following afternoon. I feel bruised all over from the journey, but when I see the hill—the town, my father's hall, the red and yellow flags fluttering on the gate house—I forget my pain.

The giants once lived here; they raised buildings and monuments made of some dazzling stone, the like of which has never been seen since in Thyrsland. Their buildings have fallen into ruin, and nobody alive knows how to fix them. And so the tall white ruins wait out the centuries, catching the sun to give the name to our town. Blicstowe: the bright place. Laid out in front of the ruins are the thatched rooves of the town itself. I know each building and its inhabitants well: the weavers, bronzesmiths, carpenters, bone workers, their wives, their muddy-faced children, the mad war-widows and the sane, bakers, potters, fishermen, lenders, counsellors of the common faith, the faithless, the homeless, the adolescent boys who dream of bearing swords alongside my sister. The roads are lined with wooden planks so that traffic may move even in muddy weather, and move it does. Carts, horses, pigs, chickens, and everywhere people. My father's people.

The town has been decorated for the wedding. Russet ribbons are wound around pillars and flutter from gable finishings, but it is too early in the year for white daisies. Our retinue thunders over the echoing bridge, up the hard-packed dirt road between the lines of oaks, and finally past the gatehouse and down to the stables. Bluebell helps me out of the cart and I stretch my legs gratefully. I glance up at the ruins: they are stained with sunset colours. My father's hall—a hulking, wood-shingled building—is stark black against the giants' stone. And there he is, standing between two of the pillars that he carved himself, smiling at me.

"Father!" I call, and he strides lithely towards me, catching me gently in his arms. His long yellow hair is streaked with grey, and age has made his blue eyes pale and his strong hands knotted. But he is still tall and handsome; he is still the first man I ever loved.

"My Rose," he says, standing back and admiring my belly. "It is wonderful to have you home, but doubly wonderful that you are here for such an occasion." He turns to Bluebell. "You spoke with Wengest?"

"Yes, Father. They will be ready to march."

A slight frown crosses his brow, but then he dismisses it. "Come inside, both of you," he says, leading me by the arm. "Gudrun is waiting to meet you, Rose. Ash arrived yesterday, and Ivy and Willow have been here a fortnight." He talks a little too fast, and I realise that he is nervous. My father—the man who sometimes comes home from battle with other men's blood embedded under his fingernails—nervous. I am caught between good-hearted amusement and pity.

We round the front of the hall, and here on the massive beams that support the doors are two carved firedrakes. My vision in Brygen returns to me. I pause to run my hand over the creature's back while Father lifts the beam and pushes the doors open. I have gone over the vision many times on the long journey today, turning the images and words over and over the way the tide turns over seaweed. Whether or not my daughter is one day queen is still an abstract thought; at the moment, she is just a bundle of squirming limbs in my belly. I will not kill Wengest, and that is the most important thing. I do not know if I have the ability to kill any man; perhaps we all do when tested. But I know that I cannot kill my husband. I like him, he is a good man. And should my crime be discovered, that would plunge his kingdom into war with my father's. So I have not spent another thought on that possibility. Instead, I have pondered on why his death now would ensure my daughter's ascension to the throne, on what could happen between now and milk-month. Of course, the handful of anxious ants in my stomach tells me that somehow Heath and I will be discovered. Other possibilities have not occurred to me and so, despite the fact that I need to ask my sister Ash about the vision, I am terrified to speak to her. Her second sight is too alert. My secrets may be uncovered.

"What is it?" Father asks, turning and seeing that I haven't followed him inside.

I smile as though nothing is wrong. "I have missed home, that's all," I say.

He takes my hand. "Home has missed you. Come. Supper is about to be served."

I hurry after Father. Bluebell stalks, sulking, four steps behind us. I am wholly prepared, on her behalf, to dislike Gudrun. We cross the vast hall, where Father's hearthband is loosely gathered, lying on benches, stoking the fire, talking softly, enjoying supper. A number of them call out to Bluebell and she breaks off to talk to them. Father drops my hand and opens the door to his state room—really just a small room with a table for private meals—and ushers me through.

The room is cosy, crowded with firelight and faces. Tapestries adorn the walls; some are shot with golden thread or are bordered with the fur of exotic animals. Along the wall beams are lined other treasures plundered from battle: cups and armbands of gold, pots and statues, ceremonial swords. The firelight is caught on the gleaming surfaces. The long carved table is laid out with baskets of fresh-baked bread, wooden bowls of pickled vegetables and strips of dried fish. I am suddenly ravenous. Around the table, on wooden benches, sit my sisters. Ash is at the far end, smiling at me. I smile in return, but move no closer. Instead, I sit between Ivy and Willow, the twelve-year-old twins. Ivy, with her magpie eyes, is pointing at my belly with a spoon, making some rude joke. Willow is shushing her. Ash is asking me how I endured the journey. But all I can pay attention to is this woman who is not one of us, Father's new wife. Gudrun of Tweoning.

She is nothing like I had imagined. I imagined somebody, I suppose, like my mother. Noble, dark-haired, eyes that betrayed steel in the spine, light in the brain. But Gudrun is softly pretty, with pale brown hair, round cheeks and bovine eyes, a gentle smile that she has turned on me.

She leans across the table and places a soft, white hand on mine. "Hello, Rose. It is truly a joy to meet you. I've heard so much about you."

How on earth can Bluebell object to this woman?

"This is my son, Wylm." Gudrun leans back and puts an arm around the middle of the boy who sits next to her. He is on the verge of manhood; his limbs seem to be growing before my eyes, straining at clothes that were probably comfortably sized just a week ago. His dark hair is lank and his hazel eyes are sullen. He manages a grudging smile, his knuckles half-hiding his mouth.

"It is a pleasure for me, too," I say. "I am very happy for my father especially." As I say it, I realise I mean it. Twelve years without my mother. He must have been so lonely, and if this woman with her soft edges and white hands can provide him the company he needs, then I cannot join Bluebell in her dislike of the situation. All things change. I touch my belly. I *know* that all things change.

A moment later, Bluebell is at the door. "Father?" she says.

"Come in, Bluebell," Father says, taking the seat between Gudrun and Wylm. "It will be our first meal as a new family."

Bluebell's eyes flicker like flame. She can barely keep her mouth from turning down. "I'm going to eat with the men," she says. "Aldric wants to discuss the march up to Is-hjarta."

There is a space of time—no longer than three seconds, though it feels longer—where tension infuses the room. Father locks eyes with Bluebell. It is a challenge, and he recognises this and, as a king, his chest expands ready to demand his will. The insult Bluebell offers is not only to him, but also to his new wife. But then he softens. Of course he understands Bluebell's resistance; he understands everything about her and his partiality is legendary: he cannot help but forgive her everything. "Very well, Bluebell," he says, glancing away.

She withdraws quickly, closing the door behind her. Gudrun studies her hands, blushing. Wylm gazes at the door with unsheathed hostility. My pulse quickens. Perhaps this is the stuff of any family disagreement, but for us it has the makings of much more significant conflict. I can see with my own eyes that one day Wylm will be a tall, strong man. The last thing a potential queen needs is a half-brother who hates her.

"Let us eat," Father says brightly.

And we do. We eat and talk, and I get to know Gudrun a little. Ivy asks me dozens of questions about babies, about Wengest, about life in Netelchester. Willow is quiet, almost shy, which makes me sad. The twins have been raised by my mother's brother and his wife, far south, since birth. My father was grieving my mother's death, Ash and I were too young to raise them, and Bluebell, frankly, would have made a mess of it. So they are our sisters, but they are also strangers. I have met them, perhaps, a dozen times.

The evening wears on, and weariness infuses my poor bones. I need to lie down. Ash catches me yawning and says, "Time for bed, Rose? I am tired too. Would you come and share with me?"

My blood tingles with ice. I cannot lie next to Ash all night: she may read my dreams. I shake my head. "No, I am fine. You go on ahead. I will wait for Bluebell." Even though Bluebell snores and her elbows invariably end up in my ribs.

"I will share with you, Ash," Ivy says, springing to her feet. "Is there room for Willow too?"

Ash looks pleased. "Of course. We may have to squeeze in, but three bodies are warmer than two."

I am falling asleep into my hands, but I stay while goodnights are said. Gudrun takes her leave, Wylm following. Father kisses her softly, murmurs something in her ear. I stand and stretch, peer out the door into the smoky hall for Bluebell. She is deep in conversation with her retainers.

Father's arm is around my waist. "You are tired, don't wait for Bluebell."

But Bluebell has looked up, seen me. She lifts her hand in a gesture that says, *wait just another short moment; I am coming.* I smile.

I turn to Father to say goodnight. I realise in a sudden hot rush that I am alone with him. It may be the only occasion for a long time. I form the question too quickly, and nearly stumble over it.

"Yldra? Do you know her?"

He flinches, almost imperceptibly, but it could be because of the abruptness of my question. "What name?"

"Do you have a sister? Or a half-sister? Yldra?"

Then he is shaking his head. "I have no sister, Rose. I know nobody of that name."

I want to say, "Are you sure?" because I sense too polished a veneer on his answer. But if he hasn't told me now, he won't tell me later. That is the nature of secrets. They do not emerge on repeated questioning; rather they burrow deeper as more lies and denials are thrown on top of them.

"I must sleep," I say, instead. "I must sleep for a hundred years, I am so tired."

"Yes, and the feast starts tomorrow." He leans down and kisses my forehead. "Goodnight, Rose."

I beckon for Bluebell, and we head for the bowerhouse.

. . .

My father is blessed with a perfectly blue sky, perfectly warm day for his wedding feast. Everyone says it is a sign from the great mother. He throws open the doors to his hall so that the sunshine can slant in on the scrubbed wooden boards and fresh rushes. Winter is over. The ceremony itself took place in the state room earlier this morning, presided over by Byrta, who has been my father's counsellor for nearly forty years. She delivered me and all my sisters, and buried my mother twelve years ago. Now solemnity is behind us, and the rest of the afternoon is given over to noisy carousing. The first full moon of the summer will rise tonight, and I have no doubt that my father's retinue will be sleeping drunk on the grass under its glow.

It is hard to be sad or anxious when all around me red and white streamers dance in the breeze. I feel light, as though my worries have drifted away a while, and I am determined not to dwell on them on this happy day. Ivy and Willow are sitting on a bench just outside the door, and I join them with a cup of spiced honey-wine and chat a little while. The smell of roasting pig rises from the hearth and circles the building, making stomachs rumble. Many of the townsfolk come up to the hall with gifts for my father and Gudrun—pots, baskets, charm dollies, cotton flowers, lucky stones—and I gather them with smiles and good wishes. My father and Gudrun move from group to group of friends and well-wishers. He barely takes his eyes from her face. Bluebell comes outside into the sunshine with two of our young cousins, who battle her with wooden swords until she pretends to be defeated and theatrically throws her long body onto the grass. Ash is safely inside with Byrta. All is well, for now.

But then the day grows cooler, dimmer. Blue washes from the sky, shadows lengthen, the scent of damp earth rises. All at once, it is too cool to sit outside, and I am starving. The noise and chatter withdraws into the hall and the great doors are hefted shut, the shutters sealed and the fire stoked. I am one of the last to enter, because I want to see where Ash is sitting, so I can choose the furthest seat from her. I end up with one of my distant uncles and his much younger wife. She is pregnant too, though barely out of childhood herself. She tells endless stories about women whose bodies were torn to pieces by childbirth, and how she hasn't slept for fear since midwinter. I grit my teeth, stealing glances at the table where all my sisters are now congregated, eating and laughing. Ash catches my eyes, beckons. I pretend not to see her. My young companion rattles on, barely stopping to put food in her mouth. With the coming dark, the morbid company, and the growing noise, my sense of contentment frays around the edges and then begins to unravel. I am so tired. I want to go somewhere dark and quiet and close my eyes. And think about Heath, even if thinking about him makes me feel desperate and frightened.

A warm hand on my shoulder. I look up, then flinch as though a snake has touched me. It is Ash.

"Rose?" she says, alarmed, pulling her hand back. In that brief touch, did she sense something? Did she read my thoughts?

I am on my feet in a moment. "I . . . Ash, I'm sorry. I'm not . . ." I intend to tell her I'm unwell, that I have to go immediately, a lie that would not convince even a child. But in that same instant the doors to the hall burst open and a man is standing there, ragged and muddy, calling for the king.

Ash turns; her eyes widen and seem to go black. The blood drains from her face.

"Ash? What is it?"

"They have underestimated the Crow King," she whispers.

Father is on his feet. Bluebell is at his shoulder. A curious, frightened silence takes hold of the wedding feast.

"My lord," the ragged stranger says, falling to his knees at my father's feet. "I have ridden night and day to pass on some grave news. The raiders are already inside the border of Bradsey. They have burned six villages, all outposts of our allies. They spare nobody, not even children. We have left it too late to slow them down. We have . . ." He trails off, exhausted. "Forgive me, my horse could go no further. I have run nearly all the way from Dunscir. They are butchers, my lord. Butchers."

I see Gudrun, her face lit by fire, still sitting at the table where a moment before she was a happy newlywed. She is terrified. Father said he would sit this campaign out, that it was a small matter, that he needed to be with his new wife and Bluebell needed her chance to lead the army alone. But now Gudrun thinks he will go away, and make her a widow again. She catches my eye, and I try to smile to offer her comfort. But I know precisely how she feels.

"We will march tonight," Bluebell says to him, and it is not a question.

Father strokes his beard. "We can be ready by—"

"You are not coming."

Aldric, one of the war chiefs, joins them. "My lord," he says to Father, "your wife sits there quaking; you have been married only a day."

Father looks from one of them to the other and, horribly, he looks old and confused. For the first time. My heart catches. Then he gathers his bearing and turns to the assembly, raising his hand. "Forgive me, my friends. I have a matter of state to attend to. Gudrun?" He beckons her and she is under his arm in a second. Ash runs after them. They leave the hall, a hundred dull murmurs in their wake.

. . .

I pace the confines of my bower while a greasy candle sputters next to the bed. I know Bluebell will come here before she leaves; her sword is still tucked under the lambswool on her side of the bed. Outside, the wedding feast continues, the revellers have spilled out of the hall under the full moon and the cloudless sky. I clutch my hands together as though to catch myself before I fall deeper and deeper into a dark place. It is really happening; Heath is really going to war. *They are butchers.* Morbid pictures have colonised my imagination. It is as though I can already feel the flush of searing heat, the hollowing out of my stomach, the unhingeing of my knees as I hear the news: *Heath is dead, he has fallen to the raiders.* All my nerves have come loose, I am helpless.

The door slams open, letting in a blast of cool evening air. I jump. It is Bluebell. As though she hasn't seen me, she strides to the bed and pulls out her sword. She is already dressed in light mail, her helm pushed down over her head so that her broken nose is hidden and her mouth looks grim under the iron's shadow.

"Bluebell?" I say.

"It is decided," she replies, without looking up. "Father is not coming."

I notice that her hands shake.

"Are you . . . nervous?" I ask.

She freezes, catches me in her frost-blue gaze. "Oh, no, Rose," she says, slowly, passionately. "I am on fire."

She sheathes the sword and turns. I call out, "Wait."

"What is it?" she says, still half-turned from me.

"There is a man . . . Wengest's nephew. He will ride with you from Netelchester. You will know him because he is fair and has no beard." My heart is thundering. "He is special to Wengest—his favourite nephew—and I do hope that he . . ."

She is impatient. She cares little for Wengest, and even less for his beardless nephew. "I have only two eyes in my head, and they must look direct in front of me. I cannot look behind for a—"

"His name is Heath," I say quickly, softly. "And he is special to *me*."

A caught breath. She turns slowly, tilts her head almost imperceptibly to the left. She blinks slowly. "Rose?"

Say nothing, say nothing. And yet, even as I scream these words in my head, my lips are moving and tears are spilling out of my eyes. My voice is thick, almost guttural. "He is the father of my child, sister."

The helm creates such shadows on Bluebell's face that I cannot read her expression. Ugly regret clogs my throat. I have surely doomed Heath, myself, the peace between Ælmesse and Netelchester.

Bluebell's voice remains even, almost cold, but not unkind. She says, "Then I will protect him so that one day she may know him." And she is gone, the door clattering shut behind her. The gust helps drown the candle flame, and I am left standing in the dark, crying with relief and cursing myself for saying anything at all.

· · ·

It is morning, not yet warm. The sun still lingers behind the rocky hill and I am walking among the giants' ruins above my father's hall. I have not slept, I have only thought. So many thoughts that they all twisted up together and made no sense. The ruins are calm and white. Here and there, brave saplings struggle against the stone foundations. The spaces between fallen stones are brimming with leaves and twigs, and captured rain that has turned brown and rank. I find a pillar that has fallen at some time in the years before me, and I sit down and slide onto my side, allowing my temple to touch the cool stone. Willing such coolness, such implacable and ancient calm, into my poor, tired brain.

My eyes are closed, but there are random impressions of colours and shapes on my eyelids. I try to watch them, but my mind skips from one hot thought to another, shattering my focus.

"Rose?"

And my skin is alight again with fear. I jolt, sitting up and opening my eyes. Ash stands a few feet away, and she looks eight years old and worried that I might shout at her. But what does it matter anymore? I told Bluebell. I no longer have a secret to hide.

"I'm so sorry," I say to her, and my voice breaks and I begin to cry.

Ash is next to me in an instant, and I press myself against her and my face twists with sobs. She rubs my back, rocks me as though I were a child and not a mother. And she says, "Rose, I already know. I've known all along."

The tears seem to fall forever.

V

Heorth-monath

Seven weeks have passed since Heath marched for Is-hjarta, and I know not whether he is alive or dead. Sometimes I believe it possible that I would sense if he had died. But I have no second sight; I have nothing but a desperate heart.

And yet the fields bloom as though hope is everywhere. The first two full moons of the warm season have come and gone: red and yellow wildflowers stretch in every direction, tight buds curl on branches, and lambs chase their mothers as though slaughter's shadow will never fall. Two nights ago, we held the hearth-month feast, to celebrate life's renewal and the great mother's benevolence. My belly has grown so full that it is an effort to put my feet on the floor in the morning. Wengest hasn't been in my bed since I returned from Blicstowe. If I were to guess, I might say that he finds my swollen body distasteful. In truth, I am glad not to see him. I am less anxious when I am not always examining his expression for knowledge of my secrets.

It is an hour before evening's fall, and any moment I expect my sister Ash to arrive. I paced at the gate house for two hours this afternoon, until my ankles grew tired and fat. I lie in my bed now, waiting for the gate watchers to call me. I should have remembered that Ash is often late, that she has little concept of time and its passing.

Ash will stay for three full moons; as a companion, an advisor, and to deliver my child. I have not spoken with her since she bid me farewell at my father's hall, when her soft eyes reassured me that all my secrets were safe, that she loved me and did not judge me for what I have done.

Faintly, I hear the signal from the gate. They have spotted Ash's retinue in the distance. I struggle to sit, put both feet on the floor and heave. And I am up. I take a breath and start to move, open my bower door and peer out.

It has grown cold. I put my hand on the threshold and sag, admitting that I will not be walking to the gatehouse. I will not wait there for Ash, nor will I bound out to meet my sister. I will stay right here in the bowerhouse, where she will come before taking me to the hall for supper.

As I turn to move back inside, I see on the stones a small wooden box. It is tucked up against the wall next to the door. I brace my back with my hand and bend to scoop it up. My name is written on it in charcoal. Black smudges transfer themselves to my fingers.

Perhaps it is a gift from one of the villagers. I have been given many warm swaddles; though usually the giver sees me in person, wanting to speak and receive a thank-you.

I close out the late afternoon cool, and return to my bed with the box. I sit with my legs crossed in front of me, and pick open the knot on the string that holds the lid on. Inside is a clay figure of a woman, no bigger than my hand. She is roundly pregnant, and wears a tiny silver knife on a thin ribbon around her neck. I am part curious, part apprehensive. It is so strange. I turn her over to look for a mark, anything that would indicate who has sent her, where she has come from. But there is nothing. The knife is set with two very small gems, and I pull it close to my face to examine them.

When I touch the tiny silver blade, I feel the first cold bolt of magic. It races up my arms and through my shoulders, and in a gasping moment is spinning in my brain.

The vision is very clear. I hold a knife, the real-size version of the miniature with its two gems in the handle. Around me is a winter's landscape. Pure white snow, and a huge spreading rowan tree with leafless branches casting skeletal shadows. Underneath the tree sits Wengest, fat and merry, drunk and hung with jewels and gold. His sword has been discarded a few feet away, and is rusted from never being used.

"I do not want to be here," I try to say, but my jaw is clamped shut and the knife is finding its own path towards Wengest's heart. My whole body lurches forward as though someone else is inside me, controlling my limbs. I strain every muscle against it, but it is no use. The knife plunges into his chest. I scream, but the sound is just an echo in my mind. Blood begins to pulse from him, staining the snow and then melting it. Steam rises, the rowan tree creaks to life. In moments, leaves are sprouting, buds are unfurling, fruit ripens fatly and drops. The profusion of life is almost grotesque, feeding on my husband's spilled blood. I know what this vision means: only with Wengest's death can my daughter flourish, can she be queen of Netelchester.

A blast of cool air hits my face. I blink slowly and the vision dissolves. I am looking, instead, at my sister Ash.

My mind lights up and, without greeting, I press the figure into her hands. "A sending," I say. "Who is it from?"

Ash's face is confused a moment, but then her fingers scrabble to grasp the object. She focuses, her eyes flutter closed. A few moments later they open again, and she shakes her head. "I tried to chase her, but she withdrew the instant she sensed me."

"She? A woman sent this?" I lean forward. "Is her name Yldra?" Even as I say this, I realise it must be true. Yldra, whoever she is, trying to convince me to kill Wengest so that my daughter will thrive. The daughter she thinks I will name Rowan.

"I had no sense of a name," Ash replies. "But it was odd . . ." She bites her lip, then smiles apologetically. "I'm afraid I am sometimes not so in control of this gift of mine, but she was familiar somehow. And unfamiliar, too."

I frown, trying to discern her meaning.

"As though," she says, "she might be related to us, but distantly."

My father's sister.

Ash is stroking my hair. "Are you well, sister? Was it a sending of ill news? Heath?"

I shake my head, the old sad longing welling up again. "No. I have no news of him," I mumble, profoundly uncomfortable with speaking of my love aloud. "It was nothing. Confusion. Trees and snow." I have not told Ash or anyone about the message these visions are sending me. I cannot bear even to say the words, *kill Wengest*, next to each other. Nor do I want to alarm my sisters about the possibility that my daughter—whom I have never considered naming Rowan—will not rule Netelchester. This possibility still fails to strike my heart strongly. Becoming a queen is, after all, not a kind thing to wish upon innocents. All I can think is that I must be in danger of being discovered, for how else could my husband's first child not succeed him? I vow to stay well clear of Wengest until the child is born.

I smile weakly at Ash. "I'm glad you are here." It is the truth.

. . .

Ash's presence brings me great joy. As summer deepens, I sleep easier at night with her beside me. I try not to think of Heath, or, at least, I try not to worry about him. I tell myself Bluebell will keep watch for me and I can ask for no greater assurance. We begin to plan the midsummer feast, raising the polite ire of Nyll and his small band of curmudgeonly trimartyrs, who grow more vocal with every seasonal festival. The predicted date of my child's birth comes and goes, and I am both glad—for a late birth will mean less suspicion directed at me—and horribly disheartened. I am so very, very tired.

VI

Milc-monath

Sleep does not come easy in these last days of pregnancy. Some reasons are material: it is simply impossible for me to get comfortable. But some are immaterial: I feel lost somehow, and guilty all the time. The dark of early morning is not a betrayer's friend. Something has woken me and I strain my ears into the dark to hear what it might be.

Voices. From the king's bower. Muffled through the wall, but voices nonetheless. Wengest is talking to somebody in his room, very late. My first thought is that he has a woman in there, and my heart grows indignant. But the second voice does not sound like a woman's. I listen for a while, trying to make out words but there are none clear enough. There is occasional laughter, but then there is quiet. The quiet stretches out. Ash breathes softly next to me. Sleep doesn't return.

I rise, curious about the voices in Wengest's bower. Is it a woman? If so, would I have the courage to confront him? I pull on a shawl and go to the door, out briefly into the starry clear night, then back in through Wengest's door. The fire is low in the hearth, just enough light for me to see that he is asleep now. His dark features are shadowed. He does not flinch when I come in, and I see that there are two empty cups on the chest of drawers. He has been drinking, but now his companion—whoever it was—has gone.

I move to back out, but my eye is caught by the dull gleam of steel. His sword.

My gaze moves, as if outside of my control, between the supine figure of Wengest and the hard blade.

Kill him before the child is born.

And I allow myself to imagine it. Not the act itself, not the resistance and gristle of his body to the blade. But the aftermath, where I am queen of Netelchester and Heath is my consort. My blood rushes with it, my good sense is in danger of being swept away.

But then I feel a strange pain in my back, down very low, and water splatters onto the rushes between my feet. Wengest stirs, so I know that I must have groaned with the sudden pain. He opens his eyes and says, "Rose, is that you?"

"The child is coming," I say.

He sits up. "Return to your sister," he says, fear and anger infusing his voice. "Men should have nothing to do with such things."

I want nothing more than to hurry back to Ash, but another pain grabs me and I have to stop and lean forward, groaning. As I do, my eye falls on a folded vellum book on the end of Wengest's bed. Wengest cannot read, and the book is clearly marked with the triangle of the trimartyrs. Nyll has been here. Nyll has been laughing with Wengest until the early hours. With the sudden clarity of anybody pulled forcibly out of her self-obsession, I see why my daughter will never be queen. It has nothing to do with Heath; it has everything to do with faith.

"Go on, off with you!" Wengest exclaims. He is out of bed now and helping me—thrusting me—towards the door. "Ash!" he calls as he slams the door open. "Tend to your sister."

All thoughts of Nyll, of Wengest, even of Heath flee from me as the pain grasps my body again. I am as confused and terrified as a pig being led to the butcher's block. I try to catch my breath and clear my mind, but the pain is far worse than I had imagined and Wengest hands me over to Ash with a barked order that he wants to hear and see nothing until the child is born and wrapped in clean linen.

At least I am back in my own bower, near my own bed. Ash bustles about me, unfolding clean cloths and offering soothing words. "Make yourself comfortable," she says.

I almost laugh. An unforgiving monster has fastened sharp jaws around my back and groin and is squeezing harder and harder. I had heard that there should be a rhythm of pain and relief, but I have no relief. Ash is concerned enough by this to feel my belly carefully. She frowns and says, "The baby is facing the wrong way. Her back is against yours."

"Is that bad? Will she die?" *Will I die?*

"No, no," Ash says, brushing my hair from my face. "She is safe, you both are. But it will hurt, Rosie. I'm sorry, but it will hurt and it will be long." She helps me onto the bed, arranging me so I am kneeling over a pile of cushions. I fear the unremitting pain, the long night ahead. I want to cry, I want to be a young virgin again who never thought of the passions of the body and all their black consequences.

. . .

The night unfurls, the sun returns and climbs high into the sky, and finally the child slides from my exhausted body. I sob with relief, and Ash sobs too. The child—hot and squirming—is a girl. A dark-haired, slate-eyed girl. I bundle her against me and offer her my breast as though I have been preparing for her arrival for my whole life. There is a pause in life, a moment of still, warm silence. A moment, perhaps, of pure happiness.

Then Ash asks me, "Do you want me to get Wengest?"

I clutch the baby jealously. She has settled to suckle. "No." She is not his, anyway. He would be a stranger in here.

"I think it would be wise to show him the child," Ash says carefully.

I gaze at her. She has dark rings under her eyes, and I realise she must be tired too. She is looking back at me with eyes as dark as mine, eyes as dark as I suspect my daughter's will be. Of course she is right. Wengest is likely in the next bower. He will have heard the moaning stop, he will have heard my daughter's keening cry. He will be waiting for Ash to tell him to come, that the bloodied sheets have been piled away and that the child and I are cleaned and covered up.

We prepare ourselves and the room, and Ash goes to fetch my husband.

In the few moments remaining, I study my daughter's face and hands, her impossibly soft cheeks and ears. She is purely mine in this last sliver of time before the king—the man who will be her father—comes to meet her. If I wasn't so exhausted, I would consider running away.

No. I would not. I know what duty dictates. The door opens and I apply a smile. Wengest looks young, but almost afraid to show his excitement. I realise that we have spent too little time together in these last few months, and we have grown strange to each other.

"It's a daughter," I say. "I hope you aren't disappointed."

"No, of course not," he replies, approaching and sitting next to me on the bed. "There will be other children."

I do not remind him that my father had five daughters and no sons at all. He is gazing at the child with soft eyes. "She is pretty like you," he says. "Dark like me."

"Like both of us," I say, hoping that I do not sound as relieved as I feel.

"I should like to name her after my mother," he says.

In an instant, I remember that his mother's name was Rowan. "No," I say. "Must we burden her with someone else's name? Can we not give her her own name?"

Wengest arches an annoyed eyebrow. "Queen Rowan was much loved by her people. You cannot deny them the joy of remembering her in the image of her grand-daughter."

I cannot resist him. Under any other circumstances, I would like the name Rowan. The rowan tree has long been associated with power and mystery.

"Come," Wengest says, his voice growing soft. "You have had her all to yourself these past nine months. Allow me one small mark of ownership." His eyes drop to her face. "She is beautiful, is she not? Perfect?"

I say nothing, imagining this serious dark creature growing into a little girl named Rowan, into a woman who will never be queen. I decide to ask Wengest directly. "You are considering taking the Trimartyr faith, are you not, Wengest?"

He studies me a few moments, a puzzled smile at his lips. "You are terribly astute, Rose. I thought you had nothing in your head but thoughts of babies."

"Nyll has you . . ." I do not say, *in his thrall.* "He has you interested?"

"I like the faith well enough, though it is a little gruesome. But a king in the trimartyr faith is appointed by Maava. No man can take his kingship without offence to the one god. It is a decision of strategy more than faith, Rose. It will make me more powerful, cement my position in my people's estimation.'

I stroke Rowan's soft head. Her eyes are falling closed. "Then Rowan will never be queen."

"If she marries a king she will. We will make an advantageous match for her. Put your mind at rest."

I do not have energy for protests. In truth, Rowan is not Wengest's child so has no right to his throne. Perhaps the next child will.

Wengest kisses my cheek softly, his beard scratching my skin. "Are you happy, Rose?"

I shake my head, teary now. "I am so very tired, Wengest. Send my sister back in. I am sorry to send you away, but I must sleep now."

He rises, tracing a soft line on the baby's cheek. "Very well," he says. "When you are feeling better, we will consult with Nyll about an appropriate feast of welcoming for the child."

I nod, crying now. My tears do not unnerve him. He merely turns his back and walks away.

. . .

Rowan is eight days old when the messenger comes. He has ridden from Is-hjarta, but not in the hard, urgent way that a bearer of bad news would ride. When he appears at Wengest's hall, he looks well-rested, cheerful, and he sends for me directly.

I leave Ash folding swaddling clothes in our bower, and take little Rowan in the crook of my arm to the hall. She has been fractious today, unable to settle to the breast or the crib. She seems happiest in motion. I rock her idly, tired beyond measurement and yet stupidly happy most of the time.

Wengest and the rider wait between the carved columns that line the outside of the hall. The doors are thrown open and inside there is the bustle of dinner's preparation, the smell of roasting meat and baking pie. When I see Bluebell's standard, my pulse quickens.

"I have news from your sister Bluebell," he says, before I have a chance to greet him.

My heart is caught up high in my chest, waiting. "She is . . . well?" It is news of Heath, I know it. Wengest is standing right next to me. How on earth will I hide my fear, my hope?

"Yes, she is. She wanted to pass on that the campaign goes well, she is unharmed and looks forward to a swift end to war in Bradsey. She wanted me to pass on, too, news that she has taken your husband's young nephew as third-in-command." Here the messenger turns to Wengest and nods his head deferentially. "You would be proud, King Wengest. He is by her side at all times."

Wengest smiles and shakes his head. "Is that so? I would not have imagined it."

I allow myself to smile too, but for different reasons. This is Bluebell's way of telling me Heath is alive, he is whole, he is by the side of the greatest protector I could wish for him.

"I thank you for your good news," I say to the messenger. "Will you stay for dinner?"

He shakes his head. "No, I will start the return journey immediately, for I have family in Dunscir who are expecting me by nightfall. Have you any message to pass on to your sister?"

I choose my words very carefully, feeling Wengest's presence close to my elbow. "Tell her I am delivered of a daughter named Rowan." I glance down at my daughter's face, and notice that she is finally asleep. "That she is a perfect beauty and a compliment to the loving bond of her parents." Here, Wengest touches my arm tenderly, assuredly; and guilt touches my heart with just the same finesse. "Tell her I am happy," I finish. "But that she and her army cannot come home soon enough."

"As you wish," the messenger says, nodding and turning. "Farewell."

"Farewell," I say.

Wengest takes my free hand and I hold it for a moment, then pull away as gracefully as I can, crossing my arms over the baby. He does not notice this small act of defiance; and we stand under the colonnade and watch the rider wind back down the hill, on his way to deliver my message of love.

DINDRANA'S LOVER

"There is in this castle a gentlewoman and this castle is hers. So it befell many years agone there fell upon her a malady. An old man said and she might have a dish full of blood of a maid and a clean virgin, that blood should be her health, and for to anoint her withal; and for this thing was this custom made."
— Sir Thomas Malory, *Le Morte D'Arthur*

Beautiful, beautiful Gabriel.

Dindrana held her arms aloft and closed her eyes as the maids dressed her. The brush of cotton on her bare skin, silk soft on her wrists, the laces drawing in across her waist and ribs. Her senses flared, heat shimmered across her skin. Because soon, Gabriel would be taking it all off her again. Reversing the flow of fabric over flesh, exposing her nipples to the evening cool, placing his warm, rough hands over her hips and buttocks.

"Done, my lady."

Dindrana opened her eyes. "Off with you," she said.

The two maids scurried away, closing the door behind them. Dindrana moved to the window and peered through the tiny mullioned pane. Outside, summer storm clouds brooded along the darkening horizon. The tallest trees were already mad in the wind. By nightfall, by the appointed hour with Gabriel, the storm would be full upon them and she would not be in her cosy chamber in her father's castle. She would be in the stables, immersed in the scent of hay and horses, enclosed in the arms of her lover, possessed by him for the first time.

Beautiful, beautiful Gabriel.

An angel's name, and an angel's face, but a stablehand nonetheless. How long had she known him and not noticed him? Fifteen years? This summer everything was different. She'd admired him from afar, then drawn closer every day, then started conversations with him, brought him small gifts of semi-precious stones. She didn't love him. Sweet Jesus, no. Love, well that was for fools and drunkards. Rather, she had become gripped by the thought of him. By his size and smell and heat and colouring, by the way his top lip flattened out when he smiled, by the sparse golden hairs on his knuckles, by the little clench at his jaw when he exerted himself. Not a night had passed in three months that she hadn't fallen asleep after imagining that forbidden embrace in liquid detail, rubbing herself against her hand while face-down on her mattress, until a gorgeous ache of pleasure shuddered through her and then extinguished to sweet smoke along her veins.

Her father was already talking about suitable husbands for her. And as Dindrana was a lady, daughter of an earl, sister of one of the King's knights, Gabriel's name would never be brought up as a potential suitor. Perhaps her eventual husband would be a crusty old man with sagging flesh and long nostril hairs. If that were the case, she was determined to have one torrid memory to warm the long nights of her future.

And so into the storm.

She pulled her cloak around her against the wind and dashed across the courtyard towards the stables. Dried leaves whirled about her feet and the long grass bent to and fro. A low rumble sounded and one or two fat raindrops spattered to the ground. She pushed open the stable door and slammed out the wind behind her. Some of the horses were restless in anticipation of the storm, switching their tails anxiously. Standing still, she waited for her eyes to adjust to the dark.

"Gabriel?" she called softly.

"Here."

She looked up. He lay shirtless on his front, leaning over the edge of the loft. His broad shoulders gleamed in the dim light. He smiled, and a bolt of heat shot from under her ribs to the cleft between her legs. She pushed her cloak back and headed for the rough wooden ladder.

"I thought you would never come," he said as she collapsed next to him in the hay.

"I'm right on time," she replied, reaching out eager fingers to touch his bare flesh.

"It feels like I've been waiting forever." He rolled on top of her and pressed his lips against hers. The tip of his tongue was in her mouth. Liquid fire under her skin. He grasped her hands and pulled them over her head, lying them gently in the hay, then began to pick at the laces at the sides of her dress. His ineptitude told her he was as new to this as she was.

"Have there been others?" she asked. "Village girls?"

"Only you," he murmured, pulling up her dress, his hand hard on the fleshiest curve of her inner thigh.

She wriggled out of her dress and he out of his trousers. His face was against her breasts.

"I love only you," he said softly.

Dindrana heard but didn't respond. She was lost on the pull of desire now anyway. The rain was heavy on the stable roof, and thunder boomed.

No. It wasn't thunder. It was the door. The door slamming open.

"Are you here, Lady Dindrana?" A male voice.

She gasped and gathered her clothes around her. The man held a torch aloft and his face was thrown into shadows, but Dindrana knew that imperious tone. Galahad. She pushed Gabriel down into the hay and peered over the edge. "What do you want?"

"I saw you leave the castle. It isn't safe to be out here in a storm."

"Leave me alone."

But he was already advancing towards the ladder. Galahad was her brother's closest friend, only fifteen years old but already one of Arthur's knights. His golden hair and rosy cheeks would have made him beautiful were he not so pious and self-righteous. The rain pounded on the roof. She hurried to rearrange her clothes, saw from the corner of her eye Gabriel trying to do the same.

"Who is up there with you?" Galahad asked. But Dindrana suspected he already knew. He had watched them with distrust over the last few weeks, and had, over meals in her father's hall, dropped a few pointed comments about chastity.

"Galahad, leave me be. I'll come inside shortly."

Too late. He was already standing over them, surveying them with a coolness that was unnatural in one so young. His free hand went to the grip of his sword.

"Gabriel?" he whispered incredulously. "The stable-boy?" He turned to Dindrana, her laces unfastened. "In the Lord's name, Dindrana, what will Percival think?"

"Please," she gasped, "don't tell Percival." Her father's endless sermons she could endure, her mother's icy displeasure, but not Percival's mute, uncomprehending disappointment.

Galahad unsheathed his sword. It glinted dimly by the lamplight.

"Which part of you has touched Lady Dindrana?" he asked Gabriel.

"Galahad, no," Dindrana protested.

"Which part, boy? I shall have to remove it."

Gabriel, terrified, merely stared at him speechlessly.

"Don't tell me, boy, that it has gone so far I shall have to make a woman of you," Galahad said.

Dindrana climbed to her feet and stayed his hand. "No. It has not gone so far."

He turned his gaze to her. "Virginity, Dindrana, is a woman's only treasure. His hands, then, shall I remove them both?"

"You shall not touch him," she said, imbuing her voice with more force than she actually felt. "Let him leave. You shall not act contrary to my wishes when you are the guest of my father."

Galahad, courteous to a fault, put his sword away. "Go," he said to Gabriel. "I shall be telling Dindrana's father of this, so you'd best go for good. You will be unwelcome anywhere in Margris from this moment on."

Gabriel stood uncertainly, reached for Dindrana. Instantly the sword was free again, swinging down and stopping a mere inch from Gabriel's hand. "You will lose it," Galahad threatened.

Dindrana and her lover faced each other for the last time.

"I'll love you always," he said.

She nodded, guilty pulse beating hard at her throat. "Go. Be safe."

He inched nervously towards the ladder, keeping a wary eye on Galahad's sword, then scrambled down and away. Dindrana drew deep breaths. The fall, from lucid heat to leaden cold was almost too much to bear.

"Dindrana, how could this be?"

She turned to face Galahad. "In the name of Christ I beg you, Galahad, don't tell Percival."

"You should not appeal to your saviour so lightly. Percival will be told as will your parents. It's what God would want me to do."

· · ·

It was as Dindrana knew it would be. Her mother's pale grey eyes almost unblinking, her mouth a sneer of disdain. Her father, pulling the wood-and-gold cross off the chapel wall and making her kneel before it, thrusting it in her face to kiss, making her hold it firm and swear, swear on Christ's bones, that she would remain a virgin until she married.

And Percival stood there, back straight as a rod, merely looking at her. Percival—strong, wise, handsome Percival. He was as dark as she was fair, and all their lives they had endured the exclamations of surprise. "Twins! And so dissimilar!" She wanted to tell him how sorry she was, how shamed she felt. But he already knew. The link they had shared since childhood was still strong, despite his protestations that it was ungodly to believe so.

Percival gazed at her, knowing everything.

. . .

She had made a promise to God, now, to keep her virginity, and she took God very seriously. But this vow seemed almost impossible to keep. Dindrana knew only a few other women her age, and none of them seemed as tortured by desire as she was. Was there something wrong with her? She prayed that the Lord would take it away, told him that she could keep her vow much more readily if only she didn't suffer with the waves of searing yearning that rose and fell within her over the coming years. Most nights found her knuckle deep in her own soft, wet flesh, pushing that spot over and over again, hoping every time that this convulsion of pleasure would be the last. But every morning it started again, tickling and spreading, warm and moist and wanting. Always wanting.

But Dindrana remained chaste.

II

Dindrana knew they were lost, long before Percival and Galahad exchanged unsure glances. Lostness had a distinct feel, a sickly veering between feeling certain and feeling adrift. The familiar passed into the unfamiliar and back again. The trees were too tall, the birdsong too distant, the sun too far.

"Are we lost?" she said at last.

"We are not lost," Percival said.

"No," said Galahad at the same moment. Neither of them turned their faces to her.

The three of them had been riding since morning, on their way to her father's winter residence. Icy rain had been falling for four hours, and the promised stop for dinner at Sir Bors's home had not eventuated, though they should have been there hours ago. As much as he tried to hide it, Dindrana could feel Percival's anxiety radiating from him in grey waves.

Despite her moleskin cloak, she was damp. Her feet were blocks of ice, and gooseflesh covered her. "I'm tired, I'm cold, and I'm hungry. We must stop somewhere. Anywhere. And soon."

Galahad slowed his horse so he was trotting beside her. "You are always too concerned with satisfying your appetite," he said just out of Percival's hearing. For the last six years, since the incident in the stables, he had taken every opportunity to remind her that he had borne witness to her moral weakness.

She steadfastly ignored him, urging her palfrey forward. "Percival," she called, catching up to him, "we should have passed Bors's house at midmorning. Soon it will be night. At the very least, we should find a busier road and ask for direction."

Galahad joined them, determined to be part of the negotiations. "We have been bearing east as we intended."

"She makes a good case," Percival sighed to Galahad. "We've missed Bors, for certain. It's long past the middle of the day, the horses are exhausted. But I hear no other hoofbeats nor wheels, I smell no smoke from a chimney or shit from a farm. And this road . . . well, it's barely a road. The mud is growing thicker, the trees closer."

"Two miles back we passed a crossroad that looked wide and well-kept. Shall we return to it?" Galahad suggested. "If the river we crossed this morning follows a sure path, then a turn southwards should bring us to water. And where there's water, there's always a town. Eventually."

They turned their horses around and headed back. The rain eased a little, and Dindrana thought she detected white sunlight trying to break through the clouds. The road south was wider but no less muddy, and led down into a leafy valley split by a mirror-silver lake. They stopped here, in a pause in the rain, rested their horses and drank water from their costrels.

Dindrana pushed back her cloak and stood at the edge of the lake, rocking back and forth on the balls of her feet to stretch her legs after hours in the saddle. Her body ached and her heart was tired, and she was not at all up to this week's fate. She was meant to be safely in her father's winter hall by nightfall, when she was to meet her prospective husband, an earl from the west country. From there Percival and Galahad were off on an adventure, searching for the mythical Sangraal, which Arthur spoke of so obsessively: the dish, it was said, which Jesus himself had eaten from at his last supper. Her own adventure would involve a life indoors, with dishes only her ageing husband had eaten from.

The lake reflected without the slightest distortion between the two leafy slopes that bracketed it. She gazed at the reflection: her own pale face and golden hair, the tiny shard of blue sky, the first bursts of autumn colour in the trees, and . . .

"Percival!" she cried, looking away from the reflection and up at the actual slope. "Look!"

Percival and Galahad both looked. Grey stone, barely above the treetops. The tower of a building.

"Church or stronghold?" Galahad asked. "There's no flag, no cross. Perhaps we are even more lost than Lady Dindrana feared."

"We are far from home, my friend," said Percival. "But we have much further to go, and much stranger things to see. Come, it's only half a mile up the hill. We'll lead the horses up. It's time we stopped for the day, sat by a fire, and ate something."

The path up the hill was narrow and overgrown. Nettles at her ankles, sour-smelling swinecress in her nostrils. Through the woods, and then the road opened out a little and they stood at the gates of a squat castle. Its tower loomed above them, half enshrouded in mist and rain. Dindrana ached to be inside by a fire with food in her belly.

They could see through the gate to an empty courtyard. The rain intensified, coming down in sheets.

"Hello!" called Galahad. "Hoy there! Open the gate! Sir Percival and Sir Galahad of the Table Round!"

Nothing. The emptiness was strange and cold. Dindrana's eyes met Percival's, and a bolt of unspoken communication passed between them. *We should leave this place.*

But then a voice called from beyond the gate. "Hoy!"

Dindrana turned to see a drably dressed soldier with a long spear approaching. They waited until he stood on the other side of the bars. "Knights of the Table Round?" he asked.

"Yes," Galahad said, proudly squaring his shoulders despite the bucketing rain. "May we trouble your master for a brief respite from the weather?"

"And who is the lady?"

Percival gave Dindrana a bewildered look before replying. "Why, she is my sister."

He rattled a set of keys on the chain at his hip, and then the gate swung inwards slowly. "Follow," said the guard.

The yard was empty, the castle buildings were in very bad repair. A whole wing was crumbling into itself, and stones were missing from the battlements. Only one stablehand came to help them with their horses, and he was a toothless old fellow who barely spoke a word of English. As he led their mounts away and they stood under cover at the side of the courtyard, a stout man with a brilliant red moustache and beard emerged from the crumbling front entrance to the castle proper.

"Welcome, welcome," he said, taking first Galahad's hand then Percival's and pumping them soundly.

"You are the master of the house?" Galahad asked.

"Yes, you could say that. What a lovely young lady. The daughter of nobility, I take it? And a maiden?"

Dindrana squirmed under his scrutiny. His eyes ran from her toes to her crown, unabashedly.

"This is my sister, Dindrana," Percival replied, the hesitation in his voice revealing his discomfort in the avid curiosity. "She is on her way to my father's residence to be married."

"Not yet married then? Your whole life awaits you." He smiled at Dindrana, and it seemed a warm and genuine enough smile. "Please come in. The rain and the cold will make you ill. We have warm food for you, and warm beds if you wish to stay for a while."

"Thank you, my lord. We don't know your name," Galahad said as they were led towards the entrance.

He stopped a moment, stroked his big red beard. "They call me Swan."

"Why is that, sir?" Dindrana asked, curious.

"Because I like to eat them I suppose. In any case, you should call me that too. This way."

Swan led them into a dark passageway, which smelled faintly of mould and damp. Dindrana felt apprehensive, though she couldn't decide why. Perhaps it was the dark. Hardly any lamps lit the hallways. The household was obviously poor. It was remote, and the mud and pine needles meant poor farmland in the surrounding area. They ascended a dank staircase and Swan gestured to his right and to his left. "A room for the gentlemen," he said, "and here a room for the lady. My most faithful maid and servant, Thea, will be in to start the fires."

"Thank you," Dindrana said, standing on the threshold of the chamber.

"Make yourself comfortable," Swan said. "We'll be eating in half an hour. Somebody will come to fetch you. Perhaps it will be me."

Percival and Galahad had already disappeared into their chamber. Dindrana waited for Swan to move, but he remained where he was, looking at her with an eager smile. "Thank you," she said again. When he still did not move, she backed into her room, closing the door gently. After a few moments she heard his footsteps move away.

She turned and looked about her. In this room, there was no trace of the creeping poverty so evident in the rest of the castle. Immaculate, gilt-woven tapestries covered the walls, a huge box-bed with a thick mattress sat in the middle, and a full-length silver-framed looking-glass hung in the corner. Dindrana glanced in the mirror. She looked a mess—wet through, with bedraggled hair and blue lips. She stripped off her wet things and hung them carefully by the fireplace, then climbed into the bed to warm up.

A quick knock at the door preceded a maid with a basket of dry kindling, who offered Dindrana a smile before kneeling before the fireplace. Soon, the fire was ablaze.

"My lady, I am Thea," she said. She was an elderly woman with thick arms. She indicated a large wooden trunk at the end of the bed. The carvings reminded Dindrana of the carvings that were sometimes dug up in the fields back home, from the people who had lived there hundreds of years ago. Intricate curves with sharp edges, a figure that looked like a serpent swallowing a child.

"You'll find clean, warm clothes in there," Thea said.

There was something warm about Thea that made Dindrana blurt out her next, anxious question. "Is this a good place? Is your master a good man?"

"I have no master," Thea said, with a smile.

"What do you mean?"

"You'll see. Enjoy the gowns." Thea slipped out, shutting the door behind her.

Dindrana threw back the covers and went to the trunk, flipped up the clasp and opened the heavy lid. Then gasped. Inside was the most incredible collection of gowns she had ever seen. In awe, she pulled out the gown on top. Blue silk, trimmed with deeper blue velvet, gilt threaded through the bodice. Another was beaded with pearls, yet another featured ermine collar and cuffs. She dug through the collection of dresses, almost laughing at the extravagance. She eyed her own wet gown hanging by the fire. It would be hours before it dried and it would soon be suppertime. On impulse she pulled out the blue silk and velvet dress and tried it on. Though it was the right length, it was far too loose across the bust. It dipped low at the front, revealing the round swelling of her white breasts. The contrast of the blue against her skin was dazzling, beautiful. She studied herself a while in the glass. Did her new husband even have sufficient eyesight to see her beauty? How might his grizzled hands look against her poreless softness? Just as Dindrana experienced desire deeply in her body, so too did she experience revulsion now. Her husband would want to touch her young body, to push himself into her and claim her virginity. And all this youthful beauty would be wasted.

Her face flushed. Embarrassed, ashamed at her vanity. Angry with her fate. She draped another of the dresses over the glass so she could no longer see herself, then settled back on the bed to rest her weary body until supper.

. . .

Swan himself came to accompany them to the dining hall. His eager smile revealed his delight at her choice of gown, although Galahad and Percival seemed less pleased with her change of clothes.

"You see your brother and I are in our own clothes," Galahad said.

"The maid said I could take a dress from the trunk. There were dozens."

"Were they all so . . . insufficient?" he muttered.

She pulled the bodice up higher on her breasts. "They were all fine gowns for special occasions. I chose the first I saw. My own clothes are wet and cold."

"As are mine and Percival's. Unlike you, Dindrana, our bodies don't speak to us more clearly than our consciences."

Dindrana fell silent. She knew that Percival stung with shame. He saw Galahad's piety as an example to him.

Swan waited a few paces ahead of them. "Here we are, my lords, my lady. The dining hall."

They entered a large firelit room. About forty people sat around on long benches, drinking and talking while waiting for the meal to be served. There was a smell of smoke and roasting meat, sweet steam and unwashed men. Dindrana felt eyes upon her, interested in her. Swan led them to the head table and sat Dindrana on his left with Percival beside her, and Galahad on his right.

"Music!" called Swan, and a trio began to play a motet. Harp, crumhorn, hand-drum. Stomping feet and loud voices joined in.

Dindrana boldly lifted her eyes and began to return some of the stares. As she did so, eyes flicking from one face to another, she grew curious. Anxious. When Swan was engaged in conversation with Galahad, she turned to Percival.

"Do you notice something unusual about the gathering?" she asked him.

He looked around. "They are quite low people. Poor."

"There are no women."

Percival scoffed. "What are you saying? I see three women. There, and there, and here at this very table." He pointed out two crones at opposite ends of the room, then indicated a woman with a hooded cape who sat catatonic at the end of their table.

"Yes, three hags older than our grandmother. There are no *young* women. No maidens, no mothers, no mistress of the castle."

"Perhaps they have moved away for the winter. This is a cold and remote part of the country."

"It seems strange. This whole place seems strange. Something is not quite right."

"Ungodly superstition, sister. Here, eat your meal."

They were served with sickly portions of pork and bread, and watery ale.

Conversation turned towards more mundane things as they ate. Dindrana choked down the meal, straining to hear conversations over the music and laughter.

"This is a well-hidden castle, Swan," Percival said. "Does it have a colourful history?"

Swan beamed with pride. "Oh yes. It's the last known residence of Saint Triscula."

Galahad's eyes lit up. "Triscula the Virgin? Here?"

"Yes. She healed the blind twins of King Bann, and helped spread the word of the true Church throughout the holy land. At the threat of rape by a pair of infidels, God spoke by striking them both with lightning, and for that she believed it was her lot never to marry and to remain a virgin. She returned here in her old age to live out her life and write her own history."

Galahad, excited as always by sanctity, began to gaze around him with renewed interest. "So Triscula may have sat here? May have eaten in this very hall?"

"Yes, my lord. Nothing much has changed here in two hundred years. Except to grow old, to fall into ruin."

Dindrana heard in Galahad's voice his customary forceful self-righteousness. "I'm appalled. Appalled that Saint Triscula's residence should fall into disrepair. We must tell the King, Percival. Have him send men and materials for repairs, for a shrine, or even a statue."

"No, no," Swan responded, shaking his head. "We're a small court. We can manage well on our own. The mistress wouldn't like the King's men being here, or other pilgrims. She wouldn't like it at all."

Percival gave Dindrana a knowing smile, then turned to Swan. "The mistress? Where is your wife, sir?"

"The mistress isn't my wife. The mistress is the true owner of this castle. However, she is extremely ill and I do what I can to keep things running on her behalf."

"Ill?" said Galahad. "I am sorry to hear that."

"Alas, sir, she has been ill for many, many years. A very long time ago she fell into a malady. We sometimes find the medicine she needs and it works for a little while and she is quite changed. Quite healthy."

"As a gentlewoman and custodian of Triscula the Virgin's shrine, she ought to have the help of the best physicians. Can we do anything? Can we speak with her?" Percival asked.

"Certainly, sir, for this is she." Swan indicated the crone who sat without moving at the end of their table. He rose and went to her, gently pulling back her hood. Her face was death-mask white, covered in festering sores. She dribbled onto herself like a simple. Swan began to speak to her in the voice one might use with a child. "See, my mistress, knights of Arthur come to pay their respect to you."

"My lady," Galahad said, standing and bowing deeply, "I am so honoured to be in the house of Saint Triscula."

The crone appeared not to have heard. Percival pulled Galahad down to his seat. "Can you not see she is all but dead, Galahad. She neither hears nor sees you."

But then the woman lifted a wasted arm, extended her hand and pointed at Dindrana.

Dindrana's blood went cold.

"Yes, my lady," said Swan. "On her way to marry. Her name is Dindrana, and she is a gentlewoman."

"The dress," the woman croaked.

"Ah, you remember that one? It was a favourite of yours." Swan grinned until it split his beard, nodding at Dindrana. "She likes you."

Dindrana forced a smile in return. Morning, and the rest of their journey, could not come soon enough.

· · ·

After the meal, while the fire roared and the rain pelted the roof, Swan stood and declared, "And now, Triscula the Virgin's finest mead. For our guests! Knights of the Table Round."

A roar of approval went up. Percival and Galahad smiled around. Dindrana leaned in to her brother and said, "Perhaps I may be excused to go to bed?"

"It would not be courteous to do so," Percival said. "We will drink with them."

She dropped her voice to a harsh whisper. "I do not like this place."

He met her eyes steadily. "I will keep you safe."

She gave him a quick smile, then Thea appeared, with a silver tray and a half-dozen silver goblets. It seemed all the wealth in the castle was invested in gowns and goblets. Dindrana took hers with a perfunctory smile, took a slow sip.

Oh, it was divine. It tasted like honey and gold, bursting sharply on her tongue and warming her chest. She took another gulp. Galahad and Percival and Swan were already involved in some kind of drinking game. Her goblet was refilled without her asking. The space grew rowdy, hot, close. The mead sang to her tongue. *Drink me*, it sang, *drink me*. The room shifted a little. She sat back in her chair, eyes closed, happy. It was the happiest mead she had ever drunk.

Swan's voice was in her ear. "Are you tired, my lady?"

"If I could drift off on this cloud . . ."

"You must feel free to go to your room and sleep. You needn't stay up with the men."

Dindrana opened her eyes. Percival and Galahad were roaring drunk. Galahad had his arms spread wide and was whirling in time with the music in front of the fire. She had not thought it possible for him to enjoy himself, and she laughed.

"What is in that mead?" she asked Swan.

"The spirit of Saint Triscula."

"Triscula the Virgin," Dindrana said. "That's what they call her."

"Yes, that's right."

She remembered Swan's joke earlier, about where his name came from. "Do they call her that because she likes to eat them?"

"You are drunk, my lady."

Dindrana shrugged. "And I am a virgin. But both problems will be reconciled in time." She pushed back her chair, stumbled to her feet. "Goodnight."

Swan cocked his head at Thea, who came and grasped Dindrana firmly under her elbow. "Come, little mistress. Your bed awaits."

. . .

"Dindrana!"

Dindrana woke sharply, eyes blinking against the glare of a lamp. Percival kneeled over her. His pupils were black liquid.

"What is it?" she asked. Her heart thudded. Were they in danger?

"Galahad. He has had a vision. A fit. He lay upon the floor and . . . he spoke in God's own tongue and when he opened his eyes he said he knew where the Sangraal was. He saw it in the eye of his mind. We leave immediately."

Dindrana could hear the rain, still pounding outside. "But Percival . . . it is night. The rain . . .This is mad."

"This is God's will. Swan has given us fresh horses. You will stay here and we will send a message to Father to come and collect you himself. Perhaps a week or ten days away."

She sat up. "No. No, I don't want to stay here. I want to come with you."

Percival was already shaking his head. Dindrana realised he was still very drunk. Beyond drunk. A little outside his own mind, as Galahad must have been when he took his prescient fit.

"Don't do this," she said, grasping his wrist. "Wait until morning. Wait until you are thinking straight."

"Can you not feel it, Dindrana? Can you not feel God's purpose? I can." He dropped his voice. "For the first time, like Galahad, I can feel it."

"I don't want to be here alone."

"These are the people of Saint Triscula. A saint will watch over you. God will watch over you." He stood, the lantern swung, making foreign shadows on his face. She almost didn't recognise him.

"I beg you, brother."

"A week. Father will come for you. I have God's work to do. Save your womanly tears." And then he was gone.

Dindrana sat up in bed, arms around her knees. She listened to the rain, then to the voices and eventually the hoofbeats. The gate creaked open and clanged shut again. A week or so, then Father would be here. She closed her eyes. She only had to last a week or so.

Dindrana finally gave in to tiredness, sliding back beneath the covers and laying her head on the pillow. Just as she was drifting off to sleep she heard footsteps on the stairwell, approaching her door. Then, unmistakably, she heard the sound of a bolt being shot and a key turning.

She had been locked in.

III

Dawn had long since broken, and Dindrana had long since been awake when her door was finally unlocked. She had tried to sleep, dozing off and on through the tangle of her fear during the night, but she had risen with the first weak glimmers of daylight and had been waiting ever since. Outside her window, the clouds had cleared to a pale, cool day.

Thea stood at her door. "Rise, Lady Dindrana," she said without expression. "The mistress wants to speak with you."

Dindrana could not contain her anger. "What is the meaning of this? Why have I been locked in? Am I not a free gentlewoman?"

"Swan will explain. You are to follow me."

"I shan't follow you anywhere unless you explain to me why I am being treated like a common prisoner," she said, trying to keep her voice from cracking with tears of fear and anger. "I have committed no crime. Why, then, am I being treated so abominably?" She could feel the blood rushing past her ears, refusing to move but terrified her outburst would be repaid with violence.

Thea merely inclined her head, as if studying a rare specimen of bird. Swan came bustling in behind her. "What's all this noise? I hope you haven't upset our guest, Thea."

"Upset me!" Dindrana cried, a hot tear escaping from her eye. "You locked me in my room!"

Swan looked genuinely bewildered. "Locked you in your room? Why, of course, we did, Lady Dindrana. For your own safety."

His response deflated her anger, turning it into embarrassment. "Oh. I see."

"We are in a remote part of the country, my lady, and thieves and beggars sometimes make their way into the castle grounds. You could see for yourself the condition the walls are in." Swan began to pace, pulling his beard nervously. "We all lock our rooms at night. I burn with shame to think that you suspected us of visiting deliberate indignity upon you. Please do not tell the mistress."

Dindrana shook her head, rubbed her teary eyes. "Don't think of it. I am tired and I am alone and afraid. I apologise for my accusations."

"But there is no need to be afraid, my lady. It will all be over in an instant, and then you will be happily lodged with us for a few days while you regain your strength."

"All be over? What do you mean?"

He continued as though he hadn't heard her question. "And then you will be served meals in your room and have everything that you could wish for as diversion."

"What are you talking about?" An edge of too-bright fear had lodged itself between his words and their possible meaning.

Swan gave her his beard-splitting grin again. "It's no big thing, my lady. Your brother agreed to it last night. I told him you could help my mistress, and he said we were allowed to press you into any kind of service necessary. You see . . . we discovered some years ago that the mistress's symptoms are relieved by something you have."

Her voice seemed to come from far away. "What is it?"

"Your blood, my lady. Just a little of it. From your right arm. Why, you wouldn't believe what good it will do her."

Heat flashed across her heart. Dindrana backed away, grasped the bed post. "No. You will not do this to me."

"It is a most charitable thing, and you will make your brother and Galahad and your King proud. Now come. Do not make me use force."

But force was necessary, for every nerve and fibre in her body resisted. They forced her off the bedpost and Swan put her over his shoulder. She broke her fingernails clinging to the doorframe, howled and screamed all the way down the dim corridors and up a narrow winding staircase. Swan sure-footedly stepped around chunks of stone lying on the stairs. It was as though the castle was rotting from within. The decaying architecture, the dank smell of centuries became as a nightmare to Dindrana. Her blood, the precious liquid that belonged in her body, hot and red and pulsing with unfulfilled passions. How desperately she wanted to keep it inside her.

At last they arrived at a circular stone room with a large mosaic pattern in the centre. Around the walls were arranged a series of intricately wrought chests of iron, scenes from saints' tales depicted on their lids and sides. A statue of a woman in black sat under the solitary window. Dindrana thought she could detect the faint scent of blood. In the centre of the mosaic sat a large grey tub. Swan wrestled her onto a stained wooden bench and Thea held her down. Thea leaned close to Dindrana's ear and said, "It will be over before you know it. I'll make your favourite pastry after. You only have to name it."

But Dindrana couldn't name her favourite pastry; she couldn't even remember it.

Then the statue under the window moved. It wasn't a statue at all; it was the mistress of the castle.

"Thea, keep her down," Swan said, and Thea did as she was told, proving too meaty and strong for Dindrana's struggle.

Swan went to the mistress and helped her to her feet, supported her as she shuffled beside him.

"Madam," Swan said to the old woman, "this is the Lady Dindrana, who is helping with your medicine."

The woman pushed back her hood and looked at Dindrana with milky, uncomprehending eyes. Dindrana was struck by how old and frail she was, two breaths away from death.

Swan smiled at Dindrana. "She will be grateful; though now she might seem unable to understand what is happening, I promise you she will be very grateful."

"You can't do this to me."

Thea lost her temper. "Hush now. It's going to happen and the more you struggle, the more ragged the cut and the longer it will take to heal. Be still."

The more ragged the cut. Dindrana took a shuddering breath and forced her body to be still. She looked the other way as they pushed up her sleeve, pulled at her arm. She braced for the pain but it didn't come.

"You are calm now, Madam," Swan said. "Sit up. First we must test your blood," he said.

"Test it?"

"Allow me to show you." He bent and gently pushed the old woman's skirts up over her knees. "Can you see these marks?"

The old woman's skin was mottled with age, but Dindrana could quite clearly see six small black spots where the skin looked burnt or rotted. "What are they?"

"We always take a pinprick of blood and test it first on her leg, where a scar would not be so easily seen. These marks are from the blood of gentlewomen who swore they were virgins, but ...." He trailed off and couldn't meet her eyes.

Dindrana was speechless.

"Lady Dindrana, I mean no blight on your reputation, but if we do not test your blood first—"

"How does their blood cause this injury?" Her heart beat fast. Perhaps she'd have the wrong kind of blood. Perhaps this awful business wasn't going to happen at all.

"It is contaminated. Only the blood of a virgin can heal my mistress. We do not know how or why it works. The cunning-man said the clean blood would be the balm for my mistress's ills, and so it has proved to be. We do not question this, we care only for her health."

Dindrana thought fleetingly of her behaviour with Gabriel in the stable loft. Galahad had saved her from spoiling her virginity. Curse him. *Curse him a million times.* And the vow she swore to her father, to her God. Right now she wished she'd broken the vow with passionate relish, because they would test her blood, and they would find her a virgin.

"Hold out your hand," Swan said.

She did so, and he pricked the end of her index finger with a pin, then touched the bloody finger gently to the old woman's leg. Dindrana watched as the tiny smudge of blood seemed to be absorbed by the skin, leaving a smooth area on the wrinkled flesh. Age had been erased.

"Good," said Swan, beaming at her. "Are you ready for what follows?"

"I have no choice." Although she was still afraid, her curiosity had begun to win out. Could it be possible that the woman would be healed not just of her sickness, but of her old age?

He clapped his hands together and Thea approached with a silver dish containing a small, sharp blade, which she placed on the wooden bench next to Dindrana. Dindrana looked anywhere but at the blade and dish. Thea now left the room and returned with bucket after bucket of steaming water for the bath. Swan watched patiently, his hand under the mistress's elbow. Nausea churned in Dindrana's stomach; the waiting was choking her.

"Madam," he said to the mistress of the castle at last, "we are ready for the transaction."

She still looked as though she understood nothing, and Swan went about the business of stripping her and laying her clothes neatly by the side of the tub. Dindrana gazed at the crone's body, her withered flesh, her sunken chest, her flat and empty breasts. She found herself musing about the monstrosity of age, recoiling from the knowledge that one day her own body would collapse and become grotesque as this woman's had. And she had never used it the way she most wanted to.

Swan made sure his mistress was comfortable and then turned to Dindrana. "Hold out your right arm and relax," he said. He took the blade and Thea positioned herself on Dindrana's right, holding the dish below her arm. Dindrana closed her eyes. She felt thumbs pressed into her soft flesh. Then the old woman made a strange hissing noise, making Dindrana jump.

"Relax," Swan said.

The old woman hissed again. An alien, unnerving sound.

"Why does she make that noise?" Dindrana asked, while, at the same moment, the knife bit through the flesh sending pain rocketing up her arm.

"You do not need to know." Swan had not said this, nor had Thea, but another female voice. It must have been the old woman but before Dindrana could turn to see, she felt darkness descending upon her and she fell into a faint.

She was immediately set upon by a nightmare: the old woman sank in her tub and it overflowed with bloody water, foaming the colour of rose petals but smelling like old tin. She grinned a hideous grin, and opened her mouth to say, "You shall die, Dindrana, that I may live." Every breath she took was a snake's hiss as she rubbed the blood into her skin.

You shall die that I may live.

The sound of her own cry woke Dindrana. It echoed in her ears as she looked around the bedchamber where she had spent the previous night. Her arm throbbed gently, but when she rolled up her sleeve to look at the wound it was dressed cleanly and bandaged. Everything was all right. She was alive and well, as had been promised. A sigh of relief, almost a laugh, passed her lips. Alive and well.

She fell back into a doze for perhaps another hour, but some thought, some niggling concern brought her back to wakefulness. The bedchamber—had they locked her in again?

Dindrana rose carefully and went to the door. It was fast, bolted from the outside. She raised a fist and banged on the door. "Swan! Unlock me." No response. She felt weak, unequal to the task of protesting, and wondered how much blood they had taken. And so tired. The bed beckoned. Sinking beneath the covers, she thought of Percival and wondered where he was, and if he could sense her distress.

The sound of footsteps woke her a second time, but on this occasion she had been sleeping for hours and it was dark outside. She sat up. A pang in her stomach informed her that she was very very hungry. Perhaps they were bringing food for her. The bolt grated against metal and the door swung inwards. Swan stood there with a lantern and a tray of food. "Your supper, my lady."

"Thank you, Swan."

He placed the lantern and the tray on top of the chest. She rose and pulled the tray into her lap. Spiced fish and bread. She began to shovel it into her mouth. "Do you have any more of that special mead?" she asked.

"No. The mistress of the house would like to thank you," Swan said, watching her.

Dindrana looked up. "Is she feeling well?"

"She is greatly improved."

"Shall I go to her?"

Swan shook his head. "She will come here. Finish your meal."

"Don't lock me in," she said.

"As you wish."

The food was hot and filling, and she felt a little stronger for having it. By the dim light of the lantern she sat and waited for the mistress of the house to come. The wind rattled at the thick windowpane, and clouds skimmed past the half-moon. At last there were footsteps, and she straightened her clothes and stood to await the lady of the house.

The door opened, and Dindrana found herself staring at a beautiful woman no older than twenty-five, with gleaming chestnut hair and skin like porcelain.

"How do you do?" she said hesitantly. "I was expecting the mistress of the house."

The woman smiled and her black eyes gleamed. "You do not recognise me then, Lady Dindrana?"

Dindrana shook her head, uncomprehending. "I'm very sorry. I have no recollection of meeting you, madam."

"Why, just this morning you granted me the enormous favour of a few drops of your blood."

Dindrana's breath caught in her throat and she felt dizzy with shock. "Surely . . . surely you're not . . ."

"The mistress of the house," the woman replied, "Lady Triscula."

Dindrana took the proffered hand without thinking. "Lady Triscula?"

"Yes, that's right."

"Named for the saint who spent her last years here?"

Triscula smiled. "I am the saint who spent her last years here."

Immediately Dindrana dropped to her knees and crossed herself. "Then what I am witnessing is a holy miracle. Forgive me, madam."

"Rise, rise," Triscula said impatiently. "It is no holy miracle. I doubt God cares much for my youth and beauty. He's always trying to take it away."

Dindrana looked up from where she knelt, a dark fear spreading in her veins. A saint, a living saint restored to youth, stood before her claiming . . . What was she claiming? That it was no holy power that had restored her? Then what kind of power?

"You are not a saint?" she said at last, not knowing what else to say.

"The Church thinks me so."

"You cured blindness."

"Not with God's help."

"You went to the holy land."

"Not to convert sinners. Rather to perform a few sins of my own."

Dindrana rose slowly to her feet, putting out a hand to the bedpost to steady herself. "In the name of sweet Jesus Christ, then, what are you?"

"Nobody of whom he would approve. I didn't come here to argue theology with you. The important issue is this: Lady Dindrana, your blood is hot and fine. Only a handful of my girls over the years have had such good blood, and we have asked all of them if they would care to stay here and keep me in supply of it."

Gazing at Triscula in wonder and fear, she shook her head. "No. No I will not. My father will be here at the end of the week."

"Your father will not find us. This is a lost place, Dindrana. Lost people end up here. We are never found."

All the breath left Dindrana's lungs. Now she longed for the normal rhythms of life. She longed for her ageing husband, her father's pious sermons, Galahad's sneering judgement. She wanted all to return to how it had been. Before . . . this.

"Please, please, I beg you. Let me go," Dindrana said.

But Triscula backed out of the chamber quickly, and Dindrana heard the bolt slide into place just as she flung herself at the door. She leaned up against it, breathless with dread. Locked in, weak, lost—her mind reeled under the weight of her problem. *What will I do?*

She pushed against the door, but of course it did not move. The bolt was on the outside, so there was no chance of forcing it open. Everybody in the castle would follow the orders of their mistress, so no hope lay in appealing to Swan or Thea or one of the other servants. Did they mean to look after her well and take a little rarely, or would Triscula want to bleed her and bleed her until there was nothing left in her veins? Her heart fluttered. By the time Percival received news of her failure to arrive, it would be entirely too late to help her. She thought about the bond they had always seemed to share and she closed her eyes and built a picture of his beloved face in her mind.

"Percival," she whispered. "Come for me. Come for me."

Then her eyes flickered open. She was mad. She couldn't rely on an imaginary meeting of minds. No, she had to act. She had to save herself.

She went to the window and pressed her face up to the glass. The weather was sodden and blustery outside, and she could see treetops shaking in the wind. Dindrana gritted her teeth as she thought of Galahad. Galahad, who had got her into this mess. Galahad with his stupid simplistic piety, always making life difficult for her. She slammed her fists against the glass and one of the tiny panes cracked, but she would never be able to loosen the lead mullions. Even if she could, the window was too tiny for her to fit through and there was at least a thirty-foot drop outside. But the action released some of her tension. She licked a trickle of blood from her knuckle where the cracked glass had cut her. Her blood, a commodity she had never thought to treasure until today. It tasted salty on her tongue. She scanned the room . . . Perhaps the tapestries . . .

Nothing behind the first or the second, but behind the third her fingers found a crack in the brickwork. A door perhaps? She pushed against it and heard stone grudgingly move against stone. Again she pushed. The doorway might lead no further than the next room, but she had to check.

The door ground open and she found herself staring into a dark passageway, too dark for its length or direction to be guessed. She took the lantern from upon the chest and held it in front of her. Downwards, it led downwards. Into where?

"It matters not," she said aloud, forcing her voice to sound brave. "I must get away from here."

Holding the lantern in front of her like a shield, she advanced down the passageway, letting the tapestry flap back into place behind her. The smell of old dirt and mould enveloped her, and she shivered from the cold. Creeping insects and lizards went about their business on the walls and stairs as she manoeuvred around them, frightened, repulsed, but still moving downwards, away from her locked chamber. The light from the lantern swung dimly around her. She picked up her skirts carefully so they didn't brush against the stone, and still the stairs wound downwards. Her heart felt like a trapped bird in her chest, desperate, cornered. At last she came to even ground. But unlike the stone slabs of stairs, below her feet now was earth. She stood for a moment looking around her. Nothing but a blank wall to her left, a short passage with a door at the end to her right. She turned right.

The door was iron, but sagging on its hinges. The air was frozen down here, so cold and dry that it seemed to make her skin itch. A rotten smell hung thickly around her. She pulled the door and stepped inside.

"Jesus preserve me," she breathed.

In the dark room, in the awful silence, lay three rows of ten dead maidens. Forgetting her own danger momentarily, she walked up the aisles between them, covering her nose from the vile stench. All were in varying states of decomposition, some little more than bones, some turned the unnatural brown of mummification.

They wore only their kirtles, and Dindrana began to suspect she knew where the dresses in the trunk in her room had come from. The table upon which each body lay was labelled. Lady Anne of Arbour. Lady Mary of Dwyllyg. Princess Ruth of Logres. All from noble blood, some of them kings' daughters. And all very, very dead.

Which was no doubt the plan for Dindrana as well.

She was frozen in her panic, her mind scrambling for a solution to this inescapable horror. She couldn't stay here among the dead maidens, but she couldn't return to her chamber. Desperately she ran around the room looking for another secret door. Nothing. At the bottom of the stairs she searched again, flung herself against the blank wall and ran her fingers over it, all in vain.

That was when she heard voices, distant and far above her. Voices that could only be coming from her room. Again she froze. They had noticed her missing. Would they come looking for her? Of course they would. Should she return and pretend she hadn't seen the roomful of dead maidens? They would never believe her.

Light glimmered near the top of the stairs. She fled in the opposite direction, into the awful crypt, extinguished the lantern and crouched in terror behind the furthest table from the door. The bones of a dead maiden were her only sentinel. The voices came closer. It was Swan and Triscula.

"Lady Dindrana," called Swan.

"We know you're down there," Triscula said, impatience tinting her voice. "Return to your room immediately."

Her own breathing seemed ragged and loud in her ears. She pulled herself into a ball, knowing it was no use but compelled by a desperate instinct to survive. Her pursuers shuffled between the dead bodies, closer and closer. Their shadows grew elongated and monstrous against the back wall.

"Come, Lady Dindrana, we will not hurt you."

She bit down an urge to laugh out loud. A roomful of dead maidens and they still expected her to believe that. Swan's hands grasped her around the shoulders and pulled her to her feet. She cried out and began to sob.

"Make her quiet," said Triscula. "I hate to hear their terror."

A sudden blow to the back of her head plunged her momentarily into blissful oblivion.

When consciousness began to seep back in, she was being dragged roughly along a passageway, her skirts trailing on the filthy ground and her knees being grazed.

"Where . . .?"

"Be quiet," said Triscula, who strode beside her.

She struggled weakly against Swan's hold, but was too dizzy to be effective. She closed her eyes and groaned, the flickering lantern light glowing dully red against her eyelids.

"There!" Swan cried as he cast her to the ground.

She opened her eyes in time to see Swan and Triscula backing away and locking a sturdy stone and iron door behind them. Her captors peered at her through a tiny, barred window.

"Enjoy your stay, Lady Dindrana," Swan said.

An unearthly yell sounded from somewhere nearby.

"What was that? Where am I?" Dindrana cried.

"You are in the dungeons and the cries are from the wretches in the other cells," Swan replied.

Dindrana looked around her, her eyes adjusting to the darkness. She was in the last cell in a row. One of her walls was deep, cold stone, the other mouldy wood with a door of bars set in it. Through those bars, she could make out the figure of a man cowering in a corner. Through the next set of bars, she could see what looked like a collection of bones. After that, everything was too dark to see.

She turned to her captors. "What are you going to do with me?" Dindrana asked.

"I think you already know," said Triscula, turning away. Swan followed her.

"What are you going to do with me?" Dindrana screamed, scrambling to her feet and closing her hands around the bars in the window.

There was no answer. Swan and Triscula disappeared from sight.

IV

At the Green Leaf Inn, among the tables of filthy peasants sopping up gravy and gulping cheap ale, Galahad shone like a golden-haired angel. He and Percival had bathed that afternoon, polished their breastplates and greaves, and now were taking a meal before continuing on their quest.

Percival weaved among the tables with two cups of apple beer. He realised that he and his companion were the focus of a great deal of attention, not all of it benevolent. It was the same wherever they went—most people revered them as Arthur's knights, but some grew jealous and hostile. Surely that was the reason he felt so uneasy this evening. Surely it was mere coincidence that he had been unable to get his sister out of his mind all day. He certainly wasn't going to reveal to Galahad the source of his disquiet. His friend was quick to judge him for any idea that may be heathen. Whatever it was that made Percival's and Dindrana's minds so closely linked could not be the work of God, according to Galahad. And perhaps he was right.

"Where are our meals?" Galahad asked as Percival sat with him.

"The innkeeper's bringing them over in a moment."

"I starve in the meantime. However, God's work must be done."

Percival nodded and tipped his cup to his lips. A fat man with only a tuft of hair approached their table with two wooden dishes, which he set before them.

"Good appetite, sirs. Are you Arthur's knights then?"

Galahad smiled his angelic smile. "Yes. We journey in his name and in God's."

"Well, I wish you nothing but good fortune," the man said deferentially.

"Thank you," said Percival, picking up his spoon.

"Good fortune has been ours already. God is with us," Galahad bragged. "We have already been accommodated at the castle that was once the residence of Saint Triscula."

The man's face darkened. "Triscula's? That's not a real place."

"I assure you it is," Galahad said. "And we stayed there."

An elderly man with a sunken face and teeth worn down to stumps overheard and came to stand by them. "It's a lost place, not a found place," he said. "Were you lost when you came by it?"

The skin on Percival's scalp prickled. "What do you mean?"

"Oh, that's a black place, sirs. Black business goes on there."

"Take it back, wretch," Galahad muttered through gritted

teeth. "It is the resting place of a saint, and the likes of you have no place in saying otherwise."

"A castle that disappears if you look away from it? That nobody can find or see? That sounds like the home of a sinner, not a—"

His sentence was cut off by the sound of Galahad's sword whisking through the air. The point stopped mere inches from the man's nose. "Say—no—more," Galahad hissed. Around them, people had stopped eating and drinking and were watching in anticipation.

"Galahad," said Percival, reaching out to stay his friend's hand.

Galahad continued as though he hadn't heard. "A saint, you hear me, a *saint* lived in that castle, and the very walls are imbued with her godliness."

The man eyed the tip of the sword closely, looked across to Percival, then back to Galahad. "I'm sorry, sir."

Percival pushed his food away and climbed to his feet. "We're going back, Galahad," he said.

Galahad turned on him, lowering his sword. "What? Surely you don't believe—"

"We're going back. We're going back to get Dindrana."

"Have you lost your wits? We are on a quest for our King and our Lord."

The quest for King and Lord . . . Percival didn't say aloud what he thought: that they had set out on a drunken conviction that Galahad had refused to shed in the light of day.

"Your sister is in the good care of the custodians of Triscula's memory," Galahad continued. "We are not going back."

Percival beat his fist on the table and roared, "I return upon this instant to that castle. Whether you accompany me or not is unimportant." Heart racing wildly, he pulled on his riding cloak and, his helm under his arm, headed for the door of the inn. Within seconds, Galahad was beside him.

"What is this madness, friend?" Galahad demanded, grabbing Percival's shoulder.

Percival shrugged him off roughly. "This madness is love for my sister. If that is a sin, then call me a sinner," he said, mounting his horse. "But do not stop me going back for her."

Galahad nodded. "Then I shall accompany you, if only to prove that you are wrong."

Percival barely heard him. Instead, the old man's words echoed in his ears.

A black place, sir.

. . .

The darkness of sleep gave way to the darkness of her prison cell, the only light reflected on the dark stone from a lantern in a bracket on the wall outside. She had dreamed of her father's house and it was too much to endure waking to this cold dungeon, her only company the rats that nibbled on the lace of her gown if she sat still, and the ravings of the lunatic in the next cell. The fear was inescapable, consuming her from the inside out. Not knowing how long she had until they came for her, to do to her what they had done to the others. Not knowing if she would ever see daylight again. It was too much to bear, and she had to pace her cell, move around, act. She spent an hour clawing at the door, hammering upon it, pushing in vain against the lock. At the same time she kept a wary eye on the bars that separated her from the next cell. The lock on that door seemed flimsy, rust-coated and bent. Pacing, pacing, pacing. In the next cell, a prisoner hung back in the gloom, quite clearly staring at her.

"What?" she asked imperiously. "Why do you stare?"

He gestured towards her with an arm that had been severed at the wrist. "I know you. I know you." He descended into his ravings again and she turned her back on him, put her hands to her head. Her terror was pulling her apart, and she realised that she had to keep herself together if she was going to escape.

Perhaps she was not going to escape.

"I know you."

She spun around, letting her anger pour forth upon the unfortunate wretch. "You do not know me. I am the daughter of an earl, and you are a lunatic criminal, you are base filth."

"No. I am only lost," he said mournfully. "Everybody here is lost."

"No matter. You do *not* know me."

She could see his head bob up and down in the darkness. "Yes. Yes. Yes."

Guilty and angry all at once, she stepped towards the door to freedom, pressed her face against the bars and gazed out along the hallway.

"Dindrana."

She whirled around. The prisoner had said her name. Tenderly, knowingly.

"How do you know my name?" But of course, Swan or Triscula must have used it when they had brought her here. She cursed herself for a fool.

"I know you," he said again. "Yes. Yes. Yes."

She stepped up to the bars between them. "Come forward. Let me see you."

He moved tentatively, frightened of her, creeping out of the gloom towards the dim light. She studied his face. At first she saw only the dirt, the filthy hair caked in mould, the lunatic's drool collecting in the corners of his beard. But then in an instant she saw beneath those things and knew him.

"Gabriel?"

He whooped and began jabbering excitedly. "Yes. Yes. Dindrana found me. I have been lost for so long."

"How can it be that you are here?" Her astonishment temporarily distracted from her fears.

"Stealing food," he said. "A long time ago. Very long time."

"And they cut off your hand?"

He shook his head and held up the stump. "Galahad."

Dindrana caught her breath. "He followed you?"

Gabriel nodded. Dindrana tried not to notice the strange emptiness in his eyes. "Followed me, cut off my hand for what I'd done. I ran and ran. I became lost. So far from home. I came here and climbed the gate. Stole from the kitchen."

"And you've been locked up in this dungeon ever since?" Unbearable guilt. All that he had suffered for the love of her.

"Yes. Many long years."

A sudden noise in the hallway alerted her to somebody's approach. She whispered urgently through the bars, "Don't let them know we are friends. Don't say a word."

She hurried away from him and soon Thea was there, bringing her food. The old woman passed bread and water through the bars, and then moved up the hallway to feed the other prisoners. Dindrana barely had appetite for the slab of hard bread. Her mind reeled from the astonishment of meeting Gabriel here. Could he help her to escape?

But he was practically senseless, and if he hadn't managed to escape in all this time—how long had the poor man been here?—then he was hardly going to be any help to her. Thea's footsteps moved away and up the stairs, and Dindrana turned at once to the bars separating her from Gabriel. He put his remaining hand out to her and she grasped it with compassion, stroking his palm with her thumb. She remembered the wildness of her youth, the irresistible pull of her yearning for him. And she felt old; she felt used up by life.

"Dear Gabriel. Look what I have done to you."

He merely stared back at her, that odd empty gaze. She remembered the last time they had been together and her blood boiled anew with rage against Galahad.

"If ever I meet him again," she whispered to herself, "I shall kill him." But somehow she knew she would never meet him again.

They came for her an hour later, bound her hands and legs and carried her once more to the blood-letting chamber. Again she blacked out during the ceremony and woke much later, weak and dizzy, her wound aching, back in her dungeon cell. The certainty that she was going to die this way had truly been impressed upon her, and she felt too frail to fight that conviction.

Gabriel slept, slumped against the bars as though he had tried to get as close as possible to her. She wept silently for all that she was going to miss in her life—love and children and the long afternoons of summer—and then she sat back and thought over the blood-letting procedure. The first time they had let her blood, they had tested it first, to be certain of her virginity. Today they had not. And why should they? She had been under lock and key since Galahad and Percival had left. She remembered those black spots on Triscula's leg, tiny patches of rotted skin that had never healed. And she thought that perhaps if she had to die, there might be a certain pleasure in knowing she would not die alone.

Gabriel was rousing from his sleep, mumbling gibberish. She gazed at his face—once so exquisite, now a filth-streaked parody of its former beauty—and she knew what she must do.

· · ·

Dindrana made her peace with her God in the few hours after her decision. Not Galahad's God—the unforgiving bully who took sadistic pleasure in judging those who loved him—but the gentle-eyed Father who watched helplessly from above as she went forward to meet her fate, who reserved a place for her in Heaven on the other side of her awful plight. She crossed herself, said "Amen" and went towards the bars that separated her from Gabriel.

"Gabriel," she whispered in the darkness. She could vaguely make out his shape sitting in the corner of his cell.

"Dindrana," he replied in his sad, empty voice.

"Come here, Gabriel. I need to ask you something."

He shuffled towards the bars. She reached through and grasped his one remaining hand. "You say you remember me. Do you remember the day you had to run away?"

He nodded. "Yes. Yes."

"What were we doing?"

He looked at her blankly.

"The day you had to run away. Remember, we met in the stables. Up in the hay. There was a storm."

Some small realisation seemed to dawn on him. "I kissed you," he said.

"Yes. You kissed me. Will you kiss me again?"

"Kiss you?" He seemed to be considering. He held up the stump of his left arm.

"I promise you won't be in trouble this time. Nobody will know. It's a secret and I won't tell anyone." She pressed her body up against the bars, allowed her fingers to touch his face. "Please, Gabriel. Please kiss me."

He pushed his face between the bars and offered her his lips. She touched them with her own, pushing down revulsion at the smell of him. He shifted forwards slightly, and she could feel the warmth of his body against her own. Her hand moved to his hair, among the matted strands, which had once shone a red-gold halo in the summer sun. Beneath her fingertips she could feel a mass of scar tissue, and wondered if a blow to the head had addled his brains, or if it had been the years locked in here, "lost" as he kept saying. The thought was too tragic to bear. She ran her other hand over his body, now weak and thin with years of maltreatment. Despite it all, despite his ill health and his witlessness, his body began to respond.

"Do you remember?" she whispered.

"Yes."

"We need to finish what we began, Gabriel."

"The door," he said, "the door is in the way."

"We'll have to manage through the bars."

He stood back a few paces and shook his head.

"The door," he said.

Exasperated, she beckoned him. "Come, Gabriel."

But she began to realise it might be impossible. Twelve iron bars between them could certainly be a powerful obstacle. She scanned the room for something to break the lock. A chunk of stone near the wall caught her eye. She picked it up and returned to the gate, hitting the lock weakly.

Gabriel was watching her. She looked up, held out the stone to him. "You try."

He timidly advanced, took the stone from her. Looked from it to the lock.

"Go on. You might be stronger than I am."

He took aim and, with a few purposeful blows, demolished the tongue of the flimsy lock. The door swung open between them. He hesitated on his side of the threshold, the stone still in his hand.

"Come," she said, beckoning him forward.

He dropped the stone and advanced. She unlaced the front of her bodice, lay back on the mouldy straw and closed her eyes. His hand moved over her skin, pushed up her skirts. She thought about the evening in the stables, the storm outside, the smell of fresh hay and horses, the way his body had felt under her fingers. She tried to keep the picture in her mind, to blot out the ghastly circumstances of this consummation, to overlay them with how it would have been had Galahad not found them.

"You are beautiful, Gabriel," she breathed, but the words were for the old Gabriel, not the sad wreck of a man he had become.

"I love you, Dindrana," he replied as his body covered hers. So different from how she had imagined it. Circumstances had robbed her of any slickness. Pain, holding her breath, trying not to hear his strange half-grunts. No gentleness, no smooth heat. And then it was done.

When he had finished, he lay on top of her very still for a long time. She stroked his hair, tenderly touched the awful scar, and prayed forgiveness for her sin.

The sound of footsteps on the stairs jolted her out of a light sleep. She sat up with a start, but Gabriel had already returned to his cell; the door was closed, the lock repositioned to appear as though it still held. She raced to the bars but dared not call out to him. He slept in his corner. He did not see her and she ached with not being able to say goodbye. Goodbye to everything . . .

Swan's voice boomed through the window to her cell. "Come, Lady Dindrana. It is time for another blood-letting."

The cell door opened and her hands were bound. Wordlessly, she followed Swan into the dark.

. . .

"I do not see the castle." Percival paced at the bottom of the hill where, last time, there had been a dark path upwards.

"It must be somewhere different. You have brought us back the wrong way," said Galahad.

"I am certain it is the right way."

"When we left you were . . . we both were . . . in a passion. Perhaps you didn't memorise the route properly."

"The old man at the inn, he said the castle can't be found if you're looking for it."

"He spoke a lot of heathen nonsense."

Percival sat down on a rock, baffled. There had been a path here. He knew it, because he had taken it. The eastern hill beside the mirror lake.

The mirror lake. He jumped to his feet and ran down to the spot Dindrana had stood when she'd first seen the castle in the reflection. He breathed, closed his eyes, then opened them and looked.

And there it was. When he turned his face up, he could see the grey tower. He returned to where Galahad waited.

"Well?" Galahad said.

"Why did we not see this before, friend?" Percival held out his palm. Where it had seemed there was only impenetrable thickets, there was actually a narrow rutted path.

Galahad looked confused, his hand went to his sword but he must have realised a sword was no defence against magic.

"Leave the horses here," Percival said. "I don't want them to hear us coming."

. . .

Her hands bound in front of her, Dindrana was led to a thick stone slab laid on top of the wooden bench in the blood-letting chamber. She recognised it immediately as the same kind of slab upon which all the dead maidens lay in the room below the stairs, and she knew that her instinct had been right—this would be her last blood-letting. She lay down, felt the stone cold through her dress, and knew she would never get up again. Dindrana trembled despite her best intentions. Stoically she faced up to her captors. "Then I am to die?"

Swan smiled down at her. "Fear not. You are probably going to be a better place." He moved about the chamber, shifting Triscula's tub so that it was close to Dindrana. He then filled it with a number of substances which he retrieved from jars in the iron chests—a thick, grey fluid, something else that resembled milk but smelled like fish, and a pitcher full of water to mix them together. Triscula entered wordlessly, shrugged a long robe of purple satin off her shoulders and slipped, quite naked, into the bath. Dindrana would never have believed that this was the same woman who had sat, shrivelled and purblind, in the same tub just a few days before.

"Madam," Dindrana said hesitantly. "I realise that tonight I will die, but I am at peace with my maker and expect to join Him soon." Her faith gave her courage, and the trembling stopped.

"You take comfort where you can, my jewel. I am not afraid of your God because if I never die I will never have to meet him."

Swan pushed up her sleeve, this time the arm closest to Triscula's tub. Thea was nowhere in sight.

"Where is the silver dish?" asked Dindrana.

"It is not deep enough. I'm bleeding you straight into my lady's bath. Your light will live on in her for years. We will not forget you."

Dindrana nodded. "Indeed, sir, I believe you will not."

Instead of turning her head away this time, Dindrana watched the proceedings. Swan unbound her hands and spread her arms apart. Her stomach was hollow and already she felt a strange floating sensation. Was it fear, or was she already being pulled towards her creator? "God be with me," she murmured, as the knife bit into the soft flesh across her wrist. She refused to black out, holding on despite her pain, despite her terror, despite her loss of blood. She was determined to see what would happen.

The blood began to trickle down her hand. Swan dug the knife in a little more. She felt an odd pop and the blood now coursed as a river, and flowed off her fingers into Triscula's bath. Each drop sizzled upon the water, turning it milky pink. Triscula relaxed into the liquid, sighing in the anticipation of the pleasure.

"Goodbye," Dindrana said, eyes growing dim.

Suddenly, a scream of pain. Dindrana smiled. Triscula screamed as though her throat would tear. The water around her was turning grey. Her skin flaked off in grey clumps.

"Help me! Get me out!"

"What is happening, my lady?"

Dindrana watched as Swan hoisted Triscula from the bath and dumped her on the stone floor. He stood by helplessly as his mistress writhed on the tiles, her skin rotting in front of his eyes. Dindrana saw a flash of white bone as Triscula's flesh fell off her bones like heavy overripe fruit, then she decided that the horrific sight was not the last thing she wanted to remember of this earth. Instead she closed her eyes and thought of Percival. She felt life ebbing from her as the blood flowed out and over her fingers, and imagined the beloved contours of her brother's face. In darkness again, but not afraid, she passed from this life into the next.

. . .

Percival did not even notice the mess of rotted flesh and bone on the floor in front of Swan. He saw only his sister, pale and still in the centre of the room.

"Dindrana!" he cried as he ran to her. He put an ear to her mouth but heard no breath, placed his hand around her soft chin but felt no warmth. His ribs wrenched. An awful emptiness entered his heart.

Galahad moved into the room and stood over Swan, inspecting with revulsion the bloody tub and the mess on the floor. "Is this your mistress? What has happened to her? I have never seen the likes—"

"Yes, yes," Swan admitted, cowering.

"But what is this . . . devilry?"

"It is Triscula, who you revere as a saint. This is all that remains of her."

"Curse your evil nonsense, man," Galahad said with a sneer. "My guts are sick of it."

Percival looked up, drew his sword. "There will be more blood."

. . .

The smouldering ruins of the castle cast a blanket of cloud over the wood. Percival's armour was besmeared with the blood of his sister's captors, Galahad's with the blood of those he believed were deep, deep in sin. They led behind them a ragged, blinking train of five prisoners rescued from the dungeons.

Percival sat heavily on the ground and put his head between his hands.

"Don't let it destroy you my friend," Galahad said. He turned to the prisoners. "Go. All of you. You are free."

One of the prisoners, a younger man with matted fair hair said, "No, sir. We are not free. We are found."

Percival could see Galahad recoil from the filthy man.

"Go on," Percival called. "Leave us be."

One by one, the men wandered off, some together, some on their own.

"Will God forgive me?" Percival asked.

"God forgives us all," Galahad replied gently. "Let us sleep with our woes and hope for clarity when dawn comes."

Percival nodded slowly.

"The Sangraal still awaits us. Once we have found it, it will wash away our sins. And our sorrows."

They curled up amongst the ferns and heather and slept. The sky wheeled above them and grew light from the east some hours later.

Many miles away, sitting on a rock by a river, Gabriel watched the rising of the golden sun in wonder as the world was born anew.

WILD DREAMS OF BLOOD

"I've never seen a bride with such sharp teeth"
— "Thrymsqvitha", *The Poetic Edda*

I

Somewhere, beneath the sound of flesh smashing into flesh, beneath the rattle of the cage, beneath the barking cheers, Sara Jones could hear music. A happy twanging song, out of sync with the chaotic rhythm of sweat and phlegm and blood. She tuned in to it, trying to follow its melody. Country music, perhaps? A woman singing. It brought a touch of the carnivalesque to the grim cavernous arena. She became more aware of the colours in the room: the bright yellow of the lights, the brilliant blue of a fighter's headband, the deep red floor.

"He's in the fence! He's in the fence!" The announcer's harsh voice slapped around the auditorium. The crowd throbbed; the heat in the room noticeably increased. The smell of men and dirt and rubber under hot lights. Sara breathed it in, her nostrils twitching. What she really wanted to smell was the iron tang of blood, but she was too far away from the action for that. The Tall Man was going down: six foot six of densely coiled muscle, but the doughy man a foot shorter with the blue headband—Blue, she called him—was pummelling him into the side of the cage. The Tall Man's feet began to slip out from under him. He had been the favourite, the one everybody had come to see win. Elimination style. An upset. Blue pounded Tall Man. Blood poured from Blue's nose, as though the effort it took to defeat his opponent had burst something in his head. Down went Tall Man. Down.

All the way down.

The hooter sounded, harsh and final.

"And there's your winner! There's your winner!" The announcer's voice was rapturous, a preacher in full ecstasy. Blue collapsed to his knees, his arms around Tall Man. They hugged, slapping each other's bare backs. Then Blue stood and raised his arms triumphant. A shapely woman—possibly the only other female body besides Sara's in the auditorium—emerged with a sash and a trophy. The season was over. The winner had been crowned.

The season was over. No more sneaking out with flimsy excuses on her tongue. The arena would close down for three months, the fighters would stay home and let their wounds heal. And Sara would go back to her wild dreams. She felt an icy itch in her stomach.

She sat in her plastic seat while the arena emptied. The music played on: harmonicas and plaintive singing. It was long past time to go home. Would Dillon be worried? Her mobile phone was still switched off in her handbag. She'd tell him the flight was late. It wasn't in Dillon's nature to investigate, and she went away for work a lot. Luckily for her, the arena was in an industrial estate just off the highway on the long drive from the airport. If she timed her trips interstate just right, she nearly always managed to see a fight on her way out or back.

Two janitors were making their way through the arena, row by row, picking up rubbish and cigarette butts. A third slopped sharp-smelling disinfectant across the floor of the cage. Sara looked around. Everyone else was gone.

Outside, the air was soft and laced with the smell of salt coming off the sea. This side of town, near the airport and the seaport, was flat and laid out with shipping yards, storage barns, and pumping stations. A plane thundered overhead. She watched its lights blinking code back to air traffic control. She'd never seen a plane fly that low over Harmony Square and she'd lived there since she was a child. It was the other side of town, other side of the highway. Manicured lawns and shopping strips. Somebody rich would whine if a plane dared to rattle their windows.

Sara's little turquoise Suzuki was the last car left in the dirt lot. While she warmed up the engine, she switched her mobile phone on. Three text messages from Dillon. *Where are you? You back safe? Let me know when you land.*

She quickly replied. *On my way.* And pulled out onto the road.

She hit the highway eight minutes later, listening to Norwegian death metal so loud it made the speakers jump. It was the only music that massaged the prickling part of her that longed for violence. Dillon had caught her listening to it once and she'd pretended it was the radio, that she'd somehow ended up on the wrong station. She was more careful now, hiding the CD deep in the back of the glove box. Not that they often took her car anywhere. Dillon was proud of his new Audi and, while a twenty-first century man in most respects, he still held onto the shred of a conviction that women weren't good drivers.

The road was eleven-p.m. quiet. She passed an occasional truck going the other way. One set of tail lights in front of her. The silent pine forest either side of the road. She drummed on her steering wheel.

Then the tail lights in front of her swerved, and she instinctively stabbed at her own brakes. The car ahead left the road at high speed, clipping the ditch and flipping, rolling into the trees. Sara had already pulled onto the shoulder before it came to rest. She cut her engine and the clattering music abruptly stopped. Silence. Her ticking engine.

She grabbed the torch from her glove box, opened the door and climbed out. The air was cold on her skin. She ran ahead the fifty metres to the other car, heart pounding. The smell of petrol. His tank had been punctured. The engine was still whirring, hot.

"Shit," she said, shining her torch inside. The car was upside down. Hanging from his seatbelt, unconscious, was Tall Man from the cage fight.

Six foot six of densely coiled muscle.

Sara looked around helplessly. No other cars. She could call emergency, but they would take too long to get out here.

Sara felt the tingle in her muscles, a foretaste of the thing she wasn't supposed to do, a guilty frisson at finally letting the dog off the leash. This was life or death, right? And nobody was watching. She rounded the front of the car and grasped its bumper bar in both hands, took a breath, and lightly flipped the car back onto its tyres. It landed with a crunch, rocked once on its suspension, then was still.

Sara wrenched open the crumpled door and half-climbed in. Reached over and unclicked his seatbelt. The smell of blood made her nose twitch.

"Wassss?" he said.

"Sh. I'm going to get you out."

She tugged and he was over her shoulder. She backed out of the car with the man worn around her neck like a burly scarf. A rough breeze tousled the long grass on the side of the road as she walked away from the wreck, which would almost certainly ignite. Her skin stood out in goosebumps. In the stony ditch beside her own car, she tucked him safely on his side. Her heart flickered and fluttered with the blue-white thrill of it. "You're safe," she said, brushing his bloody hair from his eyes with her thumb. "But I have to go."

Her feet crunched on the gravel. She started her car. A truck roared past but she didn't hear it over her music. She saw it touch its brakes as the driver spotted the crumpled car on the side of the road. Good: somebody else would call the accident in. She accelerated away, passed the truck. A bloom of orange light in her rear-view mirror told her that Tall Man's car had caught fire. Sara didn't look back.

. . .

In the harsh bright light of the roadhouse washroom, she studied herself in the mirror. A bloody smear across her pale cheek. A torn seam between shoulder and collar on her dress. Mud on her elbows. She cleaned and tidied herself. What she couldn't see in the mirror was the underneath. The hard-pumping blood, the sharp sparkling adrenaline, and the guilty fear. If anyone found out, her whole world would crumble.

. . .

"That took a long time," Dillon said, as she pushed open the door to their townhouse.

"Sorry," she said.

"Here, let me get that." He took her suitcase. "You look exhausted."

He headed upstairs while she dropped her keys on the kitchen bench and quickly glanced through the mail. Bank statements, prize homes, charities.

"There was an accident on the highway," she called, by way of an explanation for her late arrival. It wasn't a lie.

"It's okay," he called. "I've been catching up on my ironing."

She could see that. The ironing board, the smell of starch. He always started ironing right before she was due home. Her job was to notice he was doing it badly and offer to take over. She was very good at ironing shirts.

"Tell you what," she said as he emerged from the staircase, "you make me something to eat and I'll finish these shirts for you."

"Would you?"

"Of course."

He smiled, and his eyes crinkled at the corners. Five years on, and that smile could still make her heart flip over as it had that first time she'd seen him, sun in his hair, on the grass at Harmony U.

"Is a toasted sandwich okay?" he asked.

"As long as it's one of your pizza specials," she said.

"Got it."

He was in the kitchen, adding tomato paste, cheese, and pineapple to a sandwich for her. He was whistling and she thought, *he sounds merry.*

And she picked up the next shirt in the pile to give it a shake. Something fell out. Landed right between her feet. The lamplight caught its sparkle.

She bent to pick it up. It was cold between her fingers. When she stood, he was there, smiling at her.

"You'll marry me, won't you, Sara?"

. . .

Sara had crushed her grandmother's index finger at three months of age. Turned the bone to sawdust. By ten months she had broken six cots and her mother gave up and let her share the double bed. Nobody was allowed to give her wooden toys. Wood, for some reason, aroused more acutely the desire to break and crush. She fared better with stuffed teddies, which she loved to cuddle and stroke. As though their lack of resistance to the world made them safe from her unquenchable desire to smash everything to pulp.

By her third birthday, she was starting to learn self-control. As strong as she was, she still hadn't worked out the buttons on the remote control. The threat of missing *Playschool* could make her behave. Then Disney princesses taught her meek beauty. She couldn't plough her shoulder into the wall as fast in pink plastic high-heels.

But she was always aware of the dark thing inside her. It thrilled her and it frightened her, and she quickly learned to be ashamed of it; though the shame didn't make it go away. Behind the long back yard was an empty block, and she spent furtive hours every afternoon breaking branches, turning over rocks, chucking broken bricks into the iron fence. School was hard: so many other children to get along with. They had to move town four times, change schools, start over. Broken monkey bars; water bubblers wrenched off their weldings; a whiteboard eraser thrown so hard at the wall that it made a hole through the plasterboard and sailed through to the other side.

By sixth grade she was fatigued from being the new kid. She learned to be gentle. She learned to pull the rage out of her hands and arms, compress it into a white-hot ball behind her ribs. She sometimes broke a desk or a chair by accident, and gained a reputation among her teachers for being clumsy. Of course. A girl her size had to be clumsy.

That was it. She came to heel.

· · ·

Only that wasn't it. There was one other incident, wasn't there? She just didn't like to remember it. High school, bitchy teenage girls, a Queen Bee. Sara always kept her eyes down, but she nudged six foot, with red-gold hair and generous curves. She couldn't stay invisible. The rage bubbled over. It seemed so long ago, now, since she had felt that power move up through her veins and sinews . . .

Sara had seen Queen Bee just two weeks ago, across the road in the distance: she was still in the wheelchair. The clumsy-fingered churn of guilt had started all over again. Nobody had been around to witness that fight. The injuries weren't consistent with a schoolyard smackdown, so nobody believed Queen Bee and, of course, Sara denied everything.

Sara was used to denying everything.

· · ·

"It's just so old-fashioned, Mum." Sara shook the newspaper and placed it on the wrought-iron seat next to her. The oily smell of the newsprint mingled unpleasantly with the smell of tea brewing, fresh cane mulch, cut grass. Her mother's garden in Harmony Square was immaculately kept and a little old-fashioned: and so was Mother.

"I've been dreaming about the day I could put a wedding announcement in the *Harmony Times*, Sara. Don't deny me the pleasure."

"I've been getting congratulatory calls from old school friends . . . not that they were ever friends," Sara said.

"School was ten years ago. Everyone's forgiven you for being odd. They can be your friends now. A big wedding can be such a happy occasion."

Sara sat back, smiling bemusedly at Mother. "I don't want a big wedding, and I definitely don't want to invite people I used to go to school with."

Mother was perpetually prompting Sara to contact old friends or make new ones. But Sara found keeping friends difficult. Sooner or later, they sensed she wasn't telling them the whole truth about herself.

"It's silly to have your mother as your bridesmaid."

"Maid of honour. Please, Mum, don't make a huge fuss. Short engagement, just family, in the gardens next to the birch wood. Really, that's all I want."

Mother plucked a cupcake off the plate and offered one to Sara, who refused it with a raised hand.

"I can't. Wedding dress fittings coming up."

"You're beautiful exactly as you are," Mother said, but the words sounded hollow. Exactly what she was had always been a problem for both of them.

Long ago, Mother had taken to calling her unnatural strength 'your thing', a euphemism on equal footing with 'number twos' and 'monthly visitor'. When they'd moved to Harmony Square, she'd resolutely refused to talk about it anymore. "Don't let *your thing* ruin it," she'd said. "And don't mention it to anyone. We have a new beginning here."

Sara knew what Harmony Square meant to Mother. Years as a single parent, struggling on a combination of welfare and low-paid part-time jobs. Finally falling in love with her Chairman-of-the-Board boss when Sara was nine. Pete lived on the good side of the highway and invited them to share that life with him. Everything changed for them. Mother didn't have to struggle anymore. It seemed to Sara that her mother had shed twenty years off her face in the first two months in Harmony Square. Her determination never to go back to the bad side of the highway made Mother steely in a way that could be mistaken for coldness, conservative as an old lady despite her relative youth.

"I've been thinking . . ." Sara started, but stopped herself.

"Go on."

She inhaled. "I'm getting married. And usually at a wedding, there's a father of the bride. To give me away."

The tightness around Mother's mouth confirmed Sara's first instinct. Don't bring it up. Never bring it up.

But this time, instead of screeching at Sara, Mother put her teacup on the patio table with shaking hands, smoothed her hair, and said, "You have no father."

"Yes, I do. Somewhere in the world. I know you don't want me to contact him, but—"

"You have no father," Mother said, more forcefully. "I always intended to tell you the truth, and I need you to get it out of your head that there might be a loving reunion in time for your wedding. Get it out of your head."

"Mum, I—"

"When I say you have no father, I don't mean I hate him and want to forget he exists, Sara. There was nobody. Nobody. I was pregnant at seventeen and everybody assumed I was the kind of girl who got knocked up at a party. I wasn't. I didn't. I was a virgin on the day you were born."

Sara felt the tick of her heart in her throat. Mother was flushed.

"You have no father," Mother said again. "I promise you."

Her mind whirled. "Then how—"

"Don't," Mother said, a hand raised in warning. "I won't say another word. Now, more tea?"

. . .

The dreams are always in the same location. She stands outside the doors of a wooden hall, its boards stained black from years of damp and smoke. The hall faces north: the chill drifts down towards her, prickling her nostrils. A sunless place; churning clouds eat the sky. They reflect in the dark river that runs through the valley, carving its course into stony ground between thousands upon thousands of spears and swords, sprouting like saplings all around her.

In the river there are bodies. Wolves on the banks pull drowned men onto land to eat them. The smell of blood is everywhere, and Sara's dream body tingles with excitement. Bare-handed and alone, she waits. Then they come. One at a time, wading through the heavy currents of the river. Murderers, betrayers, oath-breakers. Grim men with hulking bodies and darkly glittering eyes. Some nights there are dozens, some nights there are only a few, but she knows what she must do with them, even though she doesn't know why she must do it.

The revolution inside her body is as thrilling as it is terrifying. As they approach her, raise their arms to push her out of their way and get inside the hall, she seizes them, throws them to the ground, stamps on their heads, kneels on their bellies and pummels them senseless, tears at their faces, dislocates their joints, and snaps their sinews. Something beyond rage is in control of her. It smells like animal and it pours down through her limbs with the speed of a river, the heat of lava, and the weight of iron. She shrieks and the sound echoes through the valley. It is the deathly baying of a trapped beast.

. . .

Soft, bell-like music. Sara opened her eyes and the world—the real world—rushed back in. The pale blue colours of the bedroom she shared with Dillon, the dewy sunlight through the gauzy curtains, the soft comfort of her pillows. Quiet. Order. The dream vanished with a snap, leaving only the echo of the wild chaos tingling along her veins. She took a breath. She'd had the dream hundreds of times before, but never grew used to it. Under the covers, she flexed her arm, felt the searing preternatural strength buried under her white skin. No outward sign of it gave her secret away, no muscle. If anything, she always felt as though she looked doughy; not sleek enough.

"Coffee, Sara?"

"Yes, please." Every morning when the alarm went off, Dillon got up and made coffee and toast for them both, and brought it back to bed. She hadn't made herself breakfast in two years.

He kissed her cheek. "Back in a few minutes."

She watched as he threw back the covers, the solid plane of his tanned back disappearing into black cotton boxer shorts. She smiled. Soon she would call him her husband, and the thought gave her a warm glow. Husband. Wife. New words unlocked into her vocabulary.

He looked back at her, saw her smiling. "You look happy."

"I am."

"So am I. I'm glad you're in my life."

. . .

But it had been different when he first met her. Dillon had been deeply and desperately in love—the unrequited kind—with Sara's classmate, Emily Pascoe. Emily was everything Sara wasn't: petite and slim, with glossy dark hair, and poreless olive skin. They'd all been in their third year at Harmony U together. Dillon had pressed Sara into service to help him woo Emily. Sara did everything he asked because she was deeply and desperately in love—the unrequited kind—with Dillon. Finally, Emily broke his heart and moved to the other side of the country. Dillon turned to Sara. Their close friendship grew into love.

Sara had seen Dillon's passionate side: the stormy seas that Emily had aroused in his heart. But she hadn't seen it since. She presumed she wasn't the kind of woman who aroused stormy seas. They laughed a lot together, they liked the same movies, they knew each other inside and out. He had probably never got over Emily. But she didn't ask. She was busy protecting him from her own uncomfortable truth.

. . .

Harmony Square was bordered on the north and the west with woodland. Mostly silver birches, which meant that even in the densest sections, the silver-grey trunks and yellow-green leaves held onto the sunlight. A path led through it for six kilometres, and it was a popular place to walk dogs or go jogging. Dawn and dusk were busy and safe, but Sara had timed her run badly. First, she'd finished work late. Then, she'd been stuck behind a council truck on the main street and missed every green light. Finally, she'd returned to the house to change her socks—her middle toe kept slipping uncomfortably through a hole in the seam—and the way Dillon sorted laundry meant it had taken just a fraction too long. The sun was down before she was two kilometres in, and it was only at night that the shadows in the wood gathered thickly enough to grow fear.

She hesitated, thought about turning back. But wedding dress fittings were on her mind. Sara knew she couldn't fight her generous breasts and her round hips, but she was determined at least to find the lean edge on her arms so she could wear something sleeveless in the spring sunshine.

So she kept running. She passed an elderly man with an elderly dog. He said good evening as he shuffled past. Then nobody else. Her huffing breath. Her footfalls. The occasional late-to-bed bird. Leaves falling with a soft clatter deep in the wood. Distant traffic. A soft breeze.

One foot in front of the other. She was coming to the crook in the path. In one direction, she could run an extra kilometre and come out at the river. But if she hairpinned back she'd be on her way home again: the run half over.

She rounded the crook and began the home stretch. The darkness now was comprehensive. If there was dog shit on the path, she would step on it and she simply had to accept it. If there were noises she couldn't make sense of in the woods, she simply had to ignore them. She was gripped by a powerful desire to be home at her empty house—Dillon was away for two nights on business—to have a warm shower and eat something.

Because there were footfalls. Not on the path, but in the wood. Heavy footfalls. Not lumbering. Fast and purposeful.

Sara stepped up the pace. Her heart pounded. The thing making that noise was keeping pace with her, but amongst the trees. How it found its way around low hanging branches and fallen logs in the dark was a mystery. But it was more than the footfalls that unnerved her, because Sara was strong; stronger than anyone: no masked man could knock her off her feet. It was something else, a tingling of primitive fear, a heightened sense of awareness that sent stony dread rocketing through all her limbs. A judgement was coming, something mighty and ancient. She sensed it with something beyond sight and sound. She smelled it with her gut.

At last she burst from the wood. Across the green she could see her back fence, the light left on in the upstairs bedroom. She tore across the open space, and the hulking shadow was behind-beside her. She didn't look, she kept her head down.

Through the gate, slamming it in his face. For it was a man, a huge man with an equally huge beard. Fumbled her keys. Got in the house. Locked the door. Reached for the phone.

The line was dead. She could see him through the kitchen window, scaling the six-foot back fence. Meaty hands, long muscular legs. A man-monster. If she ran out the front door, he would intercept her there. No, she would have to stay and fight. As his feet landed in her garden, the electricity fizzed. The kitchen lights browned down, then winked off: the strange unexpected silence when fridges stop humming.

Sara caught her breath. He knocked loudly on the sliding door.

Sara came out of hiding, faced him through the glass. He was in shadows, a felt hat pulled down low, a black shadow over his left eye.

"Who are you?" she demanded.

"Odin Allfather."

A slithering snake of cold discomfort and familiar longing stirred inside her.

"Go away," she said. "Go away or I'll come out there and tear your head off."

To her surprise, he smiled broadly. Not cruelly. "That's my girl."

She frowned.

"Let me in," he said. "I'm your father."

II

Sara didn't doubt he was telling the truth. Here, inside, by the light of the kerosene lamp, the resemblance between them was evident. He'd taken off his hat and now she could see the same red-gold hair, the same straight-tipped nose and generous mouth. She looked closely at his remaining eye—the other was covered with a patch—and it was the same icy blue as her eyes. Her fatherless state had meant she paid close attention to the similarities between Mother and herself. Sometimes she had imagined them, needing to feel she belonged, that she had provenance.

Here was where she came from. Without doubt. She became aware of all the tiny sounds normally hidden by electricity. The thrum of her blood pressure, the tick of the clock in the upstairs hallway, the distant traffic on the ring road that led to the city. Her skin prickled lightly.

"Why did the lights go out?" she asked him, after they had been silent, studying each other, for a long time.

"Magic."

"I see."

"I'm covered in it. It's quite a journey to get here. Don't worry. It will fade soon, and your electricity will work just fine."

"So . . . to get here from where?"

"Asgard."

"I see," she said again. Perhaps if she had been any other woman, with any other personal history, she would have thought him mad. But she had lived her whole life with supernatural strength. His explanation made the most sense of any she had conjured over the years. "And why come now?"

"You're getting married."

"You saw the announcement?" She felt just as confused as that time she had fallen off the high fence outside her Mother's house, knocking herself out for a half-second. Reality swam a little, then coalesced again.

"Yes. No. It's complicated. News comes to me of you. I gather it in strange ways."

"Magic?"

He bowed his head in a nod. "It's easier to say that than to explain. All of you here in Midgard live in ignorance, as though you are looking at existence through a pinhole."

A tickle of promise, of feeling she belonged to something vast and powerful. She tried to form words, but couldn't, so decided to stick with the basic questions. "So you came to give me away? At my wedding?"

He looked around the kitchen, eye blinking slowly. Then his gaze rested on her once more. "You're too thin."

She stifled a laugh. "You're the first person to say that to me. Ever."

"Why do you live like this? I gave you divine strength. Why have you not conquered this place?"

She swallowed hard. "Harmony Square? It didn't require conquering."

"Why have you not been all you could be? Why have you not used your strength?"

Because I was ashamed of it. But she didn't tell him that. "I couldn't use it. How would I use it? Knocking down houses for a living?" Even as she said it, the thrill of the idea shimmered across her skin. The fantasy of tearing Mother's faux-Victorian mansion down with her hands, crushing it to perfumed dust.

He shifted in his chair, shoulder flexed forward, agitated. "When I created you, I had you thrown into the future. Into a time when women were allowed to rule. Why haven't you ruled?"

Sara blinked back at him. Her heart felt compressed, icy. "What do you mean by 'creating' me?"

"I sowed my seed in a young mortal girl. I could tell with my hands on her belly that it was you: Aesir strength, mortal heart. I didn't want you to be born in Norway in 987. I wanted you to be somewhere you could make use of your strength, so I cast you 1000 years into the future."

"How?"

The corners of his mouth turned up under his shaggy beard.

"Oh. Magic."

"I'm not here to celebrate your wedding, Daughter. This Dillon Kincaid, he is not a fit husband for you."

She knew that she should have felt defensive, but instead she just felt frightened. "Dillon's very sweet. He makes me coffee every morning. We understand each other. He's perfect for me."

"Is he? Is he now?" Odin stroked his beard thoughtfully. "Then he will have to prove himself to me."

Sara bristled. "He doesn't have to prove anything to you."

Odin stood, thrust out his hand with three fingers raised. "Three tests," he said. "Mind, heart, and body."

"This is ridiculous," Sara replied, panic lighting a fire along her veins. "You can't come here after twenty-four years and—"

"A thousand years!" he roared. "A thousand years, Daughter, and this is what I'm greeted with? You hiding your strength, ironing for him, not eating so you can fit into a frilly dress? Perhaps Dillon Kincaid is worth it, but that is for me to judge."

"And if he's not? Are you going to forbid me from marrying him? You said you sent me to a more enlightened time. Fathers can't decide who their daughters marry in *my* world."

He glared at her a moment, then softened. "I'm not going to forbid you. I only want to see his worth with my own eye." He pointed to his good eye theatrically, then turned his pointing finger around. "I want you to see with your eyes."

He rose, towering over her, and put a huge hand on her shoulder. Gently, infinitely gently. "My daughter. I mean you no harm."

"Then leave me be and let me live my life." Deep down hoping, hoping he would do the opposite.

"No," he said. "You will know when the tests have started."

"Don't hurt him."

"Let things fall the way they will fall."

The lights flickered and then burned into life. Sara blinked against the sudden brightness. Odin had already turned and was stalking away, through the tiny courtyard and through the gate. Sara put her head on the kitchen table. She had never been good at thinking. Not that she was stupid: far from it. It was just that thinking—deeply thinking, connecting thoughts with feelings and understanding herself—made her so tired. She had never felt more weary than she felt now, in the wake of her father's visit.

Her father.

Sara realised she was weeping.

. . .

A week passed. Two. Sara wondered whether Dillon had already passed all his tests. He had a good mind, a good heart, and he was strong in his own way. She didn't mention Odin to anyone. Not to Dillon, who didn't know her secret strength. Not to Mother, who didn't want to know about her secret strength. Not to any of her friends at work. The wild dreams still came regularly, but now she understood what they meant. It was as though meeting her father had awakened her to the deep, lost mysteries of her own blood. The building was Odin's: Valhalla, the hall where the glorious dead could celebrate eternally. She was stopping the inglorious dead from entering.

But she never got inside it either, and the idea got under her skin and itched like an ant bite. *What if I never get inside?* She could barely articulate why it was so important to her. Her life here—in Midgard, as Odin had called it—promised her all she needed: a good home, companionship, quiet days and weeks and years. But over there—Asgard—was the rough, thrilling mystery that had called to her in her muscles since she was born.

She tried to become lucid during the dreams, to wrench open the door and go in and see the glittering firelight, hear the clatter of music, and feel the warmth of the hearth and the company. If she could glimpse the inside of that mystery, just once, then she would return to her life in Midgard and be quiet and still as she'd ever intended. But every time she put her hand on the door, she would awake, at home in Harmony Square, Dillon breathing softly and evenly next to her.

She drove out to collect Dillon late one night from work, at a building site just outside the Square. He'd designed the internal architecture of a warehouse rebuild, turning it into a retail showroom, and he'd been working long hours after electrical problems had stalled the refit.

The warehouse stood in a garden of mud and discarded building supplies. The blue-white streetlight flickered as the wind stirred the branches lining the street. Sara picked her way across to the front door, which was open. "Hello?" she called out. Her voice echoed in the big empty space.

"Sara. Up here."

She looked up to the first floor landing, to see Dillon with his hard hat on and a rolled-up architectural plan under his arm.

"Come on up," he called. "I want to show you what we've been doing."

She closed the door behind her with an echoing thump. The interior was dimly illuminated by gas lamps. "Still no electricity?" she asked, clattering up the iron stairs.

"We've had to redesign where the wiring goes. We're behind but catching up." He grasped her hand at the top of the stairs, and pulled her across to the next staircase. "The best view is from up the top."

They reached the top floor landing and stood in the semi-dark looking down.

"You have to imagine it brightly lit, and full of shiny new things. Designer furniture. Or electrical goods."

Sara squinted as though it could help her picture plasma screens and leather couches arranged artfully on the wooden walls and floorboards.

"I'm so proud of it."

She turned to him, smiling. This was his first project since his promotion. "You should be." She reached her hand up to brush his hair away from his temple and, as she did so, her engagement ring flew off.

Flew. It didn't fall. It wasn't even loose. It flew, as though it had grown wings from the back of its solitary diamond, and then plummeted in a perfect arc—down and down—towards the ground floor.

Both of them tensed, waiting for the crack as it hit the ground. Nothing.

Dillon turned and headed for the stairs. Sara hurried after him.

"Where is it?" Dillon said, scanning the floor. The gas lamps created confusing shadows.

Sara's heart sped a little. "Do you have a torch?"

Dillon unclipped the torch from his belt and began to shine it around. Together they scanned every inch of the floor with the torchbeam.

"That cost me a month's salary," he grumbled. He looked up at her. "You've lost too much weight if your ring can slide off that easily. You'll need to get it resized."

Sara said nothing. Then a gleam caught her eye. "There!" she said.

Dillon aimed the torchbeam, then crouched on the floor, shining it directly into a knothole in the floorboard, about the size of a coin. "For Christ's sake. What kind of bad luck is that?"

Bad luck. Of course he would think it was bad luck. He didn't believe in magic.

"It's under the floorboards?"

Dillon sat back on his haunches. "Underneath here is the wiring and the under-floor heating. There's a crawl space, about this high." He held his hands two feet apart. "And your engagement ring has somehow found the only way through."

"Can we pull up the floorboards?"

He shook his head. "Not without costing the contractor more money. No, I'll go through the basement entrance then into the utility hatch. I've got a pretty clear idea in my head of the floor plan, so I should be able to find it."

Now Sara understood. This was Odin's test of the mind for Dillon. Relief undid the knots in her stomach. She had never met anybody smarter than Dillon. He remembered credit card numbers and international time zones and postcodes. He could look at a route once on a map and find his way without a second glance. She smiled broadly at him. "What do you want me to do?"

"Just wait up here." He winked. "Watch me through the knothole if you like."

So she sat back on the smooth floorboards with her legs out and her palms propping her up. Was Odin nearby? Could she call out to him or speak to him? She brimmed with questions for him. But maybe it was best if she didn't ask them, in case it pitched her into lifelong yearning. She was Mother's daughter as much as Odin's; she belonged to this world as much as his. If not more.

Dillon's voice, muffled by floorboards. "I'm in."

She turned over, called through the knothole. "It's over this way."

"I know that. It's just . . . this is a bit trickier than I thought."

A flash of heat to her heart. "It's not dangerous, is it?"

"No, just tricky. It's like a maze under here. But I designed the maze, so if I can just remember where the junctions are and take it slow, I should be fine."

"Take good care." She tensed, waiting to hear his voice again. Instead she could hear bumping and slithering as he crawled through the utility space. A light buzzing feeling just under her skin. For some reason, her body was switching to alert.

Smoke. She could smell smoke.

Every sense lit up with cold electricity. "Dillon?" she called. "Dillon, I can smell smoke!"

She leaped to her feet, eyes darting madly. A thin curl of smoke emerged from between the floorboards about ten feet away, creeping closer to Dillon. She threw herself on the floor and hammered on the boards.

"Dillon!"

"Jesus Christ!" The bumping and slithering became frantic as he tried unsuccessfully to retrace the maze, backwards. Sara fumbled for her mobile phone to call emergency, but she knew she couldn't wait for a fire engine. She had to get Dillon out herself. The heat was travelling along the boards. It was under her hands, sizzling. She dropped her phone.

Sara stood, brought down her heel with heavy intent on the floor. A board cracked. She got her hands underneath it and peeled it up, as easy as another woman might peel a banana. Then she pulled another up, and another. Smoke poured out but she could see no flame.

She put her hand through the hole, coughing, frantic. "Here, Dillon! Over here!"

Calling his name was like a spell. The smoke evaporated, sucked back into the air through hidden folds. She breathed. His hand grasped her wrist. She had to remind herself not to pull him. He clambered up through the hole in the floor with wild eyes. His shoes were gone.

He stared at her. "What just happened? Where's the fire?"

"I don't know. I . . . It just . . . disappeared."

His face screwed up. "How did you . . .?" His eyes went to the hole she had torn in the floor.

"They must have been loose."

"Fucking electricians," he spat. "I could have died."

She reached into the utility space, withdrew her ring. "At least we found this." She slid it back onto her finger, her blood moving more slowly now.

He sat on the floor heavily, his head on his knees. "I could have died," he said again, under his breath.

"We should get out of here. We should call the fire brigade, just in case."

But he didn't move and she put her arms around him and clung to him, fighting tears. Dillon had failed the first test.

. . .

"My beautiful daughter. You take my breath away."

Sara spun in a slow circle. The bridal boutique was wall-to-wall with mirrors, and she saw her own statuesque body reflected infinitely around her. Smooth white skin, round shoulders, pale red hair. She was formed for midnight blue or dark crimson, but Mother wanted her in pale pink. Sara fought the conviction that she looked like a freshly picked scab. "Really? This colour, Mum?"

"It's so feminine. And you know I really don't like brides wearing white when they've been living with their fiancés for so long." Mother's mouth turned down in a ghost of disapproval, soon forgotten. "You always looked lovely in pink when you were little. The soft tones suit your skin."

Sara turned and viewed herself from all angles, craning her neck. It was a pretty colour, and Mother was often right about these things. What would Sara know about how to be a normal woman? She stooped to kiss Mother on the top of the head. "If you like this one the best . . ."

"It's your special day."

"It's special for you, too." Sara turned to the sales assistant. "This one."

The sales assistant ran about looking for pins and tape measures. Mother closed her eyes and bowed her head onto her hands.

"You okay, Mum?"

Mother looked up. "I feel old today, Sara."

"You're not old." Sara smiled. "You're still hot."

Mother tried to hide her own grin. "Well. Thank you."

"I bet Pete can't believe his luck." Pete was in his mid-sixties.

Mother pushed a stray hair off her own cheek. "Pete is a wonderful husband. And I know your Dillon will be just as wonderful." Mother's eyes grew sharp, detecting something in Sara's expression. "What? What's wrong?"

Sara shrugged. "He's been a little distant the last week or so."

"You've been away interstate again. I don't know if it's a good idea for you to travel so much. He probably feels neglected."

"No. He's not that old-fashioned." She was almost certain she was right. "I think work is on his mind." The incident at the warehouse last month had not been kind to them. Dillon had to spend many hours back at the site, making the electricians go over the wiring repeatedly, organising floor repairs, calling in the engineers again for structure and safety tests. The finish date had been pushed back, and now the star employee was losing his company money. It made him grumpy, listless. He was a man who liked to get things right. Sara also suspected he was pondering how the events of the evening had happened at all, but she never raised it with him. Life had taught her to keep her head down and not engage with the mystery. People mostly saw what they had always seen.

Mother dropped her voice. "You haven't mentioned that business about your father to him, have you?"

Sara was surprised to hear Mother raise the issue. "No. Of course not."

"Good. Because it's best forgotten."

Sara spread her hands. "It's forgotten then."

Mother smoothed her hair and looked around. "I wonder where that sales girl is?"

. . .

Sara hoped her father would come again. She wanted to tell him that she didn't care for his tests, that she was going to marry Dillon even if he failed every single one. But also, she simply wanted to see him again. She craved the weight of his arcane presence.

Then finally he returned. Dillon was working late at the warehouse and she was home alone eating a microwaved diet dinner and flicking through bridal sites on the internet. The booming knock on the door told her immediately that it was him. She rose with apprehension and longing in her heart.

"Father," she said.

"Daughter." He nodded, pulled off his hat. "I have been waiting for a chance to speak with you."

"Come in," she said, standing aside, and shutting the door after him.

He stopped at the computer desk, his hand on the back of the chair.

"Will you sit down?" she asked. She had no idea of the correct etiquette in this situation.

"No, I won't. Dillon Kincaid failed the first test and—"

"He would have been fine if you hadn't started a fire. He found the ring."

"What is a mind if it cannot hold strong under pressure?"

"He was afraid of burning to death." She was swallowing over her heartbeat. "It would make any man confused."

"I don't want you to marry 'any man'. Remember who you are."

A strong sense of disappointment gripped her. She had hoped, on seeing him again, to find a connection with him. But he seemed only interested in criticising her. The disappointment caught her off guard and she snapped. "I have only known who I am a few weeks. You have never been in my life. You can't come into it now and tell me what to do."

"I won't tell you what to do, but I can tell you what I think of your choices."

"I don't care what you think."

He threw up his hands in exasperation. "From what I see, you care what everyone else thinks."

Sara fell silent. Odin indicated the computer screen. "There is something on here you need to see."

"On the computer?"

Odin nodded. He leaned over and, with a click of the mouse, opened the webcam program.

"How do you know how to use a computer?" she asked. "They don't have them where you come from."

He held his hand over his good eye. "I see much in here," he said. "I see everything."

She peered at the computer screen.

"Sit down," he said, grasping her wrist and pushing her gently into the chair.

Sara did as she was told, then saw that there was a new file marked 'unwatched' waiting in the menu. She clicked on it, and it opened up. The video began to run. This living room, soft music playing. It was Coldplay, Dillon's favourite. A knock at the door. Then Dillon moved past the camera to answer it. The low resolution of the webcam was unkind to his face, making his cheeks look hollow.

"What is this?" Sara asked.

A firm hand on her shoulder pinned her to the seat. "Just watch."

Voices off-screen. "Hello, Dillon."

"Emily!" Puzzlement, tenderness.

"Can I come in?"

"Of course you can."

Then, standing in front of the webcam, was Emily Pascoe. Sara's erstwhile college friend. Dillon's lost love.

"What the . . . ?" Sara gasped. The lining of her heart began to glow with heat.

"Where is Sara?" Emily asked.

"Away on business. She'll be back tomorrow night. Do you want to sit down?"

"No, I won't."

Sara's senses prickled.

"Can I ask why you're here?" Dillon's shoulder was turned away from the camera, but Sara could see in his muscles that he still wanted Emily Pascoe. That he had never stopped wanting her. "I never thought I'd see you again."

Emily fixed him in her sultry gaze. "Dillon, I hear you're getting married."

"I am. Next month."

"But you and I, we have unfinished business."

Sara tensed. She waited for Dillon to deny it, to tell her that no, he was over her, that Sara was the soulmate whom he loved madly.

"Yes," Dillon said, all the slump and surrender of capitulation in his voice and body. "We do."

Emily's eyes grew dewy. She touched his shoulder, ran her fingers down his arm to his wrist. "I don't want to stop you getting married. I just want to feel your arms around me. I want you to take me against your body, just once. Then we can get on with our lives. Nobody will ever know."

Damn him. He didn't even waver. "Yes," he said. "Oh, yes."

Odin's hand tightened on Sara's shoulder. Protectively.

Emily cleared her throat loudly, stepping back. "I'm so thirsty. Could you fetch me a drink?"

"Of course." Dillon, under her spell now, hurried away. "Sit down, make yourself comfortable," he called. "I'll be . . . I'll be right back."

But before his sentence was finished, Emily had turned to the camera, dissolved and reconfigured. In her place was Odin, looking directly at Sara with a sad expression. Then he slipped out of shot. The sound of the front door closing.

Dillon returning with a glass of water. One of the glasses Sara and Dillon had bought together when they'd first moved in with each other. "Emily?" he said, puzzled. Forlorn.

The video flickered to black.

Sara could only hear her heart, beating fast but thready. Beating only because it had to.

"As I was saying, before you interrupted me," Odin said, quietly and darkly from behind her shoulder. "Dillon Kincaid failed the first test and now he has failed the second."

. . .

The grey descended and covered everything, like fog on an autumn morning. Sara hid her feelings: it was her most practised talent after all. She smiled and laughed and spoke and ate and showered and slept, but only an inch deep. Underneath the Sara that the world saw, was the Sara who had crumpled in on herself as though made of thin cardboard.

It seemed the wedding was a great machine made of cast iron cogs that turned perpetually. Inescapable. She needed a year or two to decide if she would stay with Dillon, but she had only a few more weeks. Emotional paralysis. She didn't decide to stay, she just couldn't decide to leave.

The wedding would go ahead as planned. Sometimes she told herself, perhaps he wouldn't have betrayed her completely. Perhaps he would have said this isn't right, you have to go, I love my fiancée.

But she knew. She'd always known. She was his second choice.

At night, in her dreams, she looked for Dillon. She wanted to see him come wading across the river. She searched every face for his eyes, his nose, his lips. She thought if she could tear him to pieces in her dream, then the anger would dissolve. The jealous lurch of her stomach would settle. She would be able to get on with married life.

But he was never there.

. . .

This is new, she thinks, as she becomes aware she is dreaming but there is no hall, no river, no forest of spears. The sky is deep velvet blue and she can see so many stars that her breath catches in her throat. Everything is caressed with grey-white starlight. Her bare feet are on dewy grass. Ahead of her there is a cliff, and a man sits on the edge of it. It is Odin.

She approaches. "Father? Is this a dream?"

He turns, pats the place on the grass next to him. "No. I needed to talk to you. Sit."

Sara sits. She feels the load fall from her shoulders as she leans into his hefty arm. She hangs her feet over the edge of the cliff. Below them is a raging sea, crashing and crashing on rocks. Colossal wildness, undreamed of, making her veins thrum. "Where are we?"

"Bifrost. The way between." He raises his hands and a rumble gathers across the sea. It sucks all the ambient sound out of the night, creating a vacuum in her ears. Then the deafening wail of a horn snaps the air. Sara covers her ears. Immense coloured lights unribbon into life in front of her. It is the aurora, viewed from above, and she can see that it is, indeed, a bridge, leading off to a mist-shrouded place miles and miles distant. The horn abruptly stops, leaving her ears ringing, but she can hear the low, throbbing pulse of the lights as they undulate gently.

Sara's heart squeezes. She is mortally sick of seeing existence through a pinhole.

A flapping noise drags her attention away from the lights. Two black shapes flying against the starlit sky.

"My ravens," Odin says, holding up an arm for them to land on. "Thought and Memory."

The birds land on his leather-clad arm and he chucks them under the beak, one after another, making a little clicking noise. Sara enjoys his display of tenderness.

"Go on now," he says. One bird takes off, then the other. They cross over, seem to become one. Soar up high, then plummet again, splitting back into two.

"Did you bring me here to show me all this?" Sara asks. Urgently, she hopes he will ask her to stay forever. The wedding will be off. She won't have to look at Dillon every morning and feel the pain of knowing he doesn't love her as much as she loves him.

"No," Odin says. "I brought you here to ask you whether you've decided to call off the wedding. He's failed two tests. Do you still intend to marry him?"

Sara hesitates, thinking of her mother's hands tying ribbons in her hair. Her mother who has raised her the best way she knew, even though Sara was a cuckoo. Then she realises she shouldn't hesitate; she should speak quickly. "Of course," she manages. "I love him."

A sudden bitter coldness grips her. An icy wind shoots past, tangling her hair and covering her skin in gooseflesh. Then it is gone. A dark shadow passes over them. She tries to follow it with her eyes, but it has already disappeared out to sea. She is left with a mild trepidation that keeps a little breath trapped in her lungs with every exhalation.

"You love him?" Odin asks, as though the cold shadow hadn't passed. "Even though you know how little he values you."

"He values me. He really does. You don't understand him. I've always known how he felt about Emily. It was painful to see, but not a surprise."

"He does not value you enough, Sara. You are extraordinary. You have strength beyond mortal knowledge. You have Aesir blood. You can stride across the clouds and kill with a Viking's courage. He should worship you; you are so much greater than he is."

The pride in her power is buried deep, not allowed to shine. She is afraid to let it shine, and so she speaks aloud the words she *has always spoken under her breath. "I just want a quiet life. I never asked for supernatural strength. It's been a burden, not a blessing." She puts her hand over his. "Please, can we stop this now? All this business with tests and so on? Dillon is a good man, he really is. I'll get over my jealousy and we'll have a nice life."*

Odin's single-eyed gaze searches her face, then he sighs and turns to the mist at the end of Bifrost. "It's too late."

"Too late?"

"The third test has already started."

Dread like cold iron presses on her heart. She remembers the icy shadow that passed over them, headed out across the sea. "What have you done?"

. . .

Sara woke, confused in the dark. Her ears still ringing.

No, her ears weren't ringing. Her mobile phone was ringing. The digital clock told her it was one a.m. She'd gone to bed early, before Dillon was back from work at the warehouse. The other half of the bed was neat and cold.

She snatched up the phone. "Dillon?"

"Where are you?" he snapped.

"Home in bed. Where are you?"

"Home? Then why did you call me to come here?"

"Come where?"

"Sara, what the hell is going on?"

Her heart knocked on her ribs. "Dillon, listen carefully. I didn't call you. I've been asleep. Tell me where you are now. I think you're in danger."

"In danger?"

"Where are you?" she shrieked.

A quarter-moment of silence as her fear infected him. "I'm at an industrial estate out near the airport. You said you were here with a flat tyre."

The cage-fighting arena. It had to be. "Is there a green building? With a white banner?"

"Yes. It says, 'Blood Arena'."

"Get in your car and come home. Now."

"Do you want to explain what's going—" An abrupt click. Three loud beeps. Then silence.

III

Sara wondered if he'd be dead before she got there, but then remembered that Odin had made sure she witnessed every one of Dillon's failures. *I want you to see with your eyes.* She parked the Suzuki at a crazy angle out front of the arena and stepped out. The rumble of traffic in the distance. A shower of wintry rain, harsh across the aluminium roof of the arena. The thin glow of the streetlight half a block away. She grabbed the torch from her glove box.

The door was locked, so she kicked it, bent it double, then peeled it aside. The arena was in darkness. She shone the torch around. Shadows retreated from it. Dillon paced the cage, alone.

"Dillon!" She ran down through the auditorium, past the rows of plastic seats to the centre. The room smelled of cold concrete and stale rum.

He raced to the gate. A padlock held it closed. He rattled it with all his strength. "What the fuck is happening, Sara?"

She swung her torch around, found a covered power box on the base of the cage. She hit every switch, hoping for light. Nothing.

Magic. They were covered in it. Whatever *they* were.

"Who put you in here?"

"I didn't see them properly, they covered my face. But they were big and . . ." He exhaled roughly. "I think I'm going crazy."

"What did you see?"

He blinked. Looked away, his hair falling across his eyes. "Monsters."

Sara's stomach went cold. "I'm going to get you out," she said.

"How?"

"I'm sorry you had to find out like this."

"Sara?"

She hefted the padlock in her hand, twisted it. The iron snapped like a dry twig. The gate swung open. "Come on, let's go."

Heavy, shuffling footsteps.

"How did you..?"

"Go! Now!" Then she turned her face up to the roof and shouted, "Call them off! He can't pass! We both know he can't pass!"

Dillon's face twisted with angry sobs. "Stop it, Sara! Tell me what's happening." Stubbornly, he held onto the gate. Even the imminent threat of monsters couldn't convince him to trust her.

A deep shiver loosened her gut. Fear. Suddenly it was icy cold. She shone her slender beam of light into the dark auditorium, hardly able to focus. The rain intensified on the roof, drowning out her thundering heart. A shadow moved. Her skin puckered as the light hit the monster. Only it wasn't a monster, it was a man: seven and a half feet tall, with skin so white it glowed blue. He was dressed in cloth and leather; his long black hair gleamed. His eyes met hers, and they were so pale they looked white. The freezing menace in those white eyes loosened all her nerves from their sockets.

"Frost giant," she managed to say to Dillon, before the other three stepped out of the darkness. They formed a line and filed down towards the cage. The first one, the leader, raised his hand and indicated Dillon.

"No," Sara said. "Not him. Me." She turned to Dillon and, hands beneath his armpits, lifted him aside as though he were as light as a toddler. She strode into the cage.

"No! Sara!"

But the frost giants were racing towards her now, shoving Dillon roughly aside. The gate slammed shut. Dillon tried to open it again, but a blue-white charge leapt onto his fingers and knocked him backwards. He disappeared from the stage.

"Dillon?" She ran to the side of the cage and peered down. The chainlink was cold under her fingers. Her torchbeam found him lying on the ground. She didn't know if he was dead or just unconscious. She turned, dread lined her veins with lead. Four of them surrounded her in a semi-circle. She ran her torch across their blue-white bodies. She couldn't tell them apart except that one wore a silver circle around his brow. He must be some kind of prince.

A breath. A pause.

One of the giants stepped forward and knocked the torch from her hand. It clunked to the floor and rolled to the side of the cage, caught by the chainlink. She had to fight them in the dark. Her soft, mortal body shuddered.

Sara closed her eyes and opened her arms. She remembered the dreams; her body filled with molten metal. She drew her elbows in and took a deep breath, then opened her throat and a shriek poured out of her: a tempest, a whirlpool, a piece of chaos. It echoed off the walls and ran like electricity across the ceiling. She opened her eyes, could barely see their shapes in the gloom, leaped and landed on the closest.

These creatures were nothing like the men she had fought at the river in her dreams. They were solid slabs of ice. Her knuckles split and bled as she punched him. Her opponent's blows were bruising, dazing, rattling her eyes in their sockets. But she hammered and hammered at his head until he started to crumple. They fell to the ground together. The thin reflection of blue-white torchlight turned everything into fast black shadows. Two of the others tried to haul her off him, but not before she had stamped and hammered his head to a squishy, bone-splintered paste beneath her knees and fists. One held her while the other punched her. They ploughed fists into her stomach and she held it tight as cold steel against them. The final one, the prince with the dully gleaming silver circlet, hung back watching. These were his underlings. They would soften her up so he could take her more easily. She had to get away from them and get her hands around the prince's neck, or she wouldn't survive.

She shrieked again, calling up the storm in her veins, muscles, sinews. The freezing iron clamps of their hands around her upper arms tried to pull her back, but she strained against them, shuffling forwards, until both of them lost their footing and were dragging behind her. She lifted her arms and shook hard. First one slipped off, then the other. The prince stepped forward and, in a black moment, had her head in an arm lock.

With sudden white intensity, the electricity in the room burst back on. Everything looked hyper-real, over-exposed. Music. '*Tie a yellow ribbon round the old oak tree.*' The red floor made her eyeballs ache. She struggled against the prince but the other two were crowding in now. One punched her ribs, the other her head. A mad blur of fists and blood and black hair and bright colours. Her heart pumped wildly. The pain cracked through her body. She could taste her own blood. Helpless, desperate, descending under thick water.

I am Odin's daughter. I am not weak. I do not surrender. I will be all that I can be.

Thudding blows. Ringing ears.

I can stride across the clouds and kill with a Viking's courage.

"Sara?" Dillon's voice, a long way off.

Pulling every shred of strength from every nerve and fibre of her body; pulling it out from behind shame, from behind fear; sending it rocketing up into her arms, down into her legs.

One. Sara flexes her spine, breaking the prince's hold. He stumbles, uncertain on his feet a moment. Two. She turns and heaves the other two over. They land in a heap on the floor. Three. She raises her knee and slams her heel into their heads, one, the other, one, the other. Four. She rounds on the prince, flings herself at him, brings him down to the ground. Pins him, pummels him, teeth and claws in his neck and shoulders. A blur of black and thorns and blood and breath and madness and taking him apart, taking pieces of him apart between her palms and thumbs and shrieking, shrieking, screaming all of the screams of the primal abyss . . .

Five.

Five. Breathe. Breathe.

Sara sat back, realised she had the prince's head in her hands. She let out a shout of revulsion and dropped it on the ground.

"Oh, my God."

Sara turned, saw Dillon on the other side of the cage, watching her. In that moment, she saw herself through his eyes. His quiet, compliant Sara, sitting astride a headless frost giant, among torn and bloody bodies.

"Don't look at me," she said, spitting blood through ragged lips.

But he couldn't look away.

• • •

Later, much later, they finally spoke of it. The bodies had turned to ice and melted into water. They brought their cars home. They showered. Sara tended to her wounds alone in the bathroom, with the door shut. Dillon sat, awake and upright like a coiled spring, in their bed.

The warm, soft bed where they talked and slept and made love.

"Dillon?" she said, dressed now in the pale lilac dressing gown Mother had given her for her birthday.

He seemed to shake himself. "Are you okay?" he asked.

"Bruised," she replied. "A little stiff."

"I should take you to hospital."

"No need. I'm not . . . built like other women. They didn't break anything." She perched on top of the covers next to him. "I'm sorry I never told you. I thought I could go my whole life without telling you."

"What are you? What were those things?"

She chose her words carefully. Dillon couldn't handle too many details. The very simplest brushstrokes were necessary. "My father is Odin, the Viking god. I have supernatural strength. The monsters came for you and would have killed you. They won't come back now. Odin has proved his point. I don't want to be strong, I want to be normal. I've hidden it my whole life, and I can go on hiding it. You'll never see it again. I promise."

Dillon's face worked. Eyebrows twitching, jaw clenching. "I can't un-see," he said.

"You might forget in time."

"You ripped his head off. You looked . . . crazy."

The shame of it, the weight of squirming embarrassment that he had seen her like that, made her angry. "Well, you said yes to Emily Pascoe," she snapped.

His pupils shrank to pinpoints. "How did you . . . ?"

Stalemate. They studied each other in the light from the open bathroom door.

Finally, she said, "Are we still getting married? I'll forgive you if you forgive me."

Dillon rubbed his hands over his face. Outside, the first birdsong in the birch wood. "Are you going to do that again? Ever? If I make you my wife?"

"No. No, of course not." Her heart beat fast.

He dropped his hands, fixed her in his gaze. "Who else would have us?" he sighed. "It's too late now."

. . .

The string quartet played Debussy, and the music floated on the spring breeze over the park and towards the birch wood. The sun shone, but from a long way off. Winter's chill still in the air. But no rain, and enough of the sweet smell of flowers blooming to make people smile and say, "A perfect day for a wedding."

A perfect day for *her* wedding. Sara breathed as deeply as she could against the restricting laces of her pale pink gown. She paced the small wooden deck behind the rotunda, her veil tickling her face.

Mother stopped her, grasped her hands. "Stop pacing. Everything will go just fine. Just a few more minutes."

"Is everyone here? What time is it? Is Dillon here?"

"Everyone's here. Including some people I've never seen before. But it's best for the bride to be a little late."

Sara's curiosity tingled. "People you've never seen before?"

"There's a very uncouth looking fellow up the back."

"Big beard? Eye patch?"

Mother nodded. "I presume he's a friend of Dillon's family."

"Yes," Sara lied. "He's an . . . uncle."

"He looks like a bikie." Mother smoothed Sara's veil. "All right, my darling. Deep breath. It's your special day."

Sara forced a smile. Her whole body tingled. Odin was here. She hadn't seen him in the month since the battle with the frost giants. She didn't know if he was proud of her or disappointed in her. She desperately wanted to know.

The bridal march started. The breeze freshened. Treetops rattled. Mother looked towards the birch wood with a slight frown. "They really should cull that wood," she said.

Sara's veil whipped against her throat. She followed Mother through the rotunda. Mother adjusted Sara's hem then fell behind her. Matron of Honour. They started down the short paved path between the rows of plastic seats. Head down. She stole a sideways glance. There was Odin, his own head bowed. Her breath was caught between her ribs.

She walked down towards where the celebrant stood with Dillon and his best man. Dillon smiled. She could see it was forced. He kept reassuring her that they had their whole lives to deal with their problems, but he hadn't kissed her or made love to her since the third test.

The music stopped. A hush fell. The celebrant began to speak. The wind again, fresh and high and too cold for spring. Sara risked another glance towards Odin.

He was gone.

The space between her ribs grew heavy and chill. He was gone. And why should he not go? She had made her choice. She had turned her back on her supernatural ability, she had decided to marry the man who failed every test her father had set. She had chosen to forgive Dillon his infidelity, so that he could forgive her violent secret.

Only that wasn't fair, was it? She had known it from the moment she had said it. His sin was weakness; hers was strength. And strength was not a sin. It had *never been* a sin.

The wind picked up her veil, whipped it aside and off her face, half-pulled the diamante comb from her tortured hair. Sara plucked it from her head and dropped it on the ground. It went tumbling off across the grass. Her hair fell loose. She breathed, she closed her eyes. She could hear their eyebrows lifting. The celebrant paused.

"Sorry," Sara said to the celebrant, opening her eyes. "Please continue."

Dillon watched her closely. She tried to smile and found she could only bare her teeth. He recoiled, almost imperceptibly. Her heart thudded hard in her throat.

"Do you, Dillon Kincaid, take Sara to be your lawful wedded wife . . .?" The vow rang on like a cloud passing over the sun.

"I do," Dillon said, warmth flushing his voice. "Yes, I do."

"Do you, Sara Jones . . .?"

Sara tried very hard to listen to every word, to know exactly what she was swearing to. But a black shadow caught her eye. She glanced up.

Two ravens, weaving in patterns above. She watched them, her heart lifting and falling. Her blood pulsing audibly.

She became aware of a silence. She startled, looked back at the celebrant. At Dillon. It was time for her to speak.

To swear.

To say, "I do," to Dillon and "I don't," to . . . everything else.

The ravens darted past overhead. Black wings against the pale blue sky. Disappeared into the birch wood.

Sara touched Dillon's hand, all her sorrow leaden in her fingertips. "I can't," she said.

The wind became suddenly furious. There were alarmed cries as guests held onto their hats. The treetops swirled wildly, and

Sara strode away, across the park. Then she kicked off her shoes and ran, hard, heart pumping, towards the woods.

"I'm coming, Father," she said under her breath as branches caught and tore the pink lace of her dress. Louder. Calling. "Father! Odin! I am coming! I am becoming!"

And all her body and being bent towards him, as she had been trying to do her whole life.

THE LARK AND THE RIVER

"Love is Lord of all"
— Boethius, *The Consolation of Philosophy*

I

His God caused my death, and my own gods funnelled my spirit into this yew tree to bear witness to the centuries as they travel past, dappled and shadowed in scudding sunlight. I watch as if through a veil: a veil of soft green and rain and the sound of crickets. Sometimes shapes solidify around me and I see people, coming and going through the churchyard; sometimes I am aware and alone for long, cold nights, just as though I were in my body and sitting among the tree's teeming roots. Other times, all is a jolting blur and I find myself moving fast through clouds, or working my edges into the earth and the grass. But always I am tethered here, to this tree, to this place. Always, I am tethered to Rufus.

. . .

They came on the first day of October. Autumn stained the leaves of the chestnut trees and the barley fields ripened to burnished gold. My older brother, Faran, burst into the smoky house, his long hair damp with rain, and stood in front of Father with the shifting feet of a nervous child, even though he had been on the earth twenty-four autumns before this one.

We were all scared of Father.

"What is it?" Father said.

"A pair of men up on Huntsman's Hill. I don't know who they are, but they're up to something."

Father put aside his bowl of turnip and rabbit stew, and opened his hands expectantly, impatiently, as if to say, "Well? Tell the whole story."

"They have a large instrument. Looks like a metal pair of legs," Faran continued. "They're measuring something out on the ground."

Neriende, my younger sister, said, "What are they measuring?"

"A building," Father said gruffly through his wild beard, returning to his soup.

"A church?" Mother said.

"I don't want to talk about it," Father replied, scowling grimly. A church would mean tithes and observances that he didn't want to pay.

New stone churches were going up all over England. For years, we'd done what we ought and travelled to the chapel-at-ease, four miles away at Lissford, as good Christians are meant to do. Or sometimes we forgot to travel or forgot to pray or forgot about God all together, because he wasn't as tied to our days and seasons as we needed him to be, and instead we went to the spear-stone, or the well, or the ancient yew tree, to leave offerings and tie ribbons for wishes. Our community's faith was fluid and self-serving, and we enjoyed the freedom even as we knew the creep of containment was coming in the wake of William's invasion. A church in Tiwstan: now that would make being who we were a great deal more difficult, especially my family, ruled as we were by a man who believed Christianity was a tool of authority and nothing more.

But Father said he didn't want to talk about it. And I knew better than to go against my Father's word.

Two weeks later, I saw it for myself. Four muddy days in a row, and then the sun came out proudly and the wind blew the clouds away. I had been stuck inside with the smoke and the smell of animals and my father's temper, so the good weather drew me outside. Curiosity took me up to Huntsman's Hill, where I found nothing but the shrubs and rocks that had always been there. But from there I could see down towards our village's sacred yew, the tree under which generations of my family, and the other village families, had been buried. The tree we tied ribbons on in spring, and spilled ox blood on after harvest. The tree my ancestors had been worshipping for centuries. While we had been busy with the harvest or pinned inside by rain, a team of men had cleared trees, ploughed a gap in the earth-and-hedge wall around the graveyard, pegged out long lines of rope, and dug a trench. The church would be ten feet from the yew.

I sat down, even though the damp crept through my skirt, and put my knees under my chin to gaze at the site for a long time. I had a feeling of the ground shifting underneath me. We renamed our old gods with saints' names and offered them our old libations, we celebrated Christ's ascension with a horned green man, we buried our dead with runestones as well as crosses. With a rector watching over us, we would be compelled to stay within the confines of Christianity. And it wasn't that I minded so much for myself. But my Father. My Father.

Cynric had seen the whole world turned on its head since his twenty-second birthday, when William and his Norman army had come to power in England. My father fought at that famous battle, alongside his lord Oslaf. In fact, Cynric had been Oslaf's chief retainer, a high-ranking thegn with seven hides of land here at Tiwstan.

But after the battle was settled and Oslaf had fled to Denmark, Cynric found himself with an injured leg and only two hides of land. And then, seven years later when Oslaf's property was finally bestowed upon a man from Rouen named Richart de Villeroi, Cynric's land was reduced to one. One hide to support his growing family and to make a small living that was taxed by those he considered his enemies. Cynric boiled. I knew all this because Mother had told me one time, after Father had thumped me so hard across the ear that I'd seen stars. "Your father was once a soft-hearted man, slow to anger," she'd said as she dressed the cut on my ear. "But then they took everything from him, Merewyn, and that is why we must be patient with his temper." And then she had told me to be grateful that Villeroi hardly ever came to the manor house he'd had built on the other side of Huntsman's Hill, because she was certain Father would kill him and then we'd have a *murdrum* fine on our family that we could never hope to pay.

But they hadn't taken everything from Father. A man can endure the loss of land and goods. But the foundation and comfort of his spirit? A church in the village might well take those from him too.

I gazed at the sacred yew, and a creeping fear stole into my heart. Everything was about to change.

. . .

After the trenches were dug and filled with stone rubble, the pegs and ropes disappeared and so too did the team of men. The days were growing shorter, and I knew that my Father and Faran were up to something. They spoke to each other in harsh whispers by the hearthpit after Neriende and I went to bed. Mother knew, but wouldn't say.

I heard them leave the house one night, just a week before the Midwinter feast. Neriende and I shared a bed, and so too did our two dogs and the motherless kid Neriende had adopted. I lay awake for a few minutes, then decided I wanted to see what they were going to do. I rose quietly and dressed in the dark. Neriende rolled onto my side of the bed and didn't wake. One of the dogs lifted his head, but was too cosy to follow me without explicit instruction to do so. I could hear Mother by the hearth, grinding grain for tomorrow's bread. Rather than go out through the main room and have her stop me, I crept to the small door in our bedroom that adjoined the barn. During very cold winters, Father would open it and let the animals in the house for warmth. I lifted the latch and found myself surrounded by the smell of hay, manure, and animal sweat, then a moment later I was outside in the cold, clear night.

Stars glittered against the black sky. Yesterday's rain puddles reflected the waning moon's pale blue glow. I followed their muddy footprints over the field and through the wood and across the stream. I knew where they were going, of course, but I couldn't simply turn up at the church site and ask them what they were doing, so I took a different route and found a place to hide behind an oak that had long since shivered off all its leaves. I pulled my cloak tight, but my feet ached with cold. And I watched.

Father and Faran stood at the edge of the trench, talking in low voices. Faran was wearing his fur hat, and it was pulled down so low I could barely see his eyes. Father said something to Faran and they both laughed loudly, then a few moments later were pissing in the trench. Is this what they had come out to do?

But then a shadow caught the corner of my vision, and I saw that a woman approached. She wore a long black cloak with a hood, and I knew instantly it was Seledrith, whose powerful spells and bindings were both revered and feared in the village. My father did not like Seledrith. He called her Lady Boneshadow, but never when she could hear it. And yet, here he was, meeting her at midnight on the waning moon.

I knew, then, what was going on. Father had paid Seledrith to perform some kind of magic here: something that would banish the church or curse the ground so that they couldn't or wouldn't build. I did not stay to watch. I had to get home ahead of them and, besides, my skin crackled with the cold.

As I ran home, a flurry of snow started, the first of the winter.

· · ·

The snow fell over the coming days and weeks and nobody came back to the church trench, and my father bragged of it in the village. He thought he'd won. That Tiwstan would stay as it always had been.

Meanwhile, the snow fell and fell, filling the trenches and settling in deep white drifts across the fields. It was the coldest winter I could remember, but Mother defiantly declared she remembered colder winters, even as she shivered through the long nights of howling wind and the cough in her chest grew tighter and deeper.

In the early weeks of the new year, Mother went to bed and couldn't get up again. All the blood in my body was hot and startled by how pale and ill she appeared, but Father wouldn't allow us time to be truly afraid. Neriende and I took on all her duties, as well as our own, and we also nursed her through feverish days and cough-sodden nights. Father was as remote and angry as ever, as though indignant that Mother should dare to grow mortally sick. Winter dragged on, and we all knew in our hearts that she wouldn't see spring. My sadness at her imminent loss was only a shade more intense than my fear of how life would be under the care of my father, now that Mother's calm and steady hands would not be on his shoulder.

· · ·

Snow-melt ran into the stream that flowed past the spear stone and down towards the yew. Somewhere in the mud were the seeds and bulbs that would be next month's spring blossoms. The wheel of the year was turning, and so was the wheel of life. Mother entered her final days. She was a thin shadow who lay in her bed, sleeping and wheezing, while Father spent all day outside mending fences and moving sheep from field to field, pretending nothing bad was happening.

Every evening I kissed my mother goodnight expecting it to be the last time her cheek would be warm with life. The days dragged out. Rain fell and the damp sank into her lungs and turned her cough into a bark that frayed the ends of my nerves.

Then one night, while squalling rain battered the shutters, there was a thundering knock on the door.

Neriende got such a fright she dropped her spindle. We all looked to Father, who knelt by the fire holding a spitted rabbit in the flames.

"Merewyn," he said, indicating with his shoulder that I should answer the knock.

I stood as Mother heaved with fresh coughs among the warm skins on the bed, and went to the door, unlatched it, and opened it.

A tall man stood there, in a long grey cloak, with his hood pulled up over his hair. Before I had a chance to say anything, he said, "I hear there is a woman sick in this house."

Father approached, the half-cooked rabbit held on his spear. "Are you a healer?" he asked gruffly.

The cloaked man bowed his head. "Of sorts," he said. "I can help you."

"Let him in," Neriende said, always too quick to reveal her heart to Father.

"Go away," said Father.

Faran cleared his throat. "It can't hurt," he said.

Father turned his ice-grey eyes on me. "Merewyn?"

I didn't say what I thought, which was, *She is beyond healing.* I sided with my sister and brother, because I wanted Father to go more gently with them. Faran, for all his strength, had a soft heart; and Neriende was barely out of girlhood. Between them, they made all the noise in the family. I was the quietest, but I was the strongest of spirit. I had always known it.

"Let him in, Father," I said. "He may provide us some comfort."

Father turned his back on all of us, hunched over the fire again. The man stepped inside and I shut the door on the swirling rain. He pushed off his hood to reveal thick auburn hair and dark hazel eyes. And my heart stammered as though catching a breath, because in that instant I had the impression of him being the brightest object in the dim room. I told myself it was the firelight in his hair against the drab greys and browns of our everyday life. But still, the impression stayed with me.

"I am Rufus," he said, and his name gave away his Norman birthplace as much as his accent. And yet, unlike so many others, he had taken the time to learn our language and this made me warm to him.

"She is here," Faran said, leading Rufus to where Mother lay.

Rufus knelt at her side and touched her forehead with his right hand. Immediately her coughing fit ceased, and she gasped and gazed up at him. I inched closer to watch, and found I admired greatly the breadth and shape of his fingers on my Mother's brow. The firelight caught golden threads in the hair on his wrists, and the heat coming from his body was dense and present.

"You don't need to say or do anything," he said to Mother, softly. And then he leaned close to her, almost as though he were moving to kiss her, and started to speak in his own language.

At least, that's what we all thought for the first few moments. But then recognition prickled at the back of my mind and I looked nervously to Father, whose back stiffened.

Latin. He was speaking Latin. The language of the Church.

"No!" I said, moving in to stop Rufus, just as Father threw aside the roasting rabbit and wiped his greasy palms on his tunic, ready to rip Rufus's head from his body.

Faran stood and hoisted Rufus to his feet, expertly protecting him from Father's blows under the guise of throwing the church man out.

A blur of movement and wind and rain, and Rufus was gone from our house. I was angry at him. So angry. For he had no doubt triggered for us a long evening of managing my father's horrible rage. One of us would get struck instead of Rufus: it was certain. Probably me, because I had cast the deciding vote to let him in. So like these church people to think they were doing favours, but to unwittingly do harm. The sick horror that the evening would be lived in fear and pain swirled in my belly, and I cursed Rufus. I cursed him the first time I met him.

How different things were to become.

. . .

She got better, you see. Not just a little better. The next morning, mere hours later, Mother was well again. Sitting up, asking for something to eat, breathing. Living.

Rufus healed her.

II

I wanted to thank him. That was all. Father wouldn't have it. He told us all that Mother's illness had simply run its course and Mother, Faran, and Neriende all fell in line to agree with him. Neriende tied a ribbon in the ash tree at the bottom of the field to thank the Great Mother, but nothing more was said of it. Within a few days, Mother was well enough to sit at her spinning wheel for a few hours, and complain about Neriende's bread until she decided she could now lift the grindstone and do the job herself. Life went on as it always had.

But I wanted to thank Rufus. It wasn't that I believed in his god, the god they so unimaginatively called "God". It wasn't that I disbelieved either. Gods are gods. They can't be seen, only presumed. They do things sometimes that prove they are there, and other times they do nothing and all there is for it is to wait and hope. None of us want to be alone in the world and under the heavens. But I believed that Rufus, not God, had healed Mother. He possessed a special ability and I was grateful he exercised it that night, and I wanted to tell him so.

I chose a rainy day to slip out and find him. Father and Faran were out sowing the muddy fields, and Mother and Neriende were at the loom together. I had only to feed the pigs, so I did that, and cleaned out their sty haphazardly (they were pigs, after all: they wouldn't notice), and then I headed off over the back fence and through the wood. The mud sucked at my feet and the rain fell lightly, trickling down the back of my neck and under my dress. I wasn't sure where I would find Rufus, but I thought the village a good place to start. I made my way across the stream and down towards the sacred yew.

What I saw made me stop and catch my breath. Seledrith's curse had clearly not worked. A group of twenty or so men swarmed over the site, heaving stones from a cart, cutting them and pushing them into place. I raked my damp hair out of my eyes and watched a while, in fear. Father would be ashamed that his plan hadn't worked; angry with the workers, some of whom were local to the village. He would explode. I wriggled the fingers he had seized and crushed the night Rufus had come. Mother was always afraid that Father would take his anger out into the village and kill somebody; I was far more afraid that he would kill one of us.

Eventually I noticed. Rufus was among them. His auburn hair marked him out. But I couldn't just walk up to him in front of everyone and say thank you. Father would hear of that. I hesitated, fell back a little. The rain came down.

Then he saw me. I don't know how. I was a long distance away, half-hidden in the wood's shadows. But it was as though he felt my eyes on him and glanced up to see who was watching him. Time stood still, as if all the dull-coloured workers slowed and stopped, and this magnificent tall man with his burnished hair was the only one still breathing and moving. His eyes locked with mine. He said something to the man he stood with, then he strode purposefully towards me.

This would get back to Father. I stepped backwards, alarmed. I overbalanced and had to catch myself against a tree trunk, grazing my palm. I turned to go home, cursing myself for coming out.

But then Rufus caught my shoulder gently.

"You're looking for me," he said, a statement, not a question.

I turned, gazed up at him. "My father will be angry," I said.

"God will protect you." He dropped his hand.

A hot chill ran through me. He knew nothing. "No. No, he won't."

Then Rufus smiled at me, and said, "*I* will protect you." And I felt it, so strongly and keenly. He would protect me from Father. I didn't know how, but he would. I believed it.

"A good start would be never to tell that I came to speak with you," I said.

"Then that is where we will start," he replied.

The rain still came down and we smiled at each other in the muddy woods.

"I'm Merewyn," I said. "And I came to thank you. My mother is well again."

Rufus dropped his head and closed his eyes, muttered something in Latin under his breath.

"My family think it was nothing to do with you. But I know better. She would have died that night, if not for you."

He lifted his head and met my eyes steadily. "It isn't me you should thank. It's God."

"I . . . well, why don't you thank him for me?"

Rufus laughed. "It's true then, what the Bishop says? You are all still heathens here?"

"No. We are just ourselves. There are many in the village who happily go to the chapel-at-ease and still worship the green man."

Here he frowned. "We must be one or the other. The Lord doesn't want us to be both."

A silence fell between us. The gulf between how we each saw the world opened up. I knew I should go and yet I didn't. I couldn't.

"Will you be cutting down the yew?" I asked instead.

He glanced over his shoulder and then back to me. "No. It's sacred, isn't it?"

I nodded.

"Then to worship it, you'll all have to come to the church." He smiled. "I hope you will come to the church, Merewyn."

"I expect I'll do whatever my father tells me to," I said. "Isn't that what a good daughter should do, even in your god's eyes?"

He reached out and put his hand on my wrist. The heat from his fingers was intense through my cold, sodden sleeve. "Merewyn, I would be happy to teach you about my god. I am living at the manor house, and you may call on me any time."

"The manor house? Is Villeroi here?"

He shook his head. "My uncle is still in Rouen. Though he may be joining me in a month or so to see how the church goes. But now, I must return to the church to speak to the architect. Good day."

"Good day," I said, reluctantly.

So he was Villeroi's nephew. Father would have so many reasons to hate him. I had so many reasons to fear him.

And yet, the idea of seeing him again filled me with a strange kind of succulent joy that I had never known before.

. . .

My father's temper brewed slowly and deeply as often as it bubbled over quickly and spectacularly. Often we could tell in the morning whether or not he would lash out that evening, and the day he heard that the church builders had returned was one of those days.

He left early for the market to buy a goose, but was back within half an hour with a pale face and an almost bewildered expression. The door banged open, letting in a morning draft. He regarded us all in turn and I tried not to flinch from his gaze.

"Alric Archer just told me that the church is going ahead," he said.

Faran bowed his head, and Father's attention snapped to him. "You knew," he said.

"I saw two days ago."

"And when were you going to tell me?"

"What would be the point? We didn't stop them, did we? They are coming. Whatever happens next . . ." He trailed off, glancing at Mother, my sister, and me. Something went unsaid.

"That rector won't last a year," he spat. "No Norman man is wanted here, especially not a church-monger. They're not even real men. As limp as a lady's laces."

"Not in front of the girls, Cynric," Mother said gently.

"Well, why should they not be able to laugh at the joke? These men, they cannot hold a sword or please a woman." Here he laughed cruelly, while I blushed. "What god forbids a man from taking a woman? A god who's cruel or foolish, or both. Curse them. Curse them all."

I felt my pulse quick and light at my throat. Father slammed back out of the house and we all got on as though nothing had happened, picking up our work, not speaking to each other. Faran paced, his eyes fixed on the ground.

"What did Father mean about God forbidding them to be with a woman?" I ventured finally.

"The church won't let them marry," Mother said. "Some say they must remain celibate."

I hadn't known that. How could it be possible for a man like Rufus to remain celibate? A man with so much bright energy?

Faran stopped pacing in front of Mother. "He's angry," he said, with a set to his chin I hadn't seen before. "I suppose we're all due an evening of blows and curses?"

"You should have told him," Mother said. "Better to come from his own family than a smug Christ-worshipper like Alric Archer."

Faran muttered something and he, too, slammed out of the house. The door bounced in the jam, making all the boards shudder.

Mother smiled weakly at Neriende and me. "Well," she said, "at least with only women home there will be some peace."

I turned my attention back to the hose I was darning, guilt and fear pressing behind my eyeballs.

If I am honest, Father hitting me was not my greatest fear. My greatest fear was his unhappiness, for it seemed so immense, so in danger of crushing us all, body and soul. On days where he was in a good humour—and there had been a handful since winter ended—my body would uncoil and my joints would all feel loose. His smile was a treasure so rarely glimpsed that we all delighted to look upon it. As a child, I had felt responsible for that smile, for his happiness, and also to blame for his discontent. If only I could make him happy somehow. I knew in some way that my father's misery and anger were wholly his own, and yet his good-humoured days still gave me a sense of achievement, as though I had finally fulfilled my purpose in the world.

Father was back later with his goose, then spent the day in the barn fixing the hinges on the door. His black mood was palpable through walls. We wound tenser and tenser. As I sewed, I thought of what Rufus had said. *I will protect you from your father.* Of course he had meant that he wouldn't reveal that we had spoken, but I let my frightened imagination roam in foolish places. Rufus was at least a head taller than my father, young and strong where Father was worn and grizzled. I imagined Rufus sweeping in, just as Father was unleashing his temper on me. I imagined him pushing Father aside, a column of righteous red-gold light. Or I imagined him picking me up off the floor after Father's blows, and gently tending my wounds and whispering that soft secret language that brought Mother back from the perimeter of death. I kept my mind occupied with these fantasies until dusk, when Father came in and it all started.

Mother's stew was too thin. The smell of the lavender drying was too strong, it put him off his food. Why had she not fixed his favourite shoes yet? I sat quietly in my corner of the room and watched with that sick feeling of inevitability and horror that I was so used to. Tonight it was Mother's turn to receive Father's temper. That meant that I was safe, though I took no joy in the idea. In fact, I was the one he hit the least: I was quiet, and he couldn't persecute me if he didn't know what I was thinking.

Finally, she said to him, "I will fix your shoes first thing in the morning, Cynric. Please don't trouble yourself."

And Father replied. "You idiot. I will need them first thing in the morning." He punctuated his reply with a slap around her shoulder. Mother raised her hands defensively, over her face, and Father grasped them hard and pulled them down and began to roar at her not to be a fool and an idiot and a sow and every other insult he could think of, all the while kneeing her sharply in the soft part of her thighs so she crumpled against him and had to struggle to stand. Apart from Father's cursing, the room was very quiet.

Until Faran stood and shouted. "Stop it!"

My heart went cold. Nobody had ever tried to stop Father. The edge of meaning had been reached. I knew not what would happen beyond this limit.

Father turned away from Mother, who steadied herself and adopted a tone that was meant to sound conciliatory, but was so strained across terror that it came out as a squeak. "It's all well, Faran, I will fix your father's shoes tonight and all will be well—"

"It's not all well," Faran declared, eyeball to eyeball with Father. They were both a similar stocky build, precisely the same height. "Two weeks ago, she was on death's door," Faran said in a low voice, "and now you beat her?"

"She is my wife to do with as I please."

"She is small and weak. What a brave man you are." The sarcasm was so thick and unctuous that Faran's face twisted to say it.

The next few moments were a blur. Male shouts and fists and then a horrible moment when Faran drew his knife and raised it towards Father's face.

Father stopped, a vicious snarl on his mouth. "Go on," he said. "Go on. Kill your father. Let all the gods curse you for it."

Faran stood back, sheathed the knife on his belt and said, "You will eventually find somebody to kill you, Father. But it won't be me." He turned to Mother and said. "I am leaving. If any of you had any sense you would do the same."

Mother, too frightened to speak in case the beating recommenced, said nothing. I said nothing. But Neriende clung to Faran at the door. "Don't go. Don't leave us with him!" she sobbed.

I hauled Neriende off him. "Come, sister," I said quietly. "Let him go."

Faran disappeared into the night. I didn't know if I'd ever see him again, and my heart stung. Not because I'd miss him, but because he had failed to understand that neither Neriende nor I would leave Mother unprotected. So I was angry with Faran. He had given up. He had walked away from the mess. And I had to stay in the middle of it.

Father's rage was written in every tight sinew in his neck and arms. But he didn't hit us. He sat by the fire and stared at it glassy eyed. He was still in the same position two hours later, when I went to bed.

. . .

Spring grew warm, May day came and went, and Faran didn't return. Father pressed Neriende and me into service in the fields and the barn to replace Faran, and I fell to sleep exhausted most nights. The church building continued, slowly but surely. Nobody went to the sacred yew during the day anymore: the noise and shouting made it hard to think, let alone sing a song or say a prayer. Once I went at dawn, when the night sky was bleached of its colour and the blackbirds sang in the wood. I tied a ribbon and thought of Faran, far away somewhere in the world. But the next time I came by, my ribbon was gone. I wondered if Rufus's strong fingers had untied it, and if so, what he had done with it after he took it down.

We still worshipped at the sacred well, and I know Father went often to the spear-stone that our village was named after. He believed, as villagers had for generations, that Tiw had embedded this large stone, the shape of a spear's head, as an assurance that he would always offer us his favour in battle. Was Father praying that Tiw would interfere somehow now? That he would shake the earth so the church fell down? To Father, our gods must have seemed very quiet on the matter.

On a rare day when Father had little for me to do, I went up to the rocky slopes above the wood to find some wolfsbane for Mother.

She kept a store of medicinal flowers and herbs, and her wolfsbane linament was famous in the village for numbing injuries. The sky was big and blue, stretching itself with warm-weather langour. In the distance, the river that bordered our village sparkled with reflected sunlight. Summer was coming. The flowers and bees and robins knew it. Being out and free in such weather made my heart sing. I hummed to myself as I searched for purple flowers. Hours passed and my basket filled and my hands turned pink from the sun. Then I came to the edge of the precipice and sat for a few moments looking down at the village and fields below, stretching off into the warm hazy distance to a blue horizon.

The church was a site of activity. Men moving about, noise and dust. I searched for Rufus's dark red hair, but couldn't see it. To the south of the church, my eyes found the thatched roof of Villeroi's house, the only stone building in Tiwstan. The honey-coloured bricks warmed themselves in the sun and the narrow arched windows looked out past the out-buildings—a buttery, a bower, perhaps—towards the forest and Huntsman's Hill. Was he in there? What was he doing? What did church men do? Did they spend all their time praying?

You may call on me any time.

I stood, my heart beating hard. A half-heathen girl, terrified of her godless father, with a basket of wolfsbane. I would not be welcome. There was nothing particular about me that had prompted the invitation; he just wanted to introduce me to his god. That is what Christian folk did. And yet, with all these reasons not to go, still I went.

I stopped at the gate. He was in his muddy garden, spreading grain for his chickens. I was struck again by his height, his bearing, the sun on his hair. My heart thudded. He didn't look around, but he said, "Good morning, Merewyn. Are you going to come in?"

A tiny thrill of dread ran over my body. How had he known I was there? He must have seen me from a distance.

"Yes, I am going to come in," I said, pushing open the gate.

"Does your father know you are here?" He turned now, looked at me. A challenge.

"Of course not. Are you mad? He'd murder me."

He considered me in the morning sunshine. "Then why are you here?"

"I don't know."

"I do."

My ears were filled with the sound of my pulse.

"God is calling you," he continued.

"I'm not sure that's true."

He shrugged lightly, dusted his hands together. "Come inside."

I left my basket at the door and followed him into the house. It was grander than anything I'd ever seen, with glass in the leaded windows instead of wooden shutters. The glass let narrow beams of light shine onto the rushes that covered the stone floor. Floor-to-ceiling tapestries kept the stone from reflecting cold through the house. An unpainted wooden staircase led to an upper chamber. Down in the hall, where we stood, the hearthpit smelled of cold ash. Instead of benches built into the walls, a round table sat beside the hearthpit. It was covered in a gold-embroidered cloth, and four oak chairs with carved backs were pushed up against the table.

"Will you sit and eat with me?" he said. "I have pie left over from yesterday's supper."

Eat with him? I hesitated. I shouldn't be here, but the idea of spending time with him overrode everything. "I . . . yes. Yes I will."

He pulled out a chair and motioned that I should sit, and I did. My fingers traced the threads on the embroidered tablecloth. "This is very fine," I said.

"It's my uncle's," he replied. He uncovered the remains of the pie on the bench and pulled the knife from his waistband to cut a slice. "I have nothing so fine in the world." He lifted the slice of pie onto a wooden plate and pushed it in front of me, then made another for himself. "Wine?" he asked, reaching for a corked bottle.

"Yes," I said again. I dug the spoon into the pie and took a bite. Buttery and sweet-sour. "Oh, my," I said. "This is delicious."

He returned to the table with his plate, the wine bottle and two wooden cups. "My mother taught me the recipe," he said.

I took a gulp of the sweet wine. "You don't have a cook? A housekeeper?"

"I will. When the church is built and I have my own house. But for now, I am staying here alone."

He steepled his fingers and rested his elbows on the table, and took neither a bite of his food nor a sip of his wine. He regarded me across the table with a gentle smile on his lips. I felt such a pang then, and admitted finally why I was there. I desired him. And at the same time I made this admission to myself, I had the deep and pointed realisation that I was not the first girl who had pinned her hopes on capturing his heart. Tall, beautiful, charismatic. I could not have been the only one to notice. I dropped my gaze to hide my embarrassment.

"I have news of your brother," he said.

I snapped my head back up, shocked. "You do?"

"He came to see me, the night he left. He wanted to thank me for healing your mother, just as you did. And he asked me to tell you, should I happen to see you again, that he intended to find his fortune in Byzantium with the Varangian guard. But not to tell his father. Your father."

"Byzantium." I rolled the name over my tongue. "He's never been so far."

"No?"

"None of us have. I imagine it is such a far-flung, impossibly exotic place, where flags fly in white sunlight." I shook my head. I wondered how Faran, like me a native of the mud and rain of Tiwstan, would get on. "Thank you."

"Is it true, then, that your father beats you? All of you?"

"Many fathers discipline their children."

"Faran spoke of broken bones and bruises that take months to fade."

I flinched, remembering the blood that had poured from a cut on my chin, the night before my fourteenth birthday. Father had punched me, and the ring on his finger had ripped open the skin. Mother had stitched it herself. Still, eight years later, the scar was easily visible.

"It isn't right," Rufus said.

"I know."

"I will pray for you."

Pray for me. He wanted only to pray for me. I wanted him to do to me what Garret Smith had done to me in the millet field one long, warm summer when I was eighteen. He hadn't prayed, though he had certainly called out to God a few times. With Garret, curiosity had driven me to shed my clothes in the sunlight. With Rufus, it was not curiosity, but desire. But it was a desire that could have no satisfaction, if what Mother said about church men was true. I put the spoon down and pushed the chair back. "I should go."

"There's no need for you to go."

"I shouldn't be here."

"Your father won't find out."

"No. I just . . . shouldn't be here."

He inclined his head slightly. "Yes, you should. Here is exactly where you should be. God has willed it, Merewyn. From the moment I arrived in the village, God has insisted that I look your way."

"What do you mean?"

His gaze did not waver. "I saw you, in the marketplace. On my first day here. At the sight of you, I became alert. The way I become when God's will is moving in me. Then Alric Archer told me about a sick woman that I should tend to. That was your mother. You opened the door to me. And I saw you again, in the forest. Remember?"

"I came to seek you out."

"It doesn't matter. Every time I see you, I get a . . . surge of destiny."

I swallowed hard. "And what do you think that means?"

"That God has plans for you. Through me."

I wondered that he had not interpreted the "surge of destiny" as desire, as I had, then admonished myself for my vanity.

"All will come to light when it is meant to." He finally picked up his cup and took a sip of his wine. "I won't make you stay if you are determined to go. But come to me again, when you can. I would welcome the chance to share the scriptures with you."

"I don't know any Latin." And had never desired to learn Latin, yet now it seemed a secret sensual language to share.

"I can translate some of it for you. I think it would be good for local people to hear God's word directly. Yes, do come again. But not next week. My uncle is coming, and the Bishop."

"The Bishop? To Tiwstan?"

"Twiston," he replied without blinking. "Your village is recorded by the church as Twiston. The Bishop will not tolerate the heathen name. And yes, the Bishop is coming at my invitation. Because he is . . . he is Villeroi's brother."

I was so busy thinking up a retort to his insistence the church rename our village, that I almost missed the last. "Villeroi's brother. So the Bishop is another uncle of yours?"

And at last, he dropped his gaze. A flush in his cheeks. I watched him for a moment, curious, and then realisation dawned.

"Oh," I said, "the Bishop is your father? Why didn't you just say so?" But as the words left my lips, I knew why. Church men couldn't marry. He was the Bishop's illegitimate son.

"Nobody needs to know," he said. "My mother has been well looked after."

"I won't tell anyone," I said. I saw no shame in his being illegitimate, after all.

He looked up again and smiled, and suddenly he looked much younger than I'd thought. Perhaps just a few years older than me. A flush of knowing passed through me. His father hadn't maintained a vow of celibacy. Perhaps it was not so important a rule after all.

He stood and gave me his hand to help me from my chair. His fingers were briefly, hotly, on mine, and then gone. "Here, don't forget your basket of monkshood," he said, picking up the basket I'd left by the door.

Wolfsbane. Did they have to rename everything? "Thank you," I said, turning to leave.

"We'll keep each other's secrets, Merewyn?"

I nodded wordlessly. To keep his secrets, to have him know mine, was too thrilling to utter.

III

It is strange the things I remember from here in the yew. Memories coalesce and shred apart, are stretched out of shape by time, or sometimes loom close and present, almost as though I am living them again. I remember my sister, my brother, and my mother with muted fondness; but my father with fiery love. It isn't easy to understand, but I do not strive for understanding. My existence is not solid or constant. I flicker in and out of knowledge and light and sound with no warning and no fear.

I remember walking to the market with Father, up the long hill to Lissford, just a few days after that secret meeting with Rufus. The sky was leaden with rain clouds, but the sun shone behind us on the bright green seed fields that stretched out to the east and west. I had to hurry to keep up with Father's uneven stride, but he was in a good humour. A brief shower of rain passed over us and was gone; all the while the sun shone, illuminating the drops to glistening white.

"Look you, Merewyn," he said. "It's a badger's birthday."

This was a story he'd always told Faran and me as children. When it was sunny and rainy at the same time, all the badgers in the wood celebrated birthdays. I'd believed him back then, of course, and it delighted me to hear him laugh about it now.

We trudged a little further, then the sound of a heavy cart from behind had us standing aside off the road, knee-deep in the long grass at the muddy edge of the field. Father stopped to watch the cart go past and I stood beside him, with a basket of Mother's finely woven cotton to sell at the markets.

The cart trundled over the flagstones and mud, rattling heavily. It was loaded with large blocks of stone, so I knew it was heading for the church. I also knew Father's good humour would evaporate. He cursed under his breath. We watched the cart and then resumed on our way. The clouds had moved over the sun, and I could sense imminent rain.

"Keep up, girl," he shouted over his shoulder as he stalked away.

Markets were every third Wednesday in the Lissford market square, four miles walk from Tiwstan. The cobbled square was covered in stalls with brightly coloured covers up against the soft rain. A large stone cross sat in the centre of the square and I found myself looking at it, thinking about Rufus, the church, their god. Why was there not room for all the gods? Why did theirs have to insist that ours were not real? That made no logical sense. If one was to believe in a powerful, invisible being, one could not point to other powerful, invisible beings and say, *you are under an illusion, these gods aren't real.* I was turning these ideas over in my head as Father yanked my arm and took me to the cloth merchant's stall. Father thought it less than manly to carry a basket of cloth around, but in all things was certain that only men should deal with money. While he negotiated with the merchant, I turned my back and surveyed the crowd.

A flash of auburn hair. I craned my neck. Then a group of people dispersed and Rufus was clearly in my view. With him, a well-dressed man with short hair and a neat beard. Villeroi: it had to be. His wool tunic and cloak were dyed rich shades of red and green, edged with gold braid, and fastened with gold-and-amber pins. I turned around quickly, looking anxiously at Father. The contrast of his appearance with the Norman man's was stark: his unruly beard, his dull cloak. If he saw Villeroi, it would awaken his deepest rage. He considered Villeroi a thief of land and livelihood, the reason he was selling scraps of cloth at market rather than a dozen pigs.

I sneaked another glance at Rufus and Villeroi. Rufus must have seen me, but was carefully looking the other way. "Father," I said softly, "shall we get on soon?"

"I have to buy turnips," he grunted. "The pigs got into ours." He turned and I moved slightly so I blocked his view of Villeroi, but the Norman man was too finely dressed to miss. His bright coloured clothes caught Father's eye as surely as a shining object catches the eye of a jackdaw.

"Who is that with the rector?" he asked the merchant, over his shoulder.

The merchant, a grizzled man with sunken cheeks glanced up and said, "That is Richart de Villeroi."

The temperature of my blood seemed to drop. I put my hand out instinctively, to stay father's arm. He shook me off and scowled at me.

The merchant continued, not noticing the tension between Father and me. "He's paying for the new church down in Tiwstan. The incoming rector is his nephew."

"They will all regret it, for only ill shall come of it," Father muttered through clenched teeth. "Come, Merewyn."

He strode away from the stall and out towards the road. I ran after him, stunned that he wasn't going directly to Villeroi to tear his head off. "Father, wait!" I called. "The turnips?"

"We're going home," he said.

I caught up with him, grasped his wrist again. Once more, he flung off my hand, so roughly that my arm twisted in its socket. "Leave me be!" he roared, raising his hand as though to strike me, but holding it at the last moment.

I cowered, rubbing my shoulder. In the corner of my vision, I could see Rufus's auburn hair. I stole a glance. He was looking directly at us. Father followed my gaze; his eyes locked with

Rufus's and a violent charge passed between them. Contempt was written all over Father's face; pious judgement on Rufus's. My heart slammed in my throat. That feeling I loathed but was so familiar with—a dark, horrible dread in every joint—gripped me. The moment before the storm. Father was about to lash out. But then something shifted. Father lowered his hand and smiled.

It was the most frightening thing I had ever seen him do.

He turned. "Come, girl," he said. "It's a fine thing that Villeroi is the rector's uncle. A fine thing, indeed for they will all share the same fate. I will leave them be and trust to Lady Boneshadow."

"What has she got to do with it?"

But he wouldn't answer and I knew better than to press him. I would have to speak to Seledrith myself.

. . .

Everyone knew Seledrith's hut at the edge of the wood, but few had ever been inside. The high hawthorne hedge and the overhanging oak branches blocked the sun, so no grass grew and the dust was carpeted with deadfall. A row of uneven flagstones led to the small front door. I paused a moment, soft rain making my hair and dress damp, then I knocked once, loudly.

Seledrith opened the door and eyed me. "Cynric's daughter," she said.

"Merewyn," I replied. "I'm here on my own business. Not Father's."

"Come in, then," she said, standing aside. She was a small, thin woman, dressed from head to toe in voluminous black layers. Silver bracelets hung from each wrist, jangling with charms of moons and stars. She was probably no older than Father, but the impression of advanced age was given by her scythe-like cheekbones and the sunken hollows beneath them. Her hands were pale and graceful. Perhaps she was once beautiful.

Seledrith indicated embroidered cushions next to the hearthpit where I could sit and dry out my dress. "So much rain," she said. "I've had the fire every afternoon, and here we are just a few weeks until summer."

I smiled, puzzled that the fearsome Lady Boneshadow should embroider cushions and talk so readily about the weather. The walls of the room were lined with shelves, and each shelf was neatly stocked with bottles and jars and baskets of dried flowers, feathers, herbs, sticks, and stones. The overall impression was one of order, practicality, tidy humility.

She settled next to me and stretched her bare feet out to the fire. I noticed a black tattoo on each foot: one a raven, the other a bear. "How can I help you, Merewyn, daughter of Cynric?"

"What enchantment did Father have you put on the church?"

She frowned, causing the lines around her mouth to deepen. "Here now. You said you didn't come on your Father's business."

"I meant Father didn't send me. I need to know what he has asked you to do."

"He paid me a good deal of money, child. He is likely in debt over it. If you want to know what his secret business is, you need to ask him yourself."

"Will it cause harm to people? To the rector?"

Here she narrowed her eyes. "The young rector has caught your eye?"

"He healed my mother," I replied, defensive. Was it so obvious that I had feelings for Rufus? Or was Seledrith using the soft edge of her magic to push into my mind? I shivered in my stomach.

"I have heard that story. I still don't know if I believe it."

I opened my mouth to say, *Well you did nothing to help her*, but bit it back. We hadn't gone to Seledrith for healing, because everybody knew she dealt in curses, not blessings. "I don't hold it fair, whatever god you follow, that a good favour should be repaid with a curse," I said.

She dismissed me with a wave of her hand. "He's handsome, that young man. No doubt all the village virgins will be falling over themselves for him. Don't attach yourself to him. These larks don't last."

"What do you mean by larks?"

"Let me draw you a picture," she said, picking up a cold coal from the edge of the hearthpit and applying it to the hearthstone. She sketched a bird sitting in a tree. "This is the lark," she said. Now she sketched a long flowing line that ran off the hearthpit on both edges. "And this is the river."

She paused a moment, and the rain outside intensified. A cool breeze leaked through the shutters.

"These churchmen, they are larks. They sing a beautiful song and one can't help but listen and admire it. But to follow that song slavishly is madness. The larks take to the air and their song is dispersed and lost." She poked a finger at the charcoal river. "Our ways are like the river. Ancient, eternal, part of the land and the seasons, always present and meaningful. Without the river, we die. Without larks . . . well, we have one less pretty song in the world. But we will survive."

I looked at the drawing for a long time. Although I wanted to believe what she was saying, I felt sorry for her. For every lark that flew away, another was ready to take its place. They had been singing for hundreds of years now and were building churches up and down the land; stone traps for those they charmed with their song.

"Am I to understand, then," I asked slowly, "that Rufus's association with the church means he somehow deserves to be cursed?"

Her eyebrows twitched and the mood in the room changed. She was angry with me. "I do what I am paid to do."

"What were you paid to do?"

And then she told me. Perhaps because of pride, or perhaps she wanted to scare me because I'd dared to question her. "The church, the rector—this Rufus you speak of with softness in your eyes— and all those close to him will suffer. There will be blood in the churchyard. You will see. My magic is stronger than his."

Primitive fear stirred in my blood. So here was the reason Father hadn't struck Villeroi. As Rufus's uncle, he would come under the curse himself. "I beg of you," I said, reaching for her cold hands, "remove this curse."

She flung my hands away. "I can't and I won't," she said. "You should leave before I decide to tell your father how you feel about the rector."

I climbed to my feet. "You don't know how I feel. You know nothing about me. And if you tell Father I've been to see you, I will tell him you revealed his secret."

She held her chin up defiantly, but I saw agreement in her eyes.

"Good day," I said.

"It isn't a good day," she replied. "It will be when they are all gone."

Moments later, I was outside in the pouring rain, gulping for deep breaths, knowing I needed to warn Rufus about Lady Boneshadow's curse.

. . .

Rufus had told me not to come. Not while Villeroi and the Bishop were visiting. And yet if I didn't warn him, something terrible might befall all of them before I had a chance to speak to him. Father needed me to help him fix the stable door: I had to hold it in place while he adjusted the hinges, a job that would once have belonged to my brother. So I wrestled with my problem in my mind while Father shouted and berated me for not being a tall, strong man; and took Faran's name in vain for leaving us. By the end of the day my arms were aching and my brain was too. But I had decided I could not leave Rufus unprotected from Seledrith's curse. I had to go to him.

It wasn't unusual for me to take a rambling walk on these long summer afternoons, so I left Mother and Neriende with Father's temper and strode out over the fields towards the church and Villeroi's house.

This time I did not hesitate. I swung the wooden gate in, marched up the path, and knocked hard.

Footsteps. The door opened, and a portly man of around my father's age peered out at me. He was clean-shaven, and his eyes were a ghostly grey, almost white. A fringe of greying hair surrounded a perfect bald circle on his scalp. He was dressed in a grey and white robe, the lower half splattered lightly with mud. A gold cross hung about his neck on a chain.

"I . . ." My voice had disappeared. I had expected Rufus to answer the door, not the Bishop. "I need to speak with Rufus," I managed.

"Why?"

"A matter of the church," I said, for it was true and I thought it might make him stand aside.

"Then you may speak to me." He smiled, revealing yellowed teeth. "For I am in control of this bishopric."

Then Rufus appeared at his shoulder. "What do you want, girl?" he said, and a tinge of alarm was in his voice.

"Rufus, I need to tell you something," I said.

The Bishop's eyes narrowed. "I have already directed you to tell me if it is a church matter. Young Rufus has not yet taken his ordination vows and has no official capacity to deal with church business. Certainly not while I stand in front of you. Do you understand, girl, who I am?"

I held firm. "My message is for Rufus."

The Bishop turned his eyes to Rufus, who smiled weakly. "Off you go, lass," Rufus said to me. "Your business can wait, I'm sure."

The Bishop returned his attention to me and a glaze of contempt was in his pale eyes. "You heard him. Off you go."

Embarrassment stung my cheeks. I swallowed hard, turned, and retraced my steps. By the time I got to the gate, they were both inside, the door firmly shut.

. . .

Father was in a foul mood after spending the day with my incompetence, but it was Neriende he decided to take it out on. As she was the youngest, he was the gentlest with her. His abuse came in a long tirade of needling and mocking, with only a few open-handed blows. I was glad to escape to my bed after dinner, to curl on my side and nurse my humiliation and disappointment at being dismissed so sharply by Rufus and the Bishop. How could I have misjudged the situation so badly? I had thought Rufus liked me, found something special about me. But he had spoken to me as he would speak to any village wench: so much for his "surge of destiny". Perhaps that was just a way of interesting me in his God. Well, I wasn't interested in his God and I never had been. And I never would be. Defiantly, I made a silent vow of fealty to the Mother Goddess. Yes, they could make me attend the church, but my heart was mine alone to know.

I drifted off eventually, dimly aware of Neriende slipping into bed sniffing back tears. I turned and put my arm around her and she cuddled close, but then sleep claimed me again.

And a dream came upon me. I saw Rufus, sitting on a stone seat under the arch of the church. He seemed oppressed somehow, as though the weight of that arch was sitting across his shoulders. He leaned forward, arms on knees, his embroidered robes pooled about him. But then I noticed that the roots of the yew tree were tangled about his feet, crawling around his legs, pulling him towards the earth. "Merewyn," he said, his dark eyes on mine. "Wake up."

I woke, my skin prickling, his voice still echoing in my ears. I lay there a few moments, aware of my heart and my breath. Then I rose and went to the shutter.

He was out there, leaning against the fence Father had woven of hazel wood, waiting for me.

I pulled on my cloak and went through the little door to the barn, then out into the crisp evening. The clouds were all gone, revealing a million shining stars.

"How did you do that?" I said, as I stopped in front of him.

"God's will. He works through me as his loyal servant."

"The Bishop said you weren't ordained. You are not a priest, you are a man."

"Yes, but I have worked my way through every other order and wait only for my thirtieth birthday. Let me talk to you. Walk with me."

I glanced back over my shoulder at the sleeping house. "Very well," I said. We clambered over the fence and across the fields, until we came to the edge of the woods. Finally, he spoke. "I am sorry that I dismissed you today. You must understand, the Bishop is not a forgiving man. It is better if he doesn't know you, or your name, or what you might mean to me."

I stopped, and he stopped too. "And what do I mean to you?" I asked.

"You know that. I already told you. God has marked you out to my eyes."

"God?"

"He is the great engine behind all things."

He was wrong. Love is the great engine behind all things, and in the shadowy wood I felt it stir in me. "There is a curse upon the church," I said. "A wise woman has declared that harm should come to you and to those close to you. The Bishop. Villeroi."

Rufus didn't blink. "I'm not afraid. What power does this wise woman have over God?"

"I'm afraid," I said softly. "Or at least . . . I was."

He tilted his head slightly and smiled. "And yet I am not. And nor will I ever be. You have seen what I can do. What evidence have you that her power is stronger than God, working through me?" A sniff of arrogance touched his voice, but I didn't mind. A weight lifted off my heart, for he spoke truth. Seledrith's reputation was all formed by rumour. If somebody took sick or lost an eye or fell to some misfortune, whispers swept the village that Seledrith had cursed them. But I had never seen evidence that anything other than bad luck was responsible. Rufus had healed my mother; he had called me from my sleep without words.

"How did you wake me?" I said.

He began to walk again, and I kept pace with him. "I thought about it and it happened. God willed it. This is how things have always been with me, from my childhood."

"You could do these things as a child?"

The night breeze whipped up, circled us and scattered leaves across our path.

"I grew up with my mother in a town many miles across the water. Mother made a small living baking bread, and I stayed inside and helped her and didn't venture much into the fields. But one summer, the crops were in danger of being blighted by locusts. I remember seeing the sky, grey with them, and thinking that Mother couldn't bake bread without wheat. I knew that many people were praying for an end to the locusts, but I didn't pray. Instead, I curled in my bed every night and I *willed* the locusts to die, all the while feeling the steely power of God in my innards, even though I was only six. Then one night, I dreamed that I was lying in the field, looking up at the sky and God's voice was in my mind saying, *you will have your will.* The next morning, every locust was dead."

My skin rose in gooseflesh. "Really?"

"Upon my word."

"Did anyone know you had done it?"

"I told my mother and she wrote to my father, who was the archdeacon in the next diocese. But he was not interested in me for a very long time and did not send for me. I was evidence of his sin. Years passed, I grew, and word got out in our town about my power to heal. Mother became afraid that the constant work would wear me out before my time, rob me of my childhood. So we packed up in the middle of the night and left for my father's house. Upon meeting me and witnessing my abilities first hand, he decided I was born for the church. He sent me away to be educated in the episcopal hall at Auxerre. I started in the cathedral there, carrying candles. My father told me to be discreet about my abilities, to work hard and not stand out too much. And so, from childhood, I have been on this path without deviation. A path that leads me into a future the Bishop has decided for me."

"So you don't want to be ordained?"

"I don't rightly know, Merewyn. My life is God's. I know that. Perhaps the church is the best place for me. But . . ."

He didn't speak for a long time, then. At length, I asked him, "But what?"

He sighed deeply and stopped, sagging against a tree. "I don't feel God the way my father does."

"What do you mean?"

"I feel God in my body, in my guts. I feel him here in the woods. My relationship with him is natural, almost crude. It seems the Bishop favours a relationship that is closely managed, locked up in cloisters or articulated in a million words of Latin. I sometimes wonder if he knows God at all. It is so different from the way I know God."

I smiled at him. "When you speak of God, you speak as we do of Woden or Thunor or Frig. We find them in the bright sun, not in the shadows of a church roof. We live and breathe alongside them, as the fields and the rivers live and breathe around us."

He shook his head. "There is only one God, Merewyn. Of that I am certain."

"Perhaps they are all faces of the same God."

Rufus straightened his spine and didn't answer. He gazed down at me, his eyes soft and dark.

"I never thought I would be debating theology with a pig-farmer's daughter," he said, and even though it was not meant unkindly, I bristled.

"I never thought I would be debating theology with a Norman," I countered, hotly.

"Please don't misunderstand," he continued, evenly and softly. "I merely didn't think it was possible for me to find anyone as fascinating as I find you. There is a light in you . . ." He trailed off, gazing at me.

My skin flushed warm. His body was very close and the space between us grew warm with expectation. I lifted my chin and parted my lips, and he looked at me curiously for a moment, then realised what the invitation meant.

He leaned down and kissed me, gathering my waist and spine with his hands and pressing me close against him. The passion and intensity of his kiss astonished me: I had imagined he would be tentative, that it may be his first kiss. But he kissed me hard and sweet and knowingly, and I knew he was no more a virgin than I was. My body arched against his. His lips briefly left mine to venture across my cheek, and then his warm breath was in my ear as he said, "You are so soft."

"I love you," I replied.

He stiffened.

I clung harder. But he gently pulled away. "I am sorry," he said. "I am more sorry than I can say."

I was perplexed, embarrassed. "What have I done?" I asked.

"You have done nothing but be the beautiful, open woman that you are." He turned and began to walk away. "Go home. Go to bed. Forget we kissed."

"Wait!" I called, my heart thudding. A few moments ago, I had been happy in his embrace.

"I can't," he called after him. "I can't. You know I can't."

"Can't what?"

"Love you."

I opened my mouth to answer, but despair made me speechless. *I can't love you.* I had known it all along.

. . .

I woke late the next morning, with Neriende leaning over me and shaking me gently. "Are you unwell, sister?" she said, as I blinked my eyes open and enjoyed a few brief moments of respite before I remembered the previous night, Rufus's rejection of my love.

"I . . . no, I am well."

"You've slept past breakfast."

I sat up. "Has Father gone out to the fields?"

"Yes, and Mother with him. But you promised you'd help me weed the garden beds the moment the rain let up."

"Let me have ten minutes to wake up and eat some bread," I said, forcing a smile. "The sunshine will do me good."

Neriende loved her garden, which Father had let her plant all around the house in long beds. In the high morning sunshine, we knelt together amongst the gillyflowers and periwinkles and marigolds, pulling weeds. Neriende chattered away happily while I let my thoughts return again and again to the memory of Rufus's lips on my mouth, his hands on the small of my back. I didn't hear the approaching hoofbeats.

"My, that's a fine train," Neriende said.

My head snapped up. Along the dusty track that ran thirty feet from where we kneeled, two finely dressed men, mounted on handsome horses, led a retinue of servants and horses south, out of Tiwstan. I recognised the men as Villeroi and the Bishop, and shrank into the shadows so the Bishop wouldn't see me.

But to my distress, the Bishop held up his hand for all to stop and he dismounted directly outside our house. "You there," he called to me.

I stood, smoothing my apron over my skirt. "Wait here, Neriende," I said.

"Who is that man? Why does he want to speak to us?"

"He wants to speak to me."

I approached, and the Bishop came forward. We met halfway between the horses and my house. I was aware Neriende had crept closer, but still hung back. I shooed her away with the back of my hand.

"I know your name, Merewyn," he said. His accent was thick; he stumbled over our words. In his pale irises his pupils were very small. "I ask in the village if anyone could name the dark-haired girl with blue eyes and the scar on her chin. You were not hard to find."

I remembered what Rufus had said. *It is better if he doesn't know you, or your name, or what you might mean to me.* Well, what did any of that matter now? "And why did you need my name, my lord?"

"So I could find you and speak to you, girl." He dropped his voice low, but it was steely and grim. "You should stay away from Rufus."

I didn't reply. I stood my ground and didn't drop my eyes.

"He is human," he continued. "All men of the church are human. Any of us can have our heads turned by a pretty wench, but Rufus is destined for a life much bigger than anything you or anybody else in this village can offer him. Stay away from him. Don't . . . tempt him." He spat this last command, his face crumpling into a sneer.

Still I remained silent.

His face flushed with anger. "Well? Will you stay away from him?"

By now I was enjoying too much the frustration my silence was creating. I hid a smile.

He leaned close, his rank breath hot in my face. "How dare you treat me with such insolence?" he shouted. "I am a Bishop, not a peasant farmer. You should fear me."

But growing up with my father meant I feared few other people. "I do not fear you," I said. "And if you think I have tried to tempt anyone, then you are mistaken. You waste your breath with me. I am not what you think I am."

He did not move, his face close to mine, his eyes glassy with anger and contempt.

I softened. "My lord, I wish you a safe journey."

The Bishop straightened his back. "I will not forget your name, Merewyn," he said darkly, then with a flick of his cloak, he had turned and headed back to his horse.

Neriende was at my shoulder a moment later. "The Bishop?"

"Forget you saw anything," I said, my blood cooling slowly. "They are gone, at least for now. I am tired of thinking about the church and anybody who is attached to it."

"But—"

"I won't speak of it," I said. "And nor should you."

. . .

But she did. That night. Father was angry with her because she brushed against him and made him spill his soup, and so he started pinching her arm and shouting at her that she was a worthless daughter and he wished she had never been born, and she should be more sensible and quiet like me.

"Like Merewyn?" she said, her voice thin and forced. "Merewyn who took a visit from the Bishop today?"

Father turned and I saw Neriende's face fall as she realised what she had done. I understand why she did it, and I forgive her.

"What is this about?" he asked.

My skin shrank around me. "The Bishop," I said. I couldn't think of what else to say.

"He came to see you?"

"Yes. He had me mistaken for somebody else."

Smack. The first blow, an open palm to my face. "Don't lie. Was Villeroi with him?"

I nodded. "He didn't speak to me."

"I suppose you invited him into my house. Gave him my wine."

"I barely spoke three words to him and he was on his way. It was nothing."

Another blow. This time his fist was closed. "I will decide what is nothing and what is something," Father roared. Another fist, this time to my ribs.

"Please, please," I begged, my voice cracking. "I have done you no harm, Father. Please don't hurt me."

"Of all the people in the world you could show grace to, ungrateful bitch, you chose to invite the Bishop of this accursed church into my home."

"I didn't invite him."

"He didn't come inside," Neriende piped up, but Mother hushed her and pulled her aside as father rained blows down upon me. He was beyond listening now, and I closed my eyes and tried to hold my breath against the thudding pain. He rammed me up against the wall and went to work on my ribs, shouting and swearing. Then the moment came, as it always did, when his voice softened and I knew he would soon withdraw and return to the fire, with an expression tinged by fear, but without explanation or apology.

As soon as he let me be, I slid across the wall and pushed open the door to my bedroom. Neriende hurried after me, helping me across the threshold and laying me on the bed.

"I'm so sorry," she said, over and over.

"Sh," I said, and it hurt to speak. Dark pulsating waves of pain throbbed through my ribcage.

"He has hurt you badly?"

I tried to breathe, and a sharp twinge pierced my side.

"I'll get Mother."

"No." I put out a hand. "If you want to help me, do as I say and ask no questions."

Neriende's eyes locked with mine in the dim room. "Go on," she said.

"Tell Mother I'm well and I intend to sleep it off. Don't let her in here. Don't tell them I've gone."

Neriende's voice dropped to a whisper. "Where are you going?"

"I will never say."

Neriende's face worked as though she was holding back sobs, and then she nodded once. "Go. But come back soon. Don't go forever, like Faran."

"No, I'm not going far at all." I climbed out of bed, clutching my side, and let myself into the barn, closing the door behind me carefully. I stopped, catching my breath between my teeth. I ran my hand along my ribs on my right side. The agony was exquisite. I couldn't remember the last time Father had hit me this hard. All of his frustration about Villeroi and the church must have bubbled over. In his blind rage, it probably didn't matter at all who had been standing in front of him.

I was injured, of that I was certain. And I knew only one person who could heal me.

· · ·

The pain grew more intense as I walked out across the starlit fields towards Rufus. I wish I had the power to call him with a thought, as he had called me. The air was soft with a touch of lingering warmth. An owl called in the woods. I walked, stopped, rested, walked some more. It took me twenty minutes to make the five minute journey to Villeroi's house. Candlelight flickered in the narrow windows. I hobbled up the front path and knocked loudly. There were a few moments when the night caught its breath.

Then Rufus opened the door. "Merewyn?"

"Please," I said. "I'm hurt."

He stood aside and let me in, closing the door and bolting it. I stood, dizzy from pain and exertion. He touched my lip, and his fingers came away bloody. "What happened?"

"My father," I gasped.

"By Saint Agatha's blood and bones," he breathed. Gently, he took my hand and pulled me past the big table and through a door to a small candlelit room with a mattress on the floor. He sat me on the mattress and kneeled in front of me. I smelled spices and damp wool. He reached for my lip and my jaw. I hadn't realised how injured my face was, because the pain of my broken ribs was so immense. But as his fingers touched my face, I drew in a sharp breath.

"Hold still," he said, and he bowed his head and muttered in Latin, and as he did, I could feel my jaw softening, the pain withdrawing. My body tingled with fear and wonder. What kind of man was he? Was this really his God, working through him? Or had he been born with this darkly gleaming talent, a singular man among millions? When he finished, I touched my lip and the cut was gone.

"I think my ribs are broken," I gasped.

"Take off your dress," he said to me. "I'll heal them."

"I can't," I said. "I can't lift my arms."

He set his mouth in a determined line, then helped me to my feet. With the kind of neutral expression one might wear while undressing a child, he unpinned my brooches and let my pinafore fall around my feet. He untied the laces at the front of my shift and my skin prickled in anticipation, despite the pain. With the power of his hands, he tore the front of my shift open so it could fall off my shoulders. It, too, fell to the floor, leaving me naked in front of him.

The heat in the room was immense, but gooseflesh rose all over my ribs and breasts, and the skin around my nipples puckered. My breathing was shallow and rapid. Without meeting my eyes, he reached for my ribs. His big hands softly ran from under my armpits to my waist. I shouted in pain, but he said, "Sh," very firmly, and started praying.

Softly, in the dark, his hands on my ribcage.

And miraculously the pain began to dissolve and thin, shred apart and lift away, until at last there was none at all, and I stood naked before Rufus with his hands now resting around my waist.

Feelings overwhelmed me. Gratitude, awe, desire. I saw now, very clearly, why Seledrith's curse hadn't the power to frighten him. She dealt in weeds and powders. He had a bright, lucid, godly power running through him. She could no more hurt him than a mouse could hurt a lion. "Thank you," I said.

He didn't answer. Instead, he kneeled in front of me, his hands still on my waist, and leaned in to kiss my belly. I reached for his thick, auburn hair and he pressed his whole face into my belly, leaned his weight on me and groaned.

"Rufus? Are you well?"

He looked up at me. "How am I supposed to stop myself from doing the one thing my body and my heart are thundering to do?"

"Why would you stop yourself?"

His hands slid down and around, cupping my buttocks. He lay a series of little kisses from my navel to the line of my pubic hair, then he pulled me down onto the bed and lay his full length beside me, a hand on my breast and his lips at my throat. "I would not dishonour you, Merewyn," he said.

"There is no dishonour where there is love," I said, then asked boldly, "Do you love me?"

"Yes," he breathed, "yes, I do. But I do not know where that love will lead us, and I'm afraid."

"I am not," I said, plucking at the hem of his tunic, pulling it up to reveal a hard, flat stomach. Candlelight found bright copper in his body hair. He sat up, slid out of his clothes, and caught me in his arms. Flesh against flesh in the dim, flickering light. I tipped him onto his back and sat astride him, my breasts falling softly across his face, his lips. He grasped my hands in his own and gripped them as though he were afraid of letting me go.

. . .

"I had thought one day I might marry and have children," he said, in the cool before dawn as we lay in the half-awake half-asleep between lovemaking. "Until the Pope's edict, I'd thought both were possible. I wonder how I can be a man of the church if I am not truly a man."

"Then don't be a man of the church," I said boldly. "Say no to your father"

"I cannot. At the end of the summer, I will go south for my ordination. I will come back to take up my post at the church, which should be finished by then. Villeroi means to move here and adopt the role of Lord that he has so far held in name only. He will be watching me; watching all of us. I hope to find joy in good work, but I cannot find joy with you beyond that date."

Reckless happiness gripped me. "Then we have the summer?"

"It isn't fair to you."

"You saw what my father did to me. I have long ago abandoned any idea that the world should be fair," I said.

"Then we have the summer, my love," he said.

"My love," I echoed, drifting back to sleep.

IV

We met in secret in the long summer evenings, snatching minutes when hours would have been too short. Neriende knew I disappeared sometimes in the night and she said nothing, still guilty over the beating Father had given me that night. The fear of discovery could not override the desire to be with him in the candlelit room at Villeroi's house. The intimacy we knew was not merely about the skin; it was an intimacy of the soul. I learned all the secrets in all of the rooms of his heart, just as he learned mine. Our bodies became familiar to each other, and yet the last touch before I left for the evening always ached. I grew addicted to him: the more time I spent with him, the more time I needed with him.

Once, we met in the day, by accident, at the well. Other people were around so we simply smiled and nodded, but the forbidden desire was so intense that I went through the rest of my morning chores with a hot ache between my legs. And then he called me, with his mind. *Come now*, he said.

I made an excuse and raced off through the woods, careful not to be seen. He had left the door open, and I slid in and was out of my clothes before he'd even stood up from his place at the table.

"Your body is like a slender teardrop," he said, running his hands over my waist and hips. He lifted me up, my legs around his waist, and carried me to his bed, where we spent the afternoon.

"Listen," he said as we were resting. "Close your eyes and listen. What can you hear?"

I closed my eyes and focussed my ears. "A crow calling. Robins." I smiled. "A bumblebee outside the window."

"Keep going," he said, his warm lips at the hollow of my throat.

"The wind in the treetops. Distant hoofbeats on the road."

"Can you hear the sunlight?" he asked.

I opened my eyes and smiled at him. "You can't hear sunlight."

He placed his fingers over my eyes gently, to encourage me to close them again. "Try harder."

I listened. I listened off into the summer sky. And between the bird call and the rustling leaves, I heard the sunlight, yellow-bright and fleeting.

. . .

Oh, we were foolish. We should have known nothing good would come of it. When, in all the history of love, has forbidden love ever resulted in anything good? But we didn't think of it. We lived in those brief, hot moments together, and waited through all the other cold hours, refusing to acknowledge that the end was coming as certainly as the autumn.

All the while the church went up. I saw it every time I passed it on the back path towards Villeroi's house. The tympanum arch was beautiful, carved with chevrons and leaves. But the rest of it appeared as dark and menacing as a tomb. Only two narrow windows, slits in the stone, would let any light in. When bumblebees and dandelion clocks were catching the sun across the fields, why on earth would anyone choose to worship inside the church?

But we didn't talk about God or the church, Rufus and I. There was no time. Once he had returned from his ordination and was taking mass every day at the church, there would be plenty of time for me to hear him sermonise. The summer was for words of love between a man and a woman. God would have ruined everything. I'm sure even Rufus knew that.

. . .

It was late August: long hot days that oppressed us and made our bodies slick with sweat where they touched. He said to me, "My father has written to me about my ordination."

I pressed my index finger to his lip. "No," I said. "No goodbyes."

"But I'm—"

"I don't want to know when you are going. I don't want a sad farewell. My heart cannot bear that weight."

His eyes locked onto mine and he said, "I love you, Merewyn."

But his love wasn't enough, was it? I realised I had been hoping, deep under layers, that he would change his mind about the church, about the Bishop, about what he thought God wanted for him.

I smiled and put my face up for a kiss. "Dear Rufus," I said.

"All loves, even the great ones, must eventually part," he said.

I didn't answer.

Three weeks later I arrived at his house to meet him, and he was gone. On the front step was a stone, about the size of my palm. He had painted on it a picture of the sun, and written some words on it in charcoal. I couldn't read, so I didn't know what it said, but I knew he'd left it as a gift for me. Perhaps it was his way of telling me, as he had so many times, that I should learn the meaning of these strange symbols. I slipped the stone into my pocket and sat on the doorstep, head in my hands, and cried for a time.

Then I stood and headed home, placed the stone under my bed and lay down. I didn't get up for two weeks. Finally, Father declared

I was not sick, and I was forced back into the daily routines of life. The charcoal inscription on the stone wore off and the painted sun grew dirty. Harvest time was near. The days grew shorter. Autumn was nearly upon us.

.   .   .

Just as my life lost its colour and light, the grey-brown days of autumn displaced summer's bright hues. I moved through my days like an animated doll, doing the things I'd always done, but feeling removed from it all, as though a veil of cobwebs had wrapped itself around me. Neriende guessed my pain, but only mentioned it once, while we were cooking blackberry pies ahead of Michaelmas.

"You don't smile anymore," she said.

Indeed, I didn't.

The wheel of the year turned. All Hallow's Eve was approaching, and we had word in the village that the church was finished and would be consecrated very soon. Rufus would be returning, but he would not be my Rufus anymore. Cool, remote, owned by the church. He might as well be a statue.

.   .   .

And so Tiwstan was to become a churched village. We'd had a year to grow used to the idea, and no widespread dissatisfaction or complaint spread through our community. The church was next to our sacred yew and, as Rufus rightly said, some people would come to the church for that reason alone. No doubt they would nod their heads to the tree, and maybe whisper a silent heathen prayer as they passed it, but still they would enter the church as they were required to do, and worship outwardly—perhaps even inwardly—Rufus's god. This tide had been pulling at our ankles for years, and we all knew there was no resisting it any longer. There were forty-three people living in the village, and I imagined most of them would attend the consecration.

My father would not be among them.

.   .   .

Mother woke Neriende and me that morning with an urgent air and a furtive brow.

"Cynric has gone out early to hunt for rabbits in the woods," she said. "I told him I needed skins for winter cloaks. Here, get dressed and get your shoes on."

"We are going to the consecration then?" Neriende said sleepily.

"We must. Villeroi will be there, asking names and counting heads. There's talk that he's moving here permanently. He is our lord." I could see Mother struggling between fear of her husband, and fear of a greater authority.

"He will know we've gone," I said. "When he comes back and we are not here, he'll know where we went."

"I will take his anger," Mother said. "You aren't to worry."

My pulse fluttered. I would see Rufus today. He would not meet my eye, nor would I try to meet his. But I would see him: his strong, tall body, and his bright hair. In truth, even fear of Father's temper wouldn't have kept me away.

We left the house and walked the long way to the church, avoiding meeting Father in the wood. The day was clear, but the first edge of autumn's chill was in the air. A group of people hung around the bottom of the yew tree, talking quietly. The door was open. Mother took my hand and Neriende's hand and we moved into the dim church. Candles burned in four candelabras standing at the east of the church, and from a large wooden wheel that hung from the ceiling. There was a limey smell of stone, a sweet smell of oil, and the greasy smell of candle fat. We stood together near the other villagers. Everyone somehow knew that we should talk in whispers. Then, I heard a bell. The door closed behind us.

I turned. There was Villeroi, the Bishop, and Rufus. A tonsure had been cut in his thick, red hair, and I ached a little thinking of how his hair had felt in my fingers. With them, a pair of young men swung scented incense. Moving slowly and deliberately, while the villagers watched in quiet curiosity, the church men moved about the church, marking points in holy oil, muttering in Latin, consecrating the building for God's purposes. Then they moved up to the altar and blessed it with more holy oil. Rufus stood behind it, head bowed, while the Bishop placed a long robe over his head and tied an embroidered cloak about his shoulders. The Bishop took his place at the altar, opened a book in front of him, and began to read from the gospel. In Latin.

People in the crowd shifted from foot to foot. Some stole sidelong glances at each other, amused or bored or both. The handful of folk who were already very Christian stood at the front, but their shoulders and unstill feet told that they also found the reading far too long. I didn't understand a word of it.

But then, the Bishop stood aside and indicated Rufus should step forward.

He did. He cleared his throat, and began to speak.

"It falls to me to give your first sermon, and I have chosen a homily on faith and friendship."

The boredom, the foot-shifting, ceased the moment he opened his mouth. Perhaps it was simply that he spoke our language, but perhaps everybody else could see what I already knew about Rufus: he was bright, a star in the dark. He was lovely to behold and his voice was like warm honey, as he spoke in the dim room about God's role in our community, how he would become a force that brought us together, how Rufus hoped he himself would become a friend to all of us, how the example of Jesus Christ was one of love and forgiveness. And I felt it: the first inkling that this lark's song was somehow meant for me. That if Jesus Christ was anything like Rufus, then I was happy to come to the church to learn about him, and to be part of a community. Instead of being hidden away in my father's house, waiting for the next round of beatings. Even though I couldn't love or marry Rufus, he could be part of my life through the church.

The morning seemed bright outside after the dark of the church. Villeroi stood by the door, nodding and talking to people as they left. Despite Mother's fears, there was no counting or taking of names. Mother, Neriende, and I stood under the yew and spoke for a little while with some of the other villagers. Then Mother froze and I caught the direction of her gaze.

Just outside the churchyard wall, Father stood glaring at us.

Mother's eyes darted from Father, to Villeroi, and back again.

"I'm not afraid of him. I'm not afraid of any of them!" Father roared. "Come home now, women. Come home and get what you deserve."

My cheeks flamed with embarrassment. Mother and Neriende, heads down, hurried towards Father. I glanced over to the church door. Villeroi was watching Father with a furrowed brow. The Bishop had gone back inside. But Rufus was looking at me. Directly at me. Our eyes met, the heat flared, and then he smiled.

My heart was beating so hard that it hurt.

"Merewyn!" Mother called.

I scurried away. Whatever Father did to me, it was worth it to feel Rufus's favour on me for those brief seconds.

. . .

Winter came.

Father stopped us going to church. Mother was frantic, sure that somehow we would incur angry questions from Villeroi. We had all lived so long without direct government that we weren't sure what Villeroi's presence would mean. But Villeroi travelled in and out of the village frequently, and seemed unconcerned so far with who we were. I ached to see Rufus, and I made all kinds of plans for escaping Father's surveillance, but on Sundays and saints days, he would not let us out of his sight.

And I began to understand: he didn't mind so much about whether or not we believed in our gods or Rufus's god. Certainly, too, he would be deluded to think that he could resist Villeroi's authority over us all. No, the reason he didn't want us to go was that he still hoped Seledrith's curse would come to fruition, and he didn't want his wife and children to fall foul of the curse he had paid for.

V

It was a Tuesday, early in the afternoon. I remember that clearly. Tiw's day. Our old god whose name had once been the name of our village, before the church recorded it as Twiston. I was sewing rabbit fur into my old boots to make them last another winter. Cold rain fell outside. The fire crackled and the smoke hung woody and warm in the room. Mother and Neriende were embroidering the edge of a piece of cloth together, and Father was out in the fields.

As clear as if he was standing next to me, I heard Rufus's voice in my ear. *Come to the woods where we first spoke.*

I looked around, sure that Mother and Neriende would have heard too. But they sat, busy with their own sewing, heads bowed quietly as though nothing had happened.

I put my boots aside. Stood uncertainly.

Mother looked up.

"I'm going for a walk," I said.

"In this weather?"

I nodded. Mother frowned. "Merewyn?"

"I'll be back very soon," I said. Then I was out the door before she could question me further.

I hurried along the muddy path and down to the woods, heart ticking high and hard under my ribs like a bird's. It had been months since we'd spoken, since we'd touched. Would we feel sad and strange with each other? Would the distance between our bodies feel cold, awkward?

Then I saw him and my body remembered him with a flush of warmth in spite of the cold rain. I ran to him. He heard me, turned, and caught me. Pressed me against him. Then reluctantly pushed me away.

"Where have you been?" he asked.

"Father won't let me come to the church."

We stood in the rain, gazing at each other. His bright hair fell in wet strands on his forehead and cheeks. Finally, he said, "Why has God made you so important to me if I am not to be with you?"

I didn't know how to answer. My chest felt heavy.

"The Bishop and Villeroi," he said, "they are not men to admire. I am . . . much disillusioned."

"Why did you call me out here?"

"To see if I still could. To see if the bond still holds."

"It holds," I said. "It will never break."

"You found my gift?"

"The stone? Yes. Though I don't know what it says."

He pressed his lips into a line for a moment, reluctant. I understood then that he hadn't necessarily wanted me to be able to read the inscription. That it said something he felt but was afraid of articulating.

"Please?" I asked.

"It said, 'to the woman who should have been my wife.'"

Tears sprang instantly to my eyes. The awful knowledge that I was to be separate from him forever ached hard in my guts.

"I'm sorry," he said. He reached for my hair, pushed the damp weight of it off my face. I was overwhelmed by the moment. I saw stars at the periphery of my vision. And I pressed myself into his arms and my lips onto his lips. He stiffened and began to pull away.

Then I heard my father's voice, and everything inside me went colder than the rain falling on the three of us.

He was thundering towards us, fists balled at his side, keeping his balance over slippery leaf fall and muddy ruts.

"Run," I said to Rufus.

"No, I won't run. I'll talk to him."

"No heroics. He'll kill you." And apart from the loss of Rufus, that also meant the ruin of my family.

He hesitated, eyes flicking from me to Father, and back again. Then he turned and began to run.

Father gave chase. "Come back here, French bastard." I saw him fiddling at his belt, and my blood spiked in my heart. His knife.

"Father, no! No!" I took to my heels after them, lighter on my feet than Father, whose old knee injury made him lumber. Still, he was strong and full of fury.

I reached for him and leapt, knowing I would be hurt. I grabbed at his tunic and went down. He went down too, tumbling forward across hard roots and rocks.

"Run, Rufus!" I screamed. My elbows were grazed and my hip sang with pain. I looked up and Rufus was nowhere to be seen, but Father was crawling towards me, clambering to his feet. I pulled myself up on all fours, but he put a foot in the small of my back to stop me from getting up any further.

"Father, please don't," I said, my face turned up to him.

He considered me in the mud and rain, his expression shadowy with rage. I knew it would come and I was right. He kicked me. Once in the ribs and then, when I cried out in pain, once in the head. Then he stalked away.

I gasped and dropped my head, watching drops of blood spatter from my nose and onto the fallen leaves, red and bright against the dull grey-brown.

. . .

I had to go home; there was nowhere else for me. I caught my breath in the stable, sat with my back against a sleeping cow to put some warmth back into my bones. Then in the late afternoon I crept through the door between the stable and my bedroom, stripped off my still-damp clothes and slid into bed. I had blood on my face and my whole body ached, but at least I was lying still and safe. I could hear Mother's and Neriende's voices in the next room, but not Father's deep rumble. I breathed against the pain—so much pain; pain of body and of spirit—and waited for night to fall.

But before it did, I heard knocking in the main room, and then men's voices. "Open up, we seek Merewyn."

I sat up gingerly, pulse speeding, and listened.

"She isn't here," Mother was saying. "She went out some hours ago and hasn't returned."

Muffled male voices. There were two, talking to each other. I climbed out of bed and stood at the door listening.

" . . . produce her immediately," one was saying.

"I can't if she's not here." I recognised the tone in Mother's voice: reasonable calmness, faked to cover extreme fear. They were threatening her.

I opened the door and emerged, bloody-faced and dressed only in my shift. It was Villeroi and the shire reeve. Both stood menacingly close to Mother, who saw me and sighed. Neriende had pressed herself into a corner, terrified.

"I am here," I said. "I came in through the stable, Mother."

"What do they want you for?" Mother asked.

The reeve spoke. "Stealing. A gold bracelet is missing from Lord Villeroi's home, and we have reason to believe you may have it."

"I have stolen nothing," I said.

"But you have been in Villeroi's home?"

"I . . . many months past I visited the rector there."

Villeroi smiled cruelly.

"You may search the house," I said. "You won't find anything that wasn't earned by this family through hard work and wise management."

The reeve seized my arm. "We are not fools. No doubt you have hidden it or disposed of it. You will come with us."

"Can I dress, at least?"

Villeroi pulled a cloak off the hook behind the door. One of my father's cloaks. He thrust it at me. "This will do you."

I shook off the reeve and pulled the cloak over my shoulders. My mind whirled. Why did they think I had stolen something? Had Rufus told them how often I'd been in Villeroi's house? Or had somebody seen us? My body began to shiver: big, deep shivers that started in my stomach and radiated out to my limbs, making them tremble. Black dread spread through me.

"I love you, Mother," I said.

"Merewyn!" she cried, as they marched me out of the house.

I heard Neriende crying. That was the last time I saw my home.

. . .

They took me in the back of a cart to Villeroi's estate, and locked me in one of the outbuildings. In the last of the dim afternoon light, I could see casks and barrels. I presumed it was a buttery, but perhaps it had not been attended to for some time. A tip with my toes showed me most of the barrels were empty, and there was a yeasty, dank smell trapped in the dark corners.

I sat on the cold ground with my head on my knees, full of fear and sorrow, telling myself over and over that all would be well, that Rufus would vouch for me and clear my name. The rain deepened overhead, and night came as I shivered on the floor and wondered what would happen to me. I curled on my side, pulling Father's cloak around me for warmth. It still smelled of him, and I took deep breaths, taking small comfort in the smoky, male smell.

I must have dozed, because when the door shot open it startled me awake. At first the lamplight obscured his features, but then I could see it was the Bishop. He came in, set his lamp on a wooden crate by the door and stood, arms folded, observing me.

I sat up. "Please let me go," I said. "I have stolen nothing."

"I know that," he said.

Relief flooded my veins. "Then you can tell Villeroi? I just want to go home."

"You were here though? You admitted it? You visited the rector? How many times?"

"Just a handful," I said, "over the summer. We talked about scripture."

"Do you think I'm a fool?"

"No, my lord."

"Rufus has told me this afternoon that he wants to leave the church so he may marry you." His face was hard, contemptuous.

In spite of my fear and pain, I had to work hard not to smile. "I know nothing of this, my lord," I said. "Please let me go. I am not a thief. I mean you no harm."

He crouched in front of me, his face so close I could smell his breath. "I *told* you," he said. "I told you not to charm him, tempt him. Look what you have done. He belongs in the church. He is God's to command, not yours, you devil."

Even in the dim light I could see his eyes looked mad, devoid of spirit. I said nothing, suspecting that whatever I said would make things more difficult.

"I will not allow it," he said, straightening up and seizing the lamp. "He will not marry you."

"Then let me go," I ventured. "I will live a quiet life and stay away from you all."

"You are a danger to us, now," he said simply. "I do not believe you can live quietly enough for my liking. So near to Rufus . . ."

Cold fear gripped me. "Then I will leave the village."

"I do not trust you."

"Send Rufus away."

He sighed, and his face took on a sad, resigned expression. "I do not trust him, either."

"Please. I have done nobody any harm. Let me go."

He turned and opened the door on the pouring rain. Without another word, he was gone, locking the door behind him.

. . .

Some time in the night, I heard Rufus's voice. I blinked awake. The rain was thundering now, and I wanted to be out in it, washing the blood off my face and the smell of human waste out of my clothes. I listened again, thinking he was calling me in my head. But no, his voice was right there, on the other side of the door.

"Merewyn?"

I scrambled to my feet, went to crouch by the door. "Rufus?"

"You can hear me?"

I leaned down near the bottom of the door, where the cold wind had been creeping in all night. "Yes." He would save me. He would set me free.

"I'm so sorry this has happened."

"It doesn't matter. Open the door. I want to go home."

A short silence. My heart dropped like a stone in the river.

"I don't have the key. My father is sleeping with it under his mattress."

"Can you not break the lock? Break down the door? Anything? I'm frightened. I think they intend to kill me."

"No, no. They won't kill you, my love. You must remember you speak of a nobleman and a bishop. They are not brutes."

"I think you are wrong."

"Be reassured, Merewyn. I'm sorry I cannot set you free now, but I will speak with them tomorrow. I will convince them to let you go, and to let us be together. Trust me. All will be well, just on the other side of this trial. I am sure they simply mean to scare me, but I will not be scared."

Hope skidded away from me, beyond the reach of my fingers. My stomach hollowed. No warm firelit hearth with my family, no languid summer days in Rufus's arms. Only me, alone, in the dank emptiness of the buttery. "Please, Rufus," I said, my voice breaking over sobs. "Please set me free. I can't bear another moment of it."

"But if I break down the door now, they will not listen to me tomorrow. I will tell them that God intends for us to be together. I have always known it. They will not deny God's will. Here, give me your hand."

I peered into the dark, then saw he had slid the tips of his fingers under the door. I pressed my own fingers against them. "I am afraid," I said.

"Don't be afraid. Now I must go before I am noticed missing from my bed. They are watching me closely. They think I am going to run away. But I won't leave you. God will always be on our side."

The warmth and calmness in his words soothed me. Perhaps he was right

"I will be back," he said. "Tomorrow, I hope. With good news, and your freedom."

"I love you," I said.

"I love you, too," he said. "More than I imagined it possible to love anyone."

His fingers withdrew, leaving cold damp air in their place.

· · ·

After Rufus's visit I couldn't sleep. The ground was hard and cold, Father's cloak was worn too thin, and my stomach growled with hunger. I was dimly aware of an ache in my ribs where Father had kicked me. As the rain eased and stopped, I lay wretched on the floor and waited, not knowing what I was waiting for or how long it would take.

I heard movement and low voices just before dawn. The door opened, and thin light showed me Villeroi and the Bishop.

"Where is Rufus?" I asked.

"Don't let her speak or shout," the Bishop said, and Villeroi stepped in to seize me and clap his hand so tightly over my mouth that I could barely breathe. The smell of stale sweat and lavender oil. I struggled but the Bishop put his hand hard on my shoulder and whispered harshly in my ear, "Go quietly or things will be worse."

I dragged my feet as they half-marched, half-carried me around the back of the buttery and through a gate in the fence. They were avoiding the manor on purpose so Rufus didn't wake and see them taking me. My heart burst out of my chest with fear. Surely somebody would see me. It was dawn and Huntsman's Hill had a clear view of the manor, these muddy woods they were hauling me through, the church where they were taking me. I tried to lift my head to look around, but Villeroi pinned me roughly, making my neck ache.

In the churchyard, they released me.

"Help me!" I screamed.

For the first time, I saw the rope tied around the Bishop's waist. He began to unwind it and my knees turned to water. I moved to run, but Villeroi was strong and fast, and he grasped me once again and pinned my arms behind my back, forcing me to bend forward so I couldn't see what was happening. I could tell from the roots beneath my feet that we were under the sacred yew.

I closed my eyes, making the world disappear. *Protect my soul, Great Mother.* I felt the rope slip over my neck. Everything was quick now, and rough. They didn't speak to each other and I didn't open my eyes. Burning pain on my flesh as they heaved me up by the rope. My feet lifted from the ground, even as my toes tried desperately to gain purchase. My throat blocked up and my lungs grew hard. The dark behind my eyes spangled, but then a smooth lucid blackness began to creep over me.

The pain in my body began to recede, the way it did when Rufus healed me.

A hinge swung somewhere inside me, and then released, and then I wasn't connected to it anymore. I was sailing free of it and even though I had my eyes closed I saw him come.

My father.

I saw him come, red-faced and screaming into the churchyard. I saw Villeroi and the Bishop drop the rope and saw my own body crumple to the ground. Villeroi stepped forward with his hands out to stop Father, but there was no stopping him. Villeroi had taken one too many things from him. He attacked him madly, eyes rolling, fists flying, and then a glint of steel and a river of blood. The Bishop ran to hide within the church. Time telescoped; I watched from up in the branches.

My Father, sobbing over my body, covered in Villeroi's blood.

My Father, gently picking me up and walking with me, folding his cloak—which I still wore—over my face.

He walked for a long way. A soft shower of rain moved over us, the sun shining through it. A badger's birthday.

Past the Tiw Stone.

Past the sacred well.

His legs must have been aching. But still he walked. He came to the river that marked the boundary of our village.

And he kept walking. Down the rocky bank and through the reeds and into the river. Up to his thighs, his middle, his neck, and under. The water moving through my hair, Villeroi's blood flowing off him.

Father stopped walking. He released me. He opened his arms and stayed in the river.

. . .

I blurred in and out of knowing for a long time. It seemed like an age before I saw Rufus again, and by then I was back at the tree. Villeroi's blood was long gone. Rufus was dressed in white robes and was letting people into the church. His eyes flicked to the tree and I heard him think of me. *My beloved Merewyn.*

He used the same words every time, every Sunday, every saint's day. A glance at the sacred yew, then a memory of me.

I saw Mother come, and stand there shivering by herself.

I saw her come another time with Neriende and Faran, and they said goodbye for they were going away.

I watched as years spun by and grey streaks appeared in Rufus's hair. I watched as the people I knew grew old and grave mounds were raised for them.

I watched the day that Rufus didn't arrive for the Sunday service and felt sad that I wouldn't hear him say *my beloved Merewyn* ever again, and I watched again a few days later as they buried him beneath the corner of the church.

All lovers must part. All things pass. All sorrows and horrors fade.

I am of the earth and the trees and the sky, now. But always in high summer I find myself here, with Rufus, in the churchyard and I listen hard.

And I hear the sunlight.

AFTERWORD

" . . . it's part of belonging to western civilisation."
— Kim Wilkins

AFTERWORD

A few years ago, I encountered a Facebook application called "Shite Gifts for Academics". My academic friends and I had a good time with it, sending back and forth "gifts" such as "vengeful student evaluation", "boring faculty meeting", and "sentence in outrageous academese". The one that was sent to me most often was "dorky medievalists". I remain intrigued about how comfortably, almost naturally, the adjective "dorky" modifies "medievalists". There exists an established discourse of dorky medievalism. Sometimes the dorkiness comes from engagement in overly earnest role-playing games or fannish devotion to Tolkien, or is imagined as an obsession with historical accuracy, Sheldon Cooper-style: "The tavern girl serving flagons of mead; now her costume was obviously Germanic, but in 1487 the Bavarian purity laws or *Rhineheitsgebot* severely limited the availability of mead. At best they would have had some sort of spiced wine" (*Big Bang Theory* S2E02). Dorky medievalists are dorky, it seems, because they are fervent about what appears to be a marginal interest: the Middle Ages.

But is it such a marginal interest? The Middle Ages are everywhere evident: in the days of the week, in the common invocation of crusaders, knights in shining armour, fairy-tale weddings, and fire-breathing dragons, in the names of sporting teams, in the operations of large institutions such as universities and the church. All of this everyday usage is complemented by the repeated usage across media and art forms: fiction, television, film, videogames, comic books, children's colouring books, internet memes, Viking metal, dress design, architecture, and many others. The Middle Ages have provided contemporary western culture with a vast store of images and ideas that are meaningful, relevant, and always present.

There is a tendency to see the Middle Ages as a long way off; at the far end of a spyglass. We aren't medieval; we've become modern, rational. We've superceded what we were in that "dark age". But just like a spyglass, the medieval folds up inside the modern. It inhabits us even as we try to disavow its proximity, its persistence, its always-there-ness.

Imagine a city street: urban grime, petrol fumes. Imagine a dirty alleyway with a sign that says "NO THOROUGHFARE". Now look at that second word; really look at it. "Thorough", the old way of saying through, from the Old English (i.e. pre-Norman conquest) word *þuruh*, meaning from end to end; and "fare" from *faran*, which in Old English means to journey. The sign means: no journeying through. And while all words have etymologies, ways of remembering what we've forgotten about them, this one with its archaic spelling and its constant association with the modern city, is the one that is emblematic for me of how present the medieval remains. Having an investment in the Middle Ages is not a dorky subculture thing; it's part of belonging to western civilisation.

. . .

The stories in this collection are all, in some way, responses to my ongoing extensive and passionate reading and research in the field of medieval literature and history. "The Year of Ancient Ghosts" grew out of my visit to the Orkneys, a group of islands off the north-east tip of Scotland, to research Viking culture in the area. The Orkneys are a fascinating place. They are part of Scotland, but they are very aware and connected to their Viking heritage: for instance, there is a Norwegian bible in St Magnus Cathedral. The indigenous folklore has become inflected in interesting ways by the Viking folklore that dominated the area for so many centuries under the reign of the Viking jarls. These stories often centre around the wild and dangerous sea, and why wouldn't they? Not a single island in the Orkneys is large enough to generate a land climate. They may as well be ships, constantly braced against the briny elements. I hope that I captured this sea-cold menace. And, if I may be personal and partial a moment, this novella is easily my favourite thing I have ever written.

"Crown of Rowan" is the first reprinted story in the collection. It originally appeared in the anthology *Legends of Australian Fantasy* in 2009, and it is effectively a prequel to a fantasy epic I have been working on for several years now, in between other projects. This story is set in Thyrsland, a kind of alternative version of eighth-century England. If I can characterise my writing career as a long chain of obsessions with different periods in history and their folklores, then the Anglo-Saxon period (or, if you prefer, the Old English period; but never ever say the "dark ages" to my face) seems to have become the place where my interest and imagination have come permanently to roost. I am particularly fond of Old English language and literature, and the beautiful and mighty kennings used in the poetry: the sea is the whale-road or the brine-path, monsters are marsh-treaders or shadow-walkers, bodies are made of bone-locks and sword-juice. My hope for this novella, and the novel that I can't seem to stop rewriting, is that they capture that spare and elegiac mood in some small way.

"Dindrana's Lover" first made an appearance in the 1999 anthology *Mystery, Magic, and the Holy Grail* under the title "The Death of Pamela". On re-reading to prepare it for this novella collection, I saw every flaw that the intervening thirteen years of experience have granted me, so I have rewritten it extensively here, including changing the main character's name: Pamela was not a name in use until the sixteenth-century. This story takes a scene directly from Malory's *Le Morte d'Arthur*, where Percival and Galahad leave Percival's sister (unnamed in the story) at a sinister castle and come back later to find her bled to death so that the lady of the castle may bathe in her blood and regain her youth and health. Dindrana's fate in Malory is all off-stage: for him, Percival and Galahad are the stars of the show. I have focussed on Dindrana herself. It seems to me that the "bathing in virgin blood" plot premise lends itself to questions about the virgin's own sexual desires, how they have been experienced and controlled. In this story, I have tried to capture the feel of an Arthurian romance, following Malory's example of a fourteenth-century setting rather than a more historically "accurate" era; following the Gawain poet's example of mystical places in the wilderness; but also mixing it with a little bit of bodice-ripping Gothic sensibility.

"Wild Dreams of Blood" was born digital in 2012 in *The Review of Australian Fiction*, but this is its first appearance in cold, hard print. This urban fantasy obviously has an interest in the Old Norse *Poetic Edda*, one of our most important sources for Old Norse mythology. I have written about Odin before, in my 2004 novel *Giants of the Frost*, but here is a more benevolent All Father. He is, after all, only a secondary character. The real story is in how a woman of enormous strength can learn to hide it so it doesn't offend others or expose her to ridicule, so in many ways the story is allegorical. "Why haven't you ruled?" Odin demands of his daughter, and the answer is as complex as the question appears simple. Sara Jones in this story is named after Sara Douglass, who took an interest in this story when I was writing it but sadly died before I was able to show it to her.

The final story in the collection, the last to be written and the most difficult to write, is "The Lark and the River", largely a historical romance novella with a smattering of supernatural, where the work of the Christian God is presented as potentially just as magical and numinous as the heathen rites and charms that resist the encroachment of Christianity. In a way, I am working out my own response to religion in the world: why we laugh off Thor-worshippers but nod in agreement or tolerance to, say, Catholics. The story was inspired by my visit to a tiny Norman church in Broadwell, in England's Cotswolds region. In the churchyard was a giant yew tree, a traditional sacred tree associated with death and rebirth, dated at 1400 years old. There is no record of a priest on the site before 1085, so the yew predates the church by several hundred years. In the early years of the conversion, it was quite common for Christians to build churches at old heathen sacred sites. But the conversion was not tidy, nor uncontested, and heathen practices probably continued for a very long time. That

Cnut was still having to forbid worshipping wells and trees in the early eleventh century, that William saw his invasion of England as a kind of crusade, and that the incoming Normans set about a rigorous church-building program suggests that there were still enough heathen English, or at least not-quite-Christian English, to be a problem. This church was built next to a centuries-old yew, which suggests to me that there was still some heathen activity that needed controlling in Broadwell in the late eleventh century. The world must have seemed turned on its head by the Norman conquest, new laws, new language. With this time of great upheaval in mind, I wanted to imagine a small drama, something intimate and felt at the level of a family. I sat under the yew in the churchyard, and the whole story unfolded in my imagination. I'll admit, it was a little bit magic.

And that sums up how we feel about the Middle Ages: that they are somehow a little bit magic. Our notion of the lived medieval period is so close to our notion of the fantasy Middle Ages, that sometimes the line gets blurred. The Middle Ages, before modernity and enlightenment, seem forever linked in the contemporary imagination with excess, passion, and magic. In writing about the Middle Ages, I hope I've revealed that those qualities do not just belong to *then*, but also to *now*.

. . .

Thank you, Paula Ellery for helping me pull this collection together. Your enthusiasm, wisdom, and skill in editing were invaluable. Bless you, Meg Vann for being my writing buddy for three of the five novellas within. So smart, so creative, so wise: triple threat! And bless the rest of our writing group, the Sisters, who are all so dear to me; and my wise friend Mary-Rose MacColl who helps me make writing and life fit together. Invaluable research assistance and generous G&T's were provided by Dr Marcus Harmes, who is one of the smartest people I know, and also one of the kindest. Much love to Kate Forsyth, a kindred spirit and travelling companion on the great journey we call "story". All hail Russell B. Farr, for thinking this collection was a good idea and presenting it so beautifully. Praise be to Heather Gammage, the best research assistant a writer could wish for (all errors are mine, not hers, and are entirely deliberate for writerly reasons . . . ahem). Bow low for James Blake, whom I discovered doodling illustrations of awesome in an undergraduate class four years ago, and who has interpreted my stories here with such vivid beauty. Love always to my wonderful agent and friend Selwa Anthony.

Above all, infinite gratitude and endless adoration are due to my beloved Olafr Kissybeard, Lord of the Tiny Dogs, who lets the sun in: *þonne hit wæs renig weder and ic reotugu sæt, / þonne mec se beaducafa bogum bilegde / wæs me wyn to þon . . .*

STROMNESS, YORK, BRISBANE, AND DUBLIN, 2012

ACKNOWLEDGEMENTS

"The Year of Ancient Ghosts" © Kim Wilkins 2013. Appears here for the first time.

"Crown of Rowan" © Kim Wilkins 2009. First published in *Legends of Australian Fantasy*, edited by Jack Dann and Jonathan Strahan.

"Wild Dreams of Blood" © Kim Wilkins 2012. First published in *The Review of Australian Fiction*, Vol 1, Issue 6, edited by Matthew Lamb.

"Dindrana's Lover" © Kim Wilkins 2000. First published in *Mystery, Magic, and the Holy Grail*, as "The Death of Pamela", edited by Stephanie Smith and Julia Stiles. Appears here in a substantially modified form.

"The Lark and the River" © Kim Wilkins 2013. Appears here for the first time.

AVAILABLE FROM TICONDEROGA PUBLICATIONS

978-0-9586856-6-5	Troy by Simon Brown (tpb)
978-0-9586856-7-2	The Workers' Paradise eds Farr & Evans (tpb)
978-0-9586856-8-9	Fantastic Wonder Stories ed Russell B. Farr (tpb)
978-0-9803531-0-5	Love in Vain by Lewis Shiner (tpb)
978-0-9803531-2-9	Belong ed Russell B. Farr (tpb)
978-0-9803531-3-6	Ghost Seas by Steven Utley (hc)
978-0-9803531-4-3	Ghost Seas by Steven Utley (tpb)
978-0-9803531-6-7	Magic Dirt: the best of Sean Williams (tpb)
978-0-9803531-7-4	The Lady of Situations by Stephen Dedman (hc)
978-0-9803531-8-1	The Lady of Situations by Stephen Dedman (tpb)
978-0-9806288-2-1	Basic Black by Terry Dowling (tpb)
978-0-9806288-3-8	Make Believe by Terry Dowling (tpb)
978-0-9806288-4-5	Scary Kisses ed Liz Grzyb (tpb)
978-0-9806288-6-9	Dead Sea Fruit by Kaaron Warren (tpb)
978-0-9806288-8-3	The Girl With No Hands by Angela Slatter (tpb)
978-0-9807813-1-1	Dead Red Heart ed Russell B. Farr (tpb)
978-0-9807813-2-8	More Scary Kisses ed Liz Grzyb (tpb)
978-0-9807813-4-2	Heliotrope by Justina Robson (tpb)
978-0-9807813-7-3	Matilda Told Such Dreadful Lies by Lucy Sussex (tpb)
978-1-921857-01-0	Bluegrass Symphony by Lisa L. Hannett (tpb)
978-1-921857-05-8	The Hall of Lost Footsteps by Sara Douglass (hc)
978-1-921857-06-5	The Hall of Lost Footsteps by Sara Douglass (tpb)
978-1-921857-03-4	Damnation and Dames ed Liz Grzyb & Amanda Pillar (tpb)
978-1-921857-08-9	Bread and Circuses by Felicity Dowker (tpb)
978-1-921857-17-1	The 400-Million-Year Itch by Steven Utley (tpb)
978-1-921857-24-9	Wild Chrome by Greg Mellor (tpb)
978-1-921857-30-0	Midnight and Moonshine by Lisa L. Hannett & Angela Slatter (tpb)
978-1-921857-10-2	Mage Heart by Jane Routley (hc)
978-1-921857-65-2	Mage Heart by Jane Routley (tpb)
978-1-921857-11-9	Fire Angels by Jane Routley (hc)
978-1-921857-66-9	Fire Angels by Jane Routley (tpb)
978-1-921857-12-6	Aramaya by Jane Routley (hc)
978-1-921857-67-6	Aramaya by Jane Routley (tpb)

TICONDEROGA PUBLICATIONS LIMITED HARDCOVER EDITIONS

978-0-9586856-9-6	Love in Vain by Lewis Shiner
978-0-9803531-1-2	Belong ed Russell B. Farr
978-0-9803531-9-8	Basic Black by Terry Dowling
978-0-9806288-0-7	Make Believe by Terry Dowling
978-0-9806288-1-4	The Infernal by Kim Wilkins
978-0-9806288-5-2	Dead Sea Fruit by Kaaron Warren
978-0-9806288-7-6	The Girl With No Hands by Angela Slatter
978-0-9807813-0-4	Dead Red Heart ed Russell B. Farr
978-0-9807813-3-5	Heliotrope by Justina Robson
978-0-9807813-6-6	Matilda Told Such Dreadful Lies by Lucy Sussex
978-1-921857-00-3	Bluegrass Symphony by Lisa L. Hannett
978-1-921857-07-2	Bread and Circuses by Felicity Dowker
978-1-921857-16-4	The 400-Million-Year Itch by Steven Utley
978-1-921857-23-2	Wild Chrome by Greg Mellor
978-1-921857-27-0	Midnight and Moonshine by Lisa L. Hannett & Angela Slatter

TICONDEROGA PUBLICATIONS EBOOKS

978-0-9803531-5-0	Ghost Seas by Steven Utley
978-1-921857-93-5	The Girl With No Hands by Angela Slatter
978-1-921857-99-7	Dead Red Heart ed Russell B. Farr
978-1-921857-94-2	More Scary Kisses ed Liz Grzyb
978-0-9807813-5-9	Heliotrope by Justina Robson
978-1-921857-98-0	Year's Best Australian F&H eds Grzyb & Helene
978-1-921857-97-3	Bluegrass Symphony by Lisa L. Hannett

THE YEAR'S BEST AUSTRALIAN FANTASY & HORROR SERIES
EDITED BY LIZ GRZYB & TALIE HELENE

978-0-9807813-8-0	Year's Best Australian Fantasy & Horror 2010 (hc)
978-0-9807813-9-7	Year's Best Australian Fantasy & Horror 2010 (tpb)
978-0-921057-13-3	Year's Best Australian Fantasy & Horror 2011 (hc)
978-0-921057-14-0	Year's Best Australian Fantasy & Horror 2011 (tpb)

WWW.TICONDEROGAPUBLICATIONS.COM

THANK YOU

The publisher would sincerely like to thank:

Elizabeth Grzyb, Kim Wilkins, Kate Forsyth, James Blake, Jonathan Strahan, Peter McNamara, Ellen Datlow, Grant Stone, Jeremy G. Byrne, Sean Williams, Garth Nix, David Cake, Simon Oxwell, Grant Watson, Sue Manning, Steven Utley, Bill Congreve, Jack Dann, Jenny Blackford, Simon Brown, Stephen Dedman, Sara Douglass, Felicity Dowker, Terry Dowling, Jason Fischer, Lisa L. Hannett, Pete Kempshall, Ian McHugh, Angela Rega, Angela Slatter, Cat Sparks, Lucy Sussex, Kaaron Warren, the Mt Lawley Mafia, the Nedlands Yakuza, Amanda Pillar, Shane Jiraiya Cummings, Angela Challis, Talie Helene, Donna Maree Hanson, Kate Williams, Kathryn Linge, Andrew Williams, Al Chan, Alisa and Tehani, Mel & Phil, Hayley Lane, Georgina Walpole, everyone we've missed . . .

. . . and you.

IN MEMORY OF
Eve Johnson (1945–2011)
Sara Douglass (1957–2011)
Steven Utley (1948–2013)

Lightning Source UK Ltd.
Milton Keynes UK
UKOW04f0811171117
312878UK00001B/182/P